THE VAN BIRCH INCIDENT

MARLA HOLT

eBook ISBN: 978-1-7338518-2-4

Paperback ISBN: 978-1-7338518-3-1

Cover Design by: Suite Six Studios

Edited by: Jacqueline Hritz

❦ Created with Vellum

To all the survivors

CONTENTS

Author's Note and Content Warning

Dear Reader,

Thank you so much for picking up a copy of *The Van Birch Incident*. Before you begin, I want to warn you that in this book, the main character deals with the aftermath and recovery from a sexual assault (which does not happen on the page.) Van Birch is a public figure, and the media's take on what she's going through can sometimes be brutal. At the beginning of each chapter is either a gossip article or one or more social media posts that are relevant to the progression of the story. The tone and words expressed in some of these, especially the social media posts can be difficult to read. They are based on the sort of posts I found while researching events like gamergate and cases similar to Van's. Brett Kavanaugh was going through his confirmation hearings while I wrote the first draft of this book in 2018, and the way Christine Blasey-Ford was talked about and threatened so vocally played a huge role in the scope of this book. Please be aware, that as brutal as some of the social media posts in the book are, I have tamed them down over what I read while researching. If any of this is triggering for you, please feel free to skip the bits between chapters.

I guarantee that *The Van Birch Incident* is still a slow burn romance with a happily ever after. It is even a little funny in places. However, if reading about someone else's sexual assault journey is not something you are comfortable with, please do not feel like you need to continue. You still have all my love.

XO

Marla

*L*ights flashed as Bishop helped her from the limo. Van Birch stepped onto the red carpet in her sparkly black heels and short black dress and with a huge smile drawn in red across her lips. It had taken her years to master the ability to look toward the lights but not focus on the flashes as photographers snapped pictures of her from every angle. Tonight, it was easier. Bishop held her hand as she found her balance and flashed her the grin that never failed to make her heart melt.

How had she ever found this man dangerous? Van wouldn't have wanted to cross him when it came to the music business. But he was different with her. Henry Bishop showed Van a different side than he allowed anyone else to see. She was special to him. Their relationship transcended all the other famous couples they knew. For one, it had nothing to do with publicity. What they felt for one another was genuine. And Van was starting to think that maybe it was time to end the relationship she *did* have for publicity's sake. Bishop had been suggesting it for months, but Van hadn't been ready.

She loved Bryant. He was the best fake boyfriend a girl could ask for. Handsome, with a shy smile and crooked glasses. He also lived 1500 miles away and pretty much thought of her as a sister rather than a love interest. Van cherished their friendship, but as long as she pretended to be in love with him in public, she'd never have the chance to be in love for real.

Van was pretty sure she was in love with Bishop.

She hadn't seen it coming. He was ten years older than she was, and she assumed he saw her as the annoying guitar player who never went anywhere without her reality crew and, oh, that meant you had to book twice the hotels rooms while on tour. Your team can take care of that, right Bishop dear?

But then he'd kissed her. That had been all it had taken for Van to jump his bones. That had been a year ago, and she didn't want it to stop.

Bishop squeezed her hand, and Van stepped out of his grasp, posing with him in the background. Until she had a chance to run over a plan with Phoenix and discuss it with Bryant, in public Van would play like she and Bishop were only friends.

She and Bishop would argue about it later. They always did. But she didn't know what he wanted her to do about it. Ending one relationship in the public eye and starting another without also igniting a scandal would be a delicate business. That was why they needed Phoenix's advice—only, Van had barely seen her best friend and business partner outside of yoga and business meetings lately. They had all been so busy.

She knew what Bishop would say. That they didn't need Phoenix to orchestrate a publicity stunt for them to just be together, but Van wasn't sure. Van Birch was a household name because she'd followed Phoenix's advice all these years. And America loved Bryant Wilder. They'd be heartbroken for him. And Van didn't want to be the bad guy. She put up with enough criticism as it was.

She knew there had to be a good way to make it happen, but the red carpet at a movie premier probably wasn't the best place to do it.

Bishop nudged her onward with a hand at the small of her back when paparazzi and reporters started hurling questions.

"Van, who are you wearing?"

"Is it true your dad is running for congress next year?"

"Are you and Bishop together now?"

"What about Bryant Wilder? Does he know about your affair?"

"How long have you and Bishop been an item?"

"When are you going to release your third album?"

That last question was the one that got her to hurry along. Van hadn't released new work in over two years, and she was getting pressure from all sides. The public, the fans, talk show hosts, her label. Bishop had been nagging her about that too, but there was such a thing as creative burnout, and after hustling to get her record deal, then putting out two albums less than eighteen months apart, AND touring every summer, Van was worn out. She'd told her label that if she could skip the summer tour, she'd have an album for them by the fall. That it was halfway through July and she hadn't even started wasn't something she was looking to be held accountable for.

"Van, why isn't Bryant with you tonight?" somebody shouted.

She shot them a beaming smile, and it was the only question she was going to answer. "He's working. Summer is his busy season, but he'll join me in a couple weeks for a weekend getaway."

After that it was a flurry of questions about when Van and Bryant were going to get married and if Bryant was ever going to move to L.A. and if Bishop was their third, which made Van giggle, but she just blew them all a kiss and let Bishop push her into the theater.

"For fuck's sake, they're getting bold," he growled in her ear. "Your third? Jesus Christ."

Van couldn't help her giggle. God forbid someone imply Henry Bishop was interested in a man or, you know, sharing. "Don't worry, you are so not Bryant's type."

Bishop grumbled something that Van couldn't make out, and she pushed him toward their seats. The film was an artsy something or other that Phoenix's mentor had sent them tickets to. Eve de Silva was one of the only producers in Hollywood making new movies. No remakes or reimagnings or nostalgia. She was pushing through original screenplays and making them into national sensations.

Van attending Eve's premiers gave the gossip sites an excuse to mention the movie in their articles, and it helped Van stay relevant in the off-season—especially since it had been so long since she'd released an album.

On the latest season of Van's reality show, *Pop Star*, they'd had a storyline that implied that Van might be developing feelings for Bishop, in order to create tension between him and Bryant, and also between Van and Bryant. Plus, it gave Van an excuse to play up the sexual tension between her and Bishop now that they'd started sleeping together.

Just that hint of possible attraction between Van and Bishop on TV had spawned blogs, YouTube channels, and of course, its very own ship name and hashtag. There were whole fucking teams of people arguing on Twitter whether the reality was #VanBryant or #VanBishop.

Van enjoyed playing to both sets. Last month when Bryant had been in town, they'd been on their way into a club when they'd been waylaid by paparazzi. Bryant was always nice about it and didn't mind stopping to pose with Van or answer inane questions. He even signed autographs, even though he always reminded people that he was just a contractor from Kansas and hadn't done anything to earn his fame other than date Van Birch. None of them seemed to care, and Van would always grin and blow kisses at his fans.

But when the paparazzi had begged them for a kiss? Van pulled Bryant down to her level—since he was a giant —and cupped his chin, but instead of planting one on him, she did her best Gene Simmons impression, stuck her tongue out as far as it would go, and licked up the length of his cheek. The crowd had cheered; Bryant had cracked up and pulled her into a chaste, laughing kiss. The photo was still showing up online as proof of how good they were together.

But Van had also been going out in public with Bishop more often—not a lot, since Bishop usually preferred to stay in—but enough to fuel the #VanBishop shippers and keep the rumors going until the next season of her show aired.

Tonight was one of those rare nights out, and Van was having a blast. It had been too long since she'd done anything but strategize and play house with Bishop. She missed the glitz and the glam and the showmanship. Maybe she should ask Bishop to book her some local gigs, just for fun. It had been too long since she'd been on stage. Maybe that would kick-start her motivation to write songs again.

Lately, every time Van picked up her guitar, she felt like she was running full force into a brick wall.

She might not want to talk about it exactly, but she was desperate to *want* to write songs again.

While they were waiting for the rest of the guests to make it down the red carpet and into the movie, Van texted Phoenix which shots to expect the media to pick up on. Bishop helping her out of the car, his hand on the small of her back, but also her stopping to fondly answer questions about Bryant without Bishop at her side. It was just the right amount of intrigue and razzle-dazzle to keep both #VanBryant and #VanBishop ships sailing until Van could figure out what she wanted to do next.

"What are you doing?" Bishop grunted, looking over her shoulder. Van angled her phone away. Sometimes he was way too interested in what was happening on Van's phone.

"Telling Phoenix about the third thing."

Bishop snorted.

"She doesn't think your Bryant's type either."

He leaned in too close and grazed his teeth over the

shell of her ear. "All I care about is being your type, Little Bit."

She squirmed away. Van's ears were not an erogenous zone, and he knew that.

He skimmed his fingers down her arm, a move she normally liked but, following the ear thing, only made her want him to stop touching her. Van shoved at his shoulder. "No PDAs, remember?"

"I'm ready to stop playing games, Ness."

Van wiggled her eyebrows at him. "I happen to like games."

"I'm not joking." He was using his business voice. The one that said there was no room for negotiation.

"I already told you I'd talk to Bryant about the next time he's here," she whispered at him. "What more do you want?"

"For you to work it out now."

"What, like, before the end of the movie? That would be rude."

"You wouldn't have to do anything but write a text to Phoenix. She'll take care of everything for you, just like always."

"What's that supposed to mean?"

"Just that you avoid hard work. Maybe you should ask Phoenix to write your album for you. Then at least we'd have something to sell."

"Wow." It was the only word Van could think of. She fucking hustled, and just because she was having writer's block, it didn't give him the right to be a total douche. What had crawled up his ass tonight?

"I told you, I'm done playing games, Van." He leaned in closer and whispered. "You are mine, and I'm ready for everyone to know it. And if you don't do something about it soon, I will."

Van jerked back. "Is that a threat? Because last time I checked, it was my lazy ass that was pulling in your paychecks too."

He shrugged. "There are other artists out there."

She had to stop herself from snorting. Like he would ever work for someone else. He'd made way too much money and gained way too much power as her manager. People had known of him before her, now they fucking worshiped him and his stupid man bun. "What is up with you tonight?"

"I'm tired of public Van. I want my private Van back."

She rolled her eyes and faced forward. She'd been home with him basically every night for the last two months. The only time she went out anymore was for planned publicity shots with Bryant or for yoga twice a week with Phoenix. She hadn't even hung out with Phoenix for good old-fashioned girl time in months.

She missed that.

What Van needed was time to breathe.

Then maybe the music would come to her.

Just before the house lights dimmed, she texted Phoenix, suggesting a weekend away, just the two of them.

Phoenix's response had been to ask whether Van wanted to go to Paris or the Caribbean.

At the after-party, Bishop gave any man who came near Van the evil eye, even if it was somebody they should absolutely talk to, like Gavin Mercany, who produced Van's last album, and who Van would like to produce her next.

After Bishop had scared Gavin away, Van swiped her handbag across his bicep. "What is wrong with you tonight?"

"I'm ready to go" was all he said.

Normally, Van would like to stay at a party for longer than an hour, but her Manhattan wasn't sitting well in her stomach and Bishop was on his fourth double whiskey and only getting surlier.

"Fine." Van pulled out her phone to page Mills, her driver. "You should have told me you started your period earlier."

Bishop's hand closed too tight over her elbow as he steered her toward the venue's front door. "If I said something like that to you, you would throw a fit."

"Yeah, well, the Bishop I thought I came out with tonight used to be good at talking to people. Everyone calls him a charmer." His grip tightened painfully on her elbow as they squeezed through the crowd. "But I don't know where that Bishop went and— Ow! You're hurting me."

Bishop did not let go. "Yeah, well, that Bishop went out the window when you started flirting with the paparazzi."

Van flinched back. She couldn't go far because he still had a firm grip on her arm. His hands were so big, his fingers could basically meet around her scrawny bicep.

"I haven't flirted with anyone," she said. "Or maybe you're mad because I haven't been kissing your ass all night, like I usually do."

A sneer parted Bishop's perfectly manicured dark beard. Normally, Van fantasized about his lips, but she was not into the possessiveness he'd been throwing around lately. Part of the reason she'd barely seen Phoenix or her dad or Bryant or, hell, barely even talked to Clay was because Bishop had been monopolizing her attention. It hadn't just been in a "they were in a new relationship and Van didn't want to stop jumping his bones long enough to go out for a drink with her friends" sort of monopolizing, because they'd been boning for a year. For a good portion of that time, Van had chosen to stay in with Bishop, but when she'd tried reintegrate their relationship with rest of her life these last few months, he'd resisted.

Something had changed. It was like his patience had run out with how Van lived her life. But that couldn't be right. Bishop had helped her create this life, this persona. She didn't understand why he would want to tear it down.

"I like it when you kiss my ass," he said.

Van knew he meant the words to be sexy, but the slur to his words and the growl behind them was not seductive.

"Yeah, well, after your boorish behavior tonight, it's gonna be a long time before that happens again."

Bishop harrumphed. "We'll see."

They broke free of the crowd and passed through the front doors then. Mills was waiting for them and opened the door for Van as she ducked into the back of the limo, flashing him as much of a smile as she could before Bishop crowded in behind her.

Once they were one the road, Bishop swiveled his head toward her from where he rested it against the headrest. "Now you're even flirting with the fucking driver?"

"I wasn't flirting with the driver," Van said. "I like

Mills. He's our best driver. I like to be nice to him so that he keeps being our best driver."

"Because he thinks maybe someday you'll sleep with him."

"What are you talking about?" Van asked. "The only person I sleep with is you, and I'm seriously questioning why that is at the moment."

"It's because you like my cock," he said, and Van could tell he was trying to slide into that sexy alpha mode. She sometimes liked it when he talked dirty to her and told her what to do in bed, but it didn't work if she didn't even want to be in the same car as him.

"You're such a dick," she said and scooted to the far side of the limo. She pulled her phone out of her clutch and texted Phoenix, *Definitely Paris. I need carbs more than I need rum.*

Bishop poured himself another drink and let her be on the twenty-minute ride back to her house.

Once they were inside her condo, Van headed straight for her bedroom, shed her shoes and her handbag, dropped her dress to the floor in her wake, slammed the bathroom door behind her, locked it, and turned on the shower.

She stayed under the hot water spray for a long time, hoping to wash the strange, bitter taste of this nightoff her body. Van had hoped that by the time she got out of the shower, Bishop would have passed out on the sofa or something, and she could get a peaceful night's sleep. Maybe he'd be feeling more himself in the morning. And if not, maybe Phoenix would have already booked them a weekend flight to France, and Van could escape him until he came back to his senses.

Only that's not what happened. He started banging on the door while she was half-covered in soap and still had conditioner in her hair. Bishop was yelling her name like there was a possibility she was hurting herself in here or refusing to marry him because she thought he might just be after her money ala *The Heiress*.

She rushed through the rest of what should have been a relaxing shower and pulled open the bathroom door, with her hair still dripping down her back and a towel loosely wrapped around her.

"What?"

"Don't be upset with me," he said, his words even more slurred than they'd been earlier. Van wanted to chuck the decanter of whiskey in the living room against the wall. "I'm sorry I was cranky tonight, but I love you and I'm anxious to make you mine."

Van's heart softened a little toward him as his forehead came to rest against hers. Everybody was allowed to have a bad day.

But when he tried to kiss her, Van leaned out of his reach. "Not right now, okay?" she said. "I'm just not feeling it tonight."

Bishop's hold tightened painfully on her wrist as he yanked her against him. "Well, I am."

Pop Star Files Assault Charges Against Manager

Pop star and reality-TV darling Van Birch filed charges yesterday with the L.A. County Sherriff's Department against long-time manager and rumored beau, Henry Bishop. Birch alleges Bishop sexually assaulted and raped her in her home after they attended an event together that evening.
Neither camp can be reached for comment at this moment. Neither can Birch's long-time boyfriend, Bryant Wilder. Readers know we've been following this love triangle since the most recent season of Pop Star wrapped with Bishop and Birch on screen together more than ever before.
One has to wonder how likely it was that Birch has been stringing both men along.
Which begs the question, are these assault charges genuine, or is this just another publicity stunt orchestrated by the media-savvy marketing genius, Vanessa Birch herself?
Only time will tell. Stay tuned for the latest updates.

1

*L*ight played over Van's eyelids, but she didn't open her eyes. She'd dreamed of her mother. They'd been playing guitar together. Only Van had been grown in the dream, and the rational part of her mind knew that her mother had died when Van was ten. Still, the last day had been hellish, and if she opened her eyes, she'd have to fight through the brain fog from the sedative and get out of bed. Then she would have face herself in the mirror, look at the bruises on her hips and thighs and wrists. She wasn't ready to face herself. Better to go back into the unreality of having a mother. She would have liked to have her today.

Van could almost convince herself it hadn't happened, but the media storm that was no doubt brewing would hammer that particular nail home. Van felt sure she was about to be crucified.

The door opened further, and she scrunched her eyes tighter, trying and failing to hold on to her mother's smile as footsteps crossed the room. She knew it was Phoenix standing next to her bed. Van had run to Phoenix after escaping out the damn bathroom window. She knew her best friend and business partner would have been standing guard outside Van's door like the angry bird of prey she was while Van slept. Van also hoped Phoenix had an early start on the damage control, because Van didn't want to face it. Or even think about it. She wanted to curl back into a ball and fall asleep again, but when Van tried, pain resonated through her body, and she let out a whimper.

"Van." Phoenix's voice was gentler than normal.

"No." Her voice was a hoarse croak, and she covered her head with her pillow as Phoenix sat on the edge of the bed with a sad sigh.

"Please tell me you have another one of those magic pills the hospital gave me," Van said.

That had been the only good thing that had come out of Phoenix dragging her in to report everything. She'd endured invasive examinations, a borderline insulting interview with a woman police officer, reluctant photos of her in her underwear. But at the end of all of that, a very nice nurse with a kind voice had given her a little packet with a pill inside. She said it would help with the shock.

Van wasn't sure that was the case. This weird disassociation from her body that she was feeling had to be shock, when she'd felt entirely lucid the night before, even if her hands had been shaking and her other limbs had gone numb.

It was the calm before the storm. Van could feel the anger building like clouds on the horizon on the horizon, but they were still a hundred miles in the distance. Until they reached her and she could burn, Van wanted nothing more than oblivion.

"They only gave us the one," Phoenix said.

Van shifted again, pulling herself up in bed. Phoenix helped her prop the pillows behind her back. "Do you have ibuprofen at least?" she asked as she rubbed the space over her heart. She hurt there too, like a bison was sitting on her ribs, even though there weren't any bruises there.

Bishop hadn't hit her, only held her down and tried to keep her still. She cringed and pushed the memory away, though her heart pinged with pain again. Tears gathered behind her eyes, but she blinked them away. Van hadn't cried yet. She didn't want to cry. Crying would make it real somehow, and she was afraid that if she started, she might not be able to stop.

"I'll get you some," Phoenix said. Then held out the phone that had been in her hand. "Your dad is on the phone. You should talk to him."

The room was still mostly dark because of the blackout curtains, but the clock said that it was four o'clock in the afternoon. That meant it was six pm in Kansas, where her dad lived.

"Does he know?"

"I told him," Phoenix said. She hadn't lapsed out of her gentle voice yet, and that scared Van more than anything, because Phoenix's voice was usually sharp, precise, and biting, like the sound of one of those old-time teachers rapping you over the knuckles with a ruler. It was not smart to cross Phoenix. Ever. She held grudges, and she played dirty. Usually Van was playing right along with her.

Van knew she was down, at least for today, but she had expected Phoenix to come out swinging, to rally Van with anger and outrage and action. Her calm, quiet demeanor had Van's heart slamming against her ribs.

"Just talk to him. Okay?" Phoenix said as Van took the phone.

She was gone before Van had unmuted the phone. "Daddy?" she asked, her voice cracking, making her sound like she was five instead of twenty-five.

There was a sniffle, then "Bitsy?"

Hearing the childhood nickname was all it took for the tears to start. "Daddy, I'm so sorry."

He shushed her and murmured comforting words while Van sobbed and apologized over and over again.

"Hush, hush," he kept saying. "Bitsy, it's not your fault."

It took almost ten minutes for her to calm down enough to talk. Even then, it was more because crying hurt too much than because she was out of tears.

"I think you should come home," her dad said. "You need us right now."

By "us," Van could only imagine he meant himself and Bryant. Her mom had passed when Van was ten, her stepmom had died in a car accident two years ago, and Van's so-called stepbrother, Clay, basically hadn't spoken to her since then unless he had to.

Her dad heaved in a huge breath, then sighed it out and said, "And we need you right now too."

Van's muscles tensed, and she winced. "Why? What happened?"

"Have you seen the news?"

Van hadn't seen anything since before the movie premier, though it felt like years had passed since then, not only a day. "No. Is everyone alright?" Her aching heart twinged in panic.

"Clay and I are fine. I'm with him now," he said in his steady lawyer's voice. It was the tone that walked a jury through the final arguments, the one that didn't lose focus, didn't have space for vulnerability. "We only just got cell service back, and I haven't been able to reach Bryant yet, but I'm calling him next."

Van's heart stuttered. "Why can't you get ahold of Bryant?" Bryant's house was only a ten-minute drive from the house she'd grown up in. "What happened? Why was your cell service down?'

Her dad continued in his calm tone as he said, "There was a bad storm last night. A tornado touched down in town. There was a lot of damage. The high school is gone, houses destroyed. Clay and I have been digging his neighborhood out of the rubble. Everyone here is fine, but there were families who didn't make it."

"How's the house?"

It was a selfish question in light of everything, but Van's mind was racing so quickly that it was the only coherent thought she could grasp out of the speeding melee. After making sure that her dad and Bryant—and she supposed, Clay—were alright, that house was her next priority. It was one of the most important touchstones in her life. She'd grown up there. It's where she'd lived with her mom, and after her death; it's where she'd become friends with her dad, where she'd lived when her father had married Clay's mom and suddenly she'd had an annoying older brother. Knowing that she always had that big Victorian house in Kansas to go back to when she needed a break for her life in L.A. had kept Van grounded.

The thought of going home to her dad and not being able to curl into her bed in her old room, to play her dad's baby grand piano with him—her heart was breaking all over again.

"The roof will need some work, and the guttering got ripped off, but we got off light, Bitsy."

The nickname was almost as good as her dad wrapping her in a hug from afar. Robin Birch called her that because she had always been small. Itsy Bitsy as a baby.

"I'm just glad you're alright," she said, tears gathering in her eyes again. "Because I am most definitely not okay."

"I know, honey. We'll get you home and away from all the noise."

"I'd like that. Phoenix probably already has a flight booked."

A dry, sad sigh of a laugh leaked into the phone. "You're probably right." Then her dad sighed again, and Van could picture him running his fingers over his silver beard. "Will you do me a favor and call your brother? He lost everything."

"I thought you said he was okay."

Van's heart was beating so hard, it felt like a timpani drum in her chest. Clay couldn't be hurt. They might not get along, but he was still family, sort of—even if Van had harbored a crush on him for ages. Sometimes she thought Clay might have a secret crush on her still The memory of that kiss five years ago jumped to the forefront of her mind. The one Clay had given her just before her first performance as a signed artist. That had not been a brotherly kiss, but that's all that had ever happened between them, so Van did her best to box him into the brother category in her mind. Most of the time, she failed miserably.

"Physically, he's fine. Not a scratch, which is a miracle because his house was destroyed. His work truck is gone. The tornado must have picked it up, because they haven't found it in any of the rubble yet."

Van's belly clenched as nausea washed over her for a whole new reason. Clay didn't have the resources she did. He didn't even have his mom anymore. Van had helped Clay and Bryant get their construction business off the ground when they'd finished their four years in the Army a couple of years ago. She knew they were growing, so they had to invest all of the money they made into their next project, into their ever-growing staff. Clay's work truck had been an investment, and Clay did carpentry work out of his garage. If he'd lost his tools, his vehicle, he might not be able to work, and he really could stand to lose everything.

"Oh my god. How can I help?"

"Clay will be fine. He has insurance on everything. And he and Pebbles are staying with me for now."

Van almost smiled. She'd forgotten about the dog. That had been the only time Clay had texted her in the last year. Randomly at the end of March, Clay had sent her a photo of a little gray speckled puppy with the caption, *Remember how I always wanted a dog?*

Of course, Van's response had been to squeal in delight via a series of emojis she knew would drive Clay crazy, followed by *OMG! YOU GOT ME A DOG?!!*

His answer had been somewhat along the lines of *No stupid, I got me a dog, but you can pet her if you ever come back to Wellville.*

Van had told him he could count on it.

After that? Crickets. Including when Van *had* actually been in town for her birthday. Apparently, Clay and Pebbles had spent that weekend away with *Amber*. Whoever that was. Not the same woman whose house he'd spent most of Christmas at. Daisy? Darlene? Darla?

Van had retaliated by tweeting the photo of the dog he'd sent her and tagging Clay in it so he would get 5000 notifications every day for a couple of weeks, which he would hate.

"Let me know when your flight is?" her dad asked.

"As soon as Phoenix and I can get on a plane, I imagine."

"Phoenix is coming?" He sounded surprised.

That was strange. Van hadn't traveled without Phoenix basically since they'd met. She was like Van's security blanket.

"Is that okay?"

"Of course, it's fine. Just come home, Van."

Her dad sounded so distraught, and Van wanted to go to him and let him nestle his kids under his wing like the mother hen he was.

Van and Phoenix were on a plane first thing the next morning. It was only after they were at 30,000 feet that Phoenix gave Van the rundown of how the media had been exploding while Van had been sleeping.

Bishop had denied everything, of course, even after he'd been very publicly arrested on his favorite surfing beach that morning and taken in for questioning. He'd even looked gorgeous while he was being arrested, with his perfect combination of surfer meets Hollywood beefcake. He was tall with broad shoulders and well-defined muscles. He wore his beard fashionably sculpted and his long, wavy brown hair pulled back in a man bun. He had to have somehow orchestrated his arrest on the beach, where everyone could see it happen. There would have been paparazzi everywhere as his chest glistened with salt water. In the pictures Van had seen, he'd even had an attractive dusting of sand on his arms and shoulders. He looked like a fucking Billabong ad, and Van was sure he'd done it on purpose. Clearly, he was too pretty, too unassuming, to be guilty.

God, she wished she'd had a chance to scratch his eyes out.

As far as she knew, he was still being held. That's all the detective had said when they'd let Van know they'd arrested Bishop. The police hadn't been happy when she'd told them she was leaving the state, but there was no way she was going to stay in California when Wellville was in ruins. She'd told them that her lawyers would be in touch and that they were absolutely still pursuing charges.

Van hoped Bishop rotted in prison, even as she rubbed the spot over heart again. She wasn't sure how long it would be before that stopped hurting. Considering it still stung like hell when she peed, she wanted to believe that that was reason enough to get rid of that particular pain. But nope, that bison still sat on her chest.

When Phoenix handed over Van's phone, there were close to five million Twitter notifications and almost as many emails. People were spamming the Van Birch Facebook page and the Instagram account. Van didn't even run those. Phoenix and her assistant took care of all of that. Van didn't even usually answer her own email. The only social media Van curated herself was Twitter. She wasn't about to open the app yet. After the articles and TV clips Phoenix had shown her, Van was liable to go on some angry Twitter rants of her own.

The general consensus was that she was pulling some sort of new, sick publicity stunt. While the Van Birch brand was known for doing zany things to stay on the national radar, those had been stunts like a guerilla performance beneath the Hollywood sign and orchestrating conflict for *Pop Star*. She would never fake her own rape.

This was supposed to be post-#MeToo. They, as a culture, were supposed to be listening to women now. Women and victims were supposed to be heard when they spoke out against their abusers. They were supposed to be believed. But public opinion so far was firmly planted on Bishop's side. There was no way Bishop could be guilty. He was too good, too attractive, too much fun to have done anything so heinous. And he and Van had known each other for years. Van had to be making it up, and now Bishop had to suffer the indignity of a public arrest and a police investigation while Van begged for sympathy.

"Sympathy for what?" Van yelled at Phoenix as she paced the aisle. Phoenix didn't even blanch. She had probably seen the storm clouds finally catching up to Van all morning. "My second album outsold my first by hundreds of thousands of copies. The reality show's ratings are higher than they have ever been. I am topping my game every year. Van Birch is a goddamn household name. Why the fuck would I be making this up?"

Phoenix lifted one shoulder and let it drop. She looked bored, but Van knew she was bored with the answer to the question and not with Van. Phoenix was likely feeling every single one of the things Van felt now.

"Because Bishop is a powerful, attractive man. There are whole websites dedicated him and to the two of you as a couple. The public thinks of him as your playful, loveable manager, because that's how you portrayed him on TV. They don't want to believe he's a monster."

Van collapsed back into her chair. "He's not a monster."

Phoenix raised her eyebrows. "Isn't he?"

"Maybe." Her heart thumped in her chest as she recalled the fear. The helplessness. The pain. The feeling of stepping outside her body and then the slamming back home just in time to run. "I don't know, Fe." Van sat with her head in her hands, allowing her hair to form a protective curtain around her as tears pinged at the back of her eyes. Again.

"It's okay to feel confused," Phoenix said, her hand making soothing strokes down Van's back. "You were in a relationship with him."

"Should I have seen this coming?" Van asked, curling to the side so she could rest her head on Phoenix's shoulder.

Van felt Phoenix's head shake. "I didn't always like everything about him, but I never thought he was capable of this. Most of the time, I thought he was probably good for you."

Van rolled closer into Phoenix as she remembered the

blogger who had insisted The Van Birch Incident, as it had already been branded, only proved that Bishop and Van had been sleeping together since her last tour. Then the blogger had highlighted every piece of footage from the latest season of *Pop Star* that pointed to the fact. The blogger was incredibly astute, because she had pinpointed the exact time at which Bishop and Van had started having sex. Then the blogger turned it all against Van somehow, by ending her video with, *We all know "No means no," but it's obvious Van Birch has been playing Bishop for her own ends for a year now, so I think we can all come to our own conclusions on this one.*

Because Van having a relationship, even a relatively quiet one, with Bishop meant that Van was cheating on Bryant Wilder. And America loved Bryant almost more than they loved Van. Bryant was the beautiful boy Van had grown up with in Wellville. He had dark hair that was always a little too long and chunky black glasses. When she'd known him as a teenager, he'd been too tall for his frame. But then he and Clay had joined the Army together, and both of them had filled out. Now he was broad and strong and probably just as sexy as she used to think Bishop was. As many times as they'd made out for the camera, Van couldn't drum up that sort of passion for Bryant.

She loved him fiercely and had cried in relief when Bryant had finally called her the night before to let her know that he and his house had been untouched by the tornado. She had been sick with worry for him all day. She kept imagining the quiet, studious boy who had been suspended from school for starting a fight with Rick Shroeder after she'd rejected him and he'd told the entire school that Van's tits were too small to be worth it anyway. Van hadn't even really known Bryant then; he'd just been Clay's friend that hung out at the house. When Van had asked Bryant why he'd done that, he'd shrugged and rubbed his knuckles, which were scuffed and bruised. He'd said, "You don't talk about women that way—and Clay's like a brother to me. And if you're Clay's family, you're my family."

Since that day, Van would have gladly stepped in front of a bullet for that man. In high school, Van had fantasized that her dad had fallen in love with Bryant's mom, a zany travel writer, rather than Clay's mom so that Bryant would be her actual brother. That way Clay could have been—well, whatever Clay was. Nothing to her, it turned out.

She'd called Clay anyway. Mostly because she didn't want to disappoint her dad. Clay had answered on the second ring with an impatient sounding, "Yup?"

"Clay?"

"Van, shit."

She snorted. "I guess that means you're okay then."

"Better than you, I imagine."

Van winced. He must have heard her suck in her breath, because he said, "Fuck, Van. I'm sorry. That came out wrong."

Greeeeeeaat. So Clay knew then. "Yeah, well. How's Pebbles?"

"Fine. Scared. Won't leave my side."

"Makes sense."

There was a long pause. Van could hear people shouting in the background. It sounded busy where he was. She had no way of knowing, but she imagined Clay standing in the middle of utter devastation. One foot rested with a bent knee on top of a pile of wood debris. The sun would be beating down on his taut, golden skin. A wicked hot wind would be ruffling his red-blonde hair, and he'd have a day's worth of stubble over his square jaw. His brow would be crinkled into a frown, his ice-blue eyes sparking with discontent.

It could have been the start of a movie or the cover of a romance novel, except then he'd have to have his shirt off. Under normal circumstances, Van would not object to ogling a shirtless Clay, but today, she didn't want to think about it. If she didn't already understand how fucked up she'd been by recent events, not getting hot and bothered by the idea of Clay without a shirt would definitely have been a red flag.

Van thought Clay was a dick, but a hot dick.

"Sooooo," she drew out the "O" because she had no idea what she was going to say next. "I guess I'll see you tomorrow?"

"You're coming home." It wasn't a question, but from his tone of voice, Van guessed that her dad hadn't told him *that* part. It was not like Robin Birch to leave out details.

"And you're staying with us, right?"

"For now." His voice sounded distant. "We'll see how it goes once Amber gets back to town."

Van was not fucked up enough to not roll her eyes at that. Clay was still with Amber. Spiffy.

"Well, I guess I'll cuddle Pebbles tomorrow then," Van said, then hung up really fast.

After that awkward conversation, Van was glad Bryant was the one picking them up from the airfield. Maybe once she got home, Van could pretend Clay wasn't even there.

Van snorted at her own thoughts, earning a glare from Phoenix, who was working on her tablet. Van had never been able to pretend Clay wasn't around. It was the curse of your dad marrying your fourteen-year-old crush's mom and having him move into your house. You were never not aware of his presence—or at least Van hadn't been. Not until the day he'd left for bootcamp when Van was eighteen.

"Shit," Phoenix said. "Mother-fucking shithead mother-fucker."

This was not an unusual occurrence. Phoenix might look demure and professional in her navy pencil skirt and styled red hair, but she could make a sailor blush with that mouth of hers.

"What now?" Van asked.

Phoenix flipped her tablet so that Van could see the newest hashtag trending on Twitter.

#NotBishop

Super.

Because that's how it went, wasn't it? Phoenix had already said it. Nobody wanted to think of such a nice guy as capable of such a deplorable act. But the thing was, most guys seemed like nice guys until suddenly they weren't. And there was no good way to know who to trust. Not for sure.

Van Birch Flees Home After Tornado, Sexual Assault Charges

Friday, July 13th was an unlucky day for Van Birch's hometown of Wellville, Kansas. An F-5 tornado tore through the western Kansas town Friday evening, leaving about a quarter of the population without homes. Don't worry though, sources say the Birch family home is whole and intact. Bryant Wilder's house is also untouched, and we think it's safe to say that we are all relieved this bespectacled hottie is hale and hearty and probably already looking for his next bout of fisticuffs. Notable resident and Van Birch's hunky stepbrother, Clay Noble's home was demolished.

Rumors are that Van Birch is swooping in to save the day with her reality-TV crew in tow. Birch's staff released a statement that they planned to coordinate rebuilding efforts and put a call out for donations. Raise your hand if you're hoping that means a whole season of Clay Noble and Bryant Wilder shirtless and sweating as they rebuild the town, because we are here for that. Birch's camp made no mention of the sexual assault charges the starlet filed against former manager Henry Bishop, but as Bishop was still in police custody this morning, we presume Birch plans to pursue charges from afar.

How convenient that a tornado came along at just the right time to provide the pop star an excuse to escape the scrutiny of the controversial accusations she's making against fan favorite, Bishop. We've always known Van was powerful, but we hear they are taking odds in Vegas on whether she can actually control the weather.

2

———————

eeling Bryant's arms close around her when they landed in Kansas was possibly the closest thing to comfort Van had felt in days. She didn't care that she was sore all over or that she felt like somebody had cleaved her chest open, Bryant Wilder was the one person who could make her feel better with nothing more than a hug. They swayed on the tarmac, and Van had the feeling Bryant was attempting to absorb her into himself, like that might keep her safe. "I'm so glad you're here," she said.

She could feel the camera flashes, hear Phoenix answering questions in the background, but the peace in Bryant's arms, the solace of him, was all Van could focus on.

"I'm sorry I wasn't there," he said.

"Well, I'm glad you weren't, or you'd have been in jail —again." Van reached up and smoothed a finger over the aging bruise on Bryant's chin. He'd been in the news the day before the tornado for getting into a fight at Tessa's

Nightclub. Phoenix had been furious with him, but with everything else that had happened, no one even remembered Bryant Wilder the troublemaker. All they were going to see was Bryant the doting boyfriend.

Bryant captured Van's hand and placed a kiss to the center of her palm. "It would have been worth it," he said.

"Not to me. I prefer you at my beck and call, thank you."

That forced a laugh out of Bryant's chest, and he kissed her on the forehead. "Come on, V. We've got water bottles to hand out."

Van pulled in a deep breath. Work. Right. She would do it, even if the last thing she wanted was to be in front of other people at the moment.

Bryant must have noticed her hesitation, because he squeezed her hand and said, "Hey, you know we don't have to do this, right? We can go to my place, crawl in bed, and cry our eyes out. Or we can hit Tessa's and get very, very drunk."

Van grinned despite herself. "I still want to do all of that over the next couple of days, but this afternoon isn't about me. It's about doing what I can for the people who support me."

"You sure?" He furrowed his brow, like Van might be missing something, but Van nodded.

"I'm sure." She let him usher her into the waiting car. But once they were on the road, leaving the cameras behind, Bryant slipped to his side of the bench seat and rolled his head back against the rest with his eyes closed. "Are you okay?" Van asked.

He gave her a tired smile. "It's been a rough few days," he said, running his fingers over the bruise on his jaw.

"But don't worry about me. I'm mostly sore from digging my neighbors out of their basements."

That was Bryant, selfless until the end, not worried about himself but what he could do for everyone else. Including her. He was probably exhausted. But as he rubbed his chin again, a glaze slipped over his eyes that hinted at so much more than fatigue.

Clay flipped off his phone and stared at the wall as he contemplated turning off the "Van Birch" news notification for the millionth time. Following Van's every move was the most exquisite torture. When that little email hit his inbox every night, Clay knew exactly what Van had been up to—or allegedly up to—every day. A good portion of the stories were outlandish, like suggesting Van conjured a tornado that left people dead and homeless so she had an excuse to escape L.A. The rest were little more than colorful captions to go along with paparazzi snaps. Clay would never admit it out loud, but he lived for those photos.

He unlocked his phone again just to stare at the photo of Van they'd stuck into the article about the tornado. They'd done a side-by-side with an aerial shot of the path of destruction through Wellville. In the photo of Van, she appeared completely unconcerned with the devastation. No matter that it had been taken the day before everything happened. Van and Phoenix were leaving a coffee shop in L.A. Van wore tight black leggings and a billowy white shirt that exposed one smooth, tan shoulder and a good portion of her black sports bra. The yoga mat slung over her other shoulder made it clear the girls had just finished their morning yoga, but rather than looking sweaty and frazzled, Van glowed.

She smiled, laughing at something Phoenix had said, no doubt. Clay touched a finger to Van's face, then flipped the phone off again as a pang of sadness reverberated through his chest. Van hadn't been smiling earlier that day.

She'd grinned and posed for pictures with fans while they helped hand out rations and sleeping bags at the temporary shelter at the YMCA. But Clay could see the shiny veneer for what it was—nothing more than a mask for her fans.

He had asked Bryant how she was doing when they'd had a moment alone together. Bryant, who was sporting a yellowing bruise on his jaw, had only given Clay a pained frown and shook his head. Not good then.

They'd all spent the afternoon at the shelter, then Phoenix had arranged for a taco bar to be delivered to the house for dinner. After that, Clay had made himself scarce so Robin and Van could have some time alone together. If there was ever a time when a girl needed her dad, it was probably now. They'd sat at the piano in the front room together for hours. Robin played while Van sang. That piano was where both of them went when times got hard. Clay didn't think he'd seen them there together since his mother had died two years ago.

Both times, he'd sat at the top of the stairs listening to them. Two years ago, silent tears had coursed down his cheeks as he'd listened to them mourn with music. That night he had been such an unfathomable mixture of bereaved and angry and jealous that Van and Robin still had each other while he had no one that he couldn't bring himself to do what he really wanted to do—which was retrieve his old guitar from his high school bedroom and join them. Part of him hadn't felt welcome. The tie that had bound him to Robin and Van was gone, and he'd been reeling so hard from the loss of his mother that he'd assumed for a few weeks that with her death, he was going to be alone in the world.

Robin had proved him wrong. Even Van moved forward as if their relationship hadn't changed, and eventually Clay realized that if he had joined them that night, they probably would have welcomed him with open arms and tearful smiles.

Tonight, though, he knew both Robin and Van needed this time together. Clay was so grateful that Van still had Robin to come home to. And he had Pebbles to keep him company. She lay by his side for two hours while he stroked her soft puppy ears and just listened as his heart broke.

Clay had never felt more helpless. After all the steps he'd taken to protect Van from the stupid guys she dated in high school... Hell, after the steps he'd taken to protect her from him. It wasn't like the Army had been a new idea to Clay. He'd been considering it since he was seventeen. He'd only stayed and gone to community college to make his mom happy, but he'd finally enlisted at twenty because he couldn't get Van out of his head. He'd been finding it more and more difficult to ignore his feelings for her. The sort of feelings that he absolutely was not allowed to have for her.

And he hadn't wanted to hold her back.

Clay knew that if he'd been able to date her, he would

have asked her to stay in Kansas. To stay with him. For him. It wouldn't have been fair to Van. She'd been destined for so much more. So Clay had enlisted in the Army and taken himself out of the equation entirely.

They'd only stopped playing an hour ago, and it was coming up on midnight. Clay had been torturing himself reading the different accounts in the media of what had happened and scrolling through pictures of her smiling. He even laughed at the one of her licking Bryant's face, even as he wished for the millionth time that there was a way for him to trade places with his best friend and not be a creepy bastard or a shitty friend.

But what was a man who was in love with a woman he could never have supposed to do?

It wasn't like Clay hadn't tried to forget her. He'd fucked. He'd dated. He currently had a girlfriend that he genuinely liked. It didn't change how much he still loved Van.

He covered his eyes with his arm. He should be asleep.

Clay hadn't really slept since the storm. He was exhausted, physically and emotionally. But how was he supposed to sleep when he'd lost everything but his dog and the clothes on his back? He was so full of restless energy; he wanted to fix everything. There wasn't much he could do yet. Helping clear away the rubble and debris eased some of the restlessness. It's what he'd been doing the last two days until it had been time to go to the shelter. Meeting those people, some who were injured or who had lost loved one on top of losing their homes. It had almost made everything worse. Handing out blankets and bottled water felt like slapping a band-aid on a gushing artery, and Clay felt petty for complaining about living in Bryant's ill-fitting clothes.

He looked forward to putting the town back together. Rebuilding the houses that had been blown apart and setting Wellville to rights might ease this feeling that the world had shifted beneath him without his permission. Maybe he'd wake up one day and find he wasn't walking perpendicular to the ground but on it once more.

Clay had a feeling that rebuilding other people's houses wasn't going to do that for him. That only having *his* home back would. That wasn't going to happen. Clay had put everything he had into building that house the first time. The insurance would only cover the cost of his mortgage, leaving him nothing left to rebuild with. He truly had lost everything.

Clay had never been more thankful for the time and expense he and Bryant took to put a basement in every one of the few new houses they'd built since starting their company. Clay was alive because of that basement, and so were so many other people across the town. It had been the ones in the slab houses that hadn't made it.

The storm had come on like most summer storms do, purple clouds gathering in the western sky. They'd had the guys pack it in early and lock everything down so they wouldn't lose tools if the winds got high.

The sky grew dark just as everyone left the job site. Clay had been planning to go to the grocery store since he was down to cottage cheese and a two-year-old jar of pickles in the fridge. But he'd been worried about Pebbles. There had only been a couple of bad storms this year, and she'd curled up by his side, shaking, through both of them.

He hadn't wanted the pup to be alone, so he'd headed straight home.

Clay used his garage for carpentry work, and as he screeched to a stop in his driveway and hopped out of his truck, the rain slammed down on his shoulders. He sprinted up the front porch steps just in time to miss the hail. The weather app on his phone went off at the same time the tornado sirens sounded.

Pebbles ran with him into the basement where Clay tucked the shaking dog beneath him and crouched. The unmistakable sound of a freight train barreled down on top of them. His knees ached from kneeling on the concrete, and Pebbles whined as the storm raged on, but neither moved, even hours after silence fell. Eventually, he must have fallen asleep, because when Pebbles licked his cheek, he woke to faint, dusky gray light shining in the egress windows.

Clay had to clear away debris to make it up the basement stairs. He'd convinced himself that he'd have a house when he made it free. When he emerged into what should have been the laundry room, there was nothing but open sky. The sun was just breaking over the horizon, and every house within two blocks had been flattened along with the trees. Some cars still sat covered in splintered wood in the driveways, but Clay couldn't see his truck anywhere.

A few of his neighbors had also picked their way out of their basements, so he and Pebbles made themselves useful, helping the families get out and scavenge what they could. Clay tried to check on Robin, his only family left in town, but Clay's phone was dead, and nobody else had signal.

He worked for hours. Clay's throat burned with thirst, and his stomach felt like it was caving in on itself, but barely anybody had any food, and what had been found had gone straight to the kids. No one complained.

About mid-morning, Robin's black SUV pulled up in front of the rubble that used to be the house Clay had built with his own two hands. He parked in the middle of the street. Nobody cared. It was chaos. Robin wrapped Clay in the longest, warmest hug he'd ever received from anyone that wasn't his mother.

"I was so worried about you, son," he said. Clay could hear the tears biting at the back of Robin's throat. "I had just about steeled myself to drive out here and uncover your body."

"I'm sorry," Clay said, unable to hold back the grief that tugged at the back of his eyes. Robin had been the only father figure he had ever known. And even if he and Clay's mom had problems sometimes, and they'd been distant this past year, Clay still respected the hell out of him. He hadn't meant to worry Robin, and the water in his eyes and tight strain in Robin's jaw got to Clay like nothing else. "I was helping everyone, and my phone is dead."

Robin pulled back and wiped the tears from Clay's cheek like he was five, even as he let his own fall freely. "I know you were," he said. "Don't be sorry. It's the right thing to do."

Then he sucked in a deep breath and stood beside Clay surveying the devastation. Robin swiped at his eyes with his wrist. "Who else needs help?"

Clay shrugged. "Everybody, but I've been trying to help the families with kids first."

They spent the day helping neighbors dig out whatever of value was left in the rubble. Robin drove whoever needed a ride to a family member's house or to one of the shelters that had been set up, while Clay did most of the heavy lifting.

Robin let Clay charge his phone in his SUV, and not long after lunch, a sandwich bar that Robin had funded out of his own pocket was set up on somebody's former front door and a couple of saw horses.

As the sun started to dip in the sky, phones started coming to life with voicemails and text notifications. Robin excused himself and took refuge next to his car to call Van. Clay shot Bryant, his only other close friend in the city, a text before he texted Amber back to let her know he was fine. There was no response from Bryant after a few minutes, and Clay told himself that it was just because Bryant's phone was dead. But the dread and worry he'd been battling all day rose with every minute that went by without an answer.

Clay circled Robin's SUV, about to demand they go check on Bryant as the real world began to settle back down on his shoulders. He needed to call the crew and see how they and their families were doing. He needed to get Marie, their office girl, to start sourcing rebuilding supplies, because they were about to have more business than they could handle. And then there was all the bullshit he was going to have to do personally to rebuild his life from the ground up.

A ball of anxiety formed in Clay's stomach at the thought of how much debt he was about to get into—again—when he saw Robin's face.

Robin's mouth was hitched in a sneer, and his eyes

held a murderous gleam. He was already red and sweaty from being out in the hot July sun, but his flush of fury was impossible to miss.

Clay froze. The flush on Robin's face deepened as he listened to whatever was happening on the phone.

"What—?" Clay started, but Robin held his hand up.

"I want to talk to her," he said. When Robin had used that tone of voice on Clay as a teenager, it was all he could do not to cower and hop to. The man was a svelte, tennis-playing attorney with salt and pepper hair, but he could have been a drill sergeant with the way he commanded respect.

"I need you to check if she's awake," he said. "Now."

It was afternoon in L.A. by now too, but it didn't surprise Clay that Van was still in bed with the way she could party sometimes. Or maybe she was sick; that would better explain the scowl on Robin's face but not the anger.

Clay had been about to ask when a loud crash sounded behind them as one of his neighbors tried to unearth his car. Phoenix—Clay assumed Robin was speaking to Phoenix— must have asked, because Robin explained what the noise was.

Clay couldn't help himself anymore, "Robin, what's going on?"

But Robin shook his head and said into the phone, "There was a tornado here last night, Fe. A bad one."

Clay cocked his head to the side. Since when had Robin called Phoenix, "Fe?"

"I'm fine," he said. "We haven't gotten ahold of Bryant yet. Clay isn't hurt, but he lost his house along with about half the town."

Robin spent the next couple of minutes assuring Phoenix they were alright, before finishing with "I'm more worried about Van." Then he moved the phone to the side and said to Clay, who was tense with dread, "Something happened between Van and Bishop last night, and Van's been sedated."

Clay's heart dropped into his stomach, which was already somewhere around the vicinity of his toes. "Where is she?" he asked. His voice a rasp of its usual tone as his mind rapid fired all the different reasons why someone would be sedated. None of which were good.

"She's at Phoenix's."

Good. They were away from the public eye, and even if Phoenix didn't like Clay, he respected the fact that she was as mean as a mountain cat and twice as fierce. She'd claw Bishop's eyes out before she let him anywhere near Van again—whatever had happened.

Clay was about to ask what happened when Robin's attention switched back to the phone at his ear. Clay watched his eyes well up and heard Robin's voice crack as he said Van's childhood nickname into the phone.

Clay gave them their privacy and planted himself on the curb in front of where his house had stood. Pebbles, who'd been sleeping in the shade of the sandwich table, loped over and collapsed next to him. Clay rubbed her silky ears as he searched for the latest news on his phone.

He didn't believe the first article he read. He decided they were exaggerating. But after three more articles all in the same vein, Clay's blood was boiling. He'd always thought he'd live a long, humble midwestern life, working hard, settling down with some woman eventually. Clay had always thought he wanted to be a family man. But as he locked his phone and glanced up at Robin, Clay knew he was going to spend the rest of his life in prison for murdering Henry Bishop.

Robin talked Clay down, at least for the moment. An hour later, Van called to check in on Clay, and he was awkward and stupid on the phone, because it should have been the other way around. Clay should have called her first.

Today they'd given one another the perfunctory sibling hug when she arrived and hadn't said two words to one another since.

The last article he'd read just now had been a thesis on how Van had been cheating on Bryant with Bishop, and when Bishop had broken things off with her, Van had concocted the rape story to get back at him. Clay stroked the top of Pebbles's head, thinking about how the first part was true at least. Bishop and Van hadn't exactly been secretive about their infatuation with one another over the last few months. It infuriated Clay that she would do that to Bryant, even though Bryant pretended he wasn't bothered. Not that he'd have much room to criticize. Bryant had had his fair share of one-night stands—mostly with men—in the last few years.

It was a cowardly thing to do, Bryant using his bisexuality as an excuse to cheat on Van. As if Van wasn't enough for Bryant all on her own. Clay wanted to kill him every time it happenedThe two of them had their own set of rules when it came to their relationship, and in the end, it wasn't any of Clay's business. There had never been any room for Clay to start a relationship with Van, so Bryant had won the friendly competition for Van's heart before it had even started. Any time Clay had tried to talk to

Bryant about his long-distance relationship with Van, Bryant shut it down, so Clay had given up trying to ask a long time ago.

A soft knock at his door startled Clay from his thoughts. Both he and Pebbles sprang up when they saw Van standing in his doorway. She'd changed out of her skinny jeans into a pair of running shorts, but she still wore the long-sleeved black t-shirt, even though it still had to be ninety degrees outside. Her eyes were sunken, and she wore the vacant expression Clay knew from the days after his mom died.

Pebbles hopped off the bed and wiggled her excited puppy dance around Van's feet while Clay congratulated himself on not being caught in his underwear.

Van's eyes slid over his shirtless chest and down to his gym shorts and bare feet, then back up to his face. "I'm sorry, you were sleeping. I'll just—" Van turned to go.

Clay crossed the room in three strides. "Not yet. Stay." He tugged on her wrist.

Van winced and flinched away, cursing under her breath.

Clay raised his arms so his hands were visible and stepped clear of the doorway. "Sorry. Sorry. Come in, please."

Van rubbed at her wrist and took a tentative step into the room as Pebbles circled her feet.

"I can't remember the last time I was in here," she said, looking around the space.

It was more or less unchanged from when Clay was a teenager. There was a double bed with a simple blue duvet. A quilt that one of Van's aunts had made lay folded at foot. Baseball and football trophies sat on the dresser.

Clay's guitar—the old one—was propped in the corner. Not the nice one he'd splurged on after his deployment. That one hadn't survived the storm.

Van stopped when she stood in the middle of the room and scrunched her toes into the rug. "It looks the same."

Clay approached with caution, hands casually at his sides. "Mom and Robin didn't change your room either."

Van's room, at the other end of the hall, was lighter than the deep blue and dark trim in his room. Everything in her room was white and bright and airy with pops of hot pink and black and gold. Clay had always thought of them as her colors.

"I miss your mom." Van folded her arms over her chest and rubbed her shoulders like she was cold as she turned in a circle, still surveying his teenage boy decor. "If she was still here, she's who I would have wanted to talk to tonight."

She revolved to face Clay, and she looked so lost and so small. That's when he saw them. Her sleeve had ridden up, revealing a ring of angry purple bruises around her wrist. His instinct was to grab her forearm and pull her wrist up to eye level to examine the marks more closely.

Clay settled for taking a small step closer and snagging her fingers in his. She stiffened but didn't jerk away. He pulled her arm straight, and like a rag doll, she let him. When Clay pushed back her sleeve, she looked over her shoulder instead of at the bruises that were still angry and raised.

"What is this?" Clay asked. He knew, but somehow seeing the evidence made it more real than any gossip column on the internet.

Van slipped from his grasp and collapsed backwards onto the bed.

"What do you think it is?" she said to the ceiling.

Clay sat beside her. "Where else did he hurt you?"

Van sniffed, and that's when Clay noticed the silent tears streaking from the corners of her eyes back into her hair. One hand moved to the hem of her shirt, the other to the waistband of her shorts. His mind struggled to interpret her actions as she bared her midriff to him.

How many times had Clay fantasized about this exact situation? Van on his bed, undressing for him, but not like this. Not when her stomach and hips were peppered with fingerprint shaped bruises. Not when a handprint nearly the size of his own marked the swell of her hip.

"Jesus, Van." His fingers itched to trace the outside of the biggest bruise as he imagined the pain of it, but he didn't dare touch her.

Her breath hitched on a sob in her throat, and her voice was thick with tears when she said, "I told him no."

Clay lifted his hands, signaling that he was going to hug her, she gave a brief nod, and he gathered her into his arms then. He held her as she cried. Every now and then she'd say things like, "I'm so stupid," or "I thought he loved me." Clay shushed her and stroked her silky hair until she quieted. Still she clung to him, her arms around his neck, her head resting on his shoulder.

Clay eased back onto the pillows, covered her with the handmade quilt, and kissed the top of her head.

He had never seen Van like this. She didn't do broken and vulnerable. She was sassy, defiant, independent, bold. But as she dozed on him, she felt tiny and delicate. She couldn't weigh more than a hundred pounds.

"He was drunk," she said against Clay's neck. She'd been so quiet, he'd thought she'd fallen asleep, but the tickle of her whispered words over his throat said otherwise.

"That's not an excuse."

Van didn't seem to hear him. "We'd been bickering all night, and he'd started saying the weirdest things, and when I argued back—" she cut herself off from voicing what happened next.

Clay's grip tightened on her reflexively, as if he could protect her from the memories even as rage burned inside him. "I'm so sorry, Van."

"He wanted me to move in with him. Was trying to get me to break it off with Bryant. And I was going to. I thought I loved him. I thought—" This time her words were choked off by another sob, and Clay understood why she'd wanted his mom. She wasn't just dealing with trauma. Van was heartbroken.

"That monster didn't deserve you," Clay said. "And you deserve so much better than this."

She snuggled further into his tear-damp chest. "Thank you for being nice to me."

The words were out of Clay's mouth before he could stop them. "Of course. I love you."

Her ear lay right over his heart, so there was no way she didn't notice how his heart rate jumped from lazy to pounding the second he realized what he'd said.

To cover it up, Clay gave her the lamest lie, "Besides, what are brothers for?"

Van snorted and said in a voice that was much closer to her usual snarky tone, "Can we just agree that we are never going to have that kind of relationship?"

Clay didn't exactly need the reminder that his affections were one-sided. They might be sharing an intimate moment, but he had zero pretensions when it came to Van's regard for him. Clay was the guy who cramped her style as a teenager and was only tolerated because her producers liked to toss him into a few episodes of her show each season.

Tonight was an anomaly.

"Well, I'm here for you, if you need me," Clay said.

They lapsed into silence after that. Van fell asleep. Eventually, Clay drifted off too. At some point, the creak of the door awakened him, and Clay half rose to find Robin peeking his head inside. Robin's eyes softened when they landed on Van. He nodded at Clay, then closed the door.

When Clay woke the next morning. Van was gone.

Pop Star Turned Humanitarian

In the last week, singer and reality-TV show star Van Birch has appeared on major news networks to publicize relief efforts for hometown, Wellville, Kansas. One-quarter of the moderately sized Kansas town's population is now without homes, and the local high school was destroyed only weeks before the school year was meant to resume.

Birch is drumming up sympathy along with enough financial support to rebuild a majority of the town before winter. She has partnered with corporate sponsors and longtime boyfriend and contractor Bryant Wilder to organize enough construction crews to get the work done fast.

So far, Birch has been grimly mute on the topic of pending sexual assault charges against former manager Henry Bishop.

Bishop has denied all charges, citing a lover's spat, and is currently out on bail pending further investigation from the Los Angeles County Sheriff's Department.

Meanwhile, Birch has been photographed palling around town with Wilder. Despite the obvious recent hiccups in their relationship and the lingering bruise from Wilder's recent bar brawl, the pair seems happy to be reunited. Take a look at the photos and tell us what you think. Does a smiling, besotted Van Birch seem like a recently wronged woman, or is this dust up with Bishop just another of her many publicity stunts?

---

3

*T*he main floor of her dad's house had become command central over the last two weeks. They should probably have rented an office space, but Van's producer liked the house as a setting. The studio had lent them interns to keep everything organized, so Van wasn't complaining about saving an extra thousand a month.

Not that money was really an issue, but she *was* footing a huge part of this bill herself. It was one-hundred percent worth it, but agreeing to pay the wages of all the temporary construction workers they were going to need was no joke. It made Van a little queasy to transfer that much money out of her account and into the relief fund Phoenix had set up. You'd think by now she'd be used to having money, but she wasn't.

Van had been doing remote interviews from the front room next to her dad's piano. She was positioned so her dad's baby grand stood behind her, poetically musical she supposed, but a stark contrast between what her family still had and what so many others had lost.

Van's entire production crew had moved into the historic hotel downtown. The only damage that place had suffered was the loss of its sign and a few windows. Her producers were eating this activity up. It was supposed to be a minimal filming season as she'd intended to be writing her new album, but all this hustle and bustle made for better TV.

Van was nowhere near ready to write her album.

The idea to stay in Wellville and help the city rebuild had come to her during the night she'd spent in Clay's room. She'd always meant to help out; aside from being with her dad, that was part of the reason she'd come home in the first place, but the idea that *she* could stay to see it all through hadn't occurred to her until she was drifting off to sleep in Clay's arms and she realized that she didn't want to leave.

Clay had been really nice to her—probably better than he'd ever been, and she'd cried all over him even though he'd basically just lost everything. Van had never felt so guilty, but she also hadn't slept as well as she'd slept that night since then. Van kind of wanted to try sleeping next to him again. For science.

Van had woken Phoenix up at dawn that morning and relayed her evil plan. Despite her cranky, pre-yoga snarl, Phoenix was all over it.

Helping her town recover, giving those families back their homes, was worth the nightmare of coordinating with insurance companies and demanding corporate sponsors. Van's days this past two weeks had resembled little more than a series of frantic phone calls interrupted by trainer-mandated workouts.

She usually spent her evenings with Bryant, dancing and drinking and eating three bites of food before she collapsed into Bryant's bed and started all over. Van had a mission right now, a purpose, and that felt good.

That she was avoiding going back to L.A., back to her condo, and back to the possibility of running into Bishop on the street, which was something no one had had the guts to bring up to her.

Van had stayed mum on the topic, not that it had stopped even the top reporters on cable news networks from trying to direct her toward discussing Bishop. Off the air they'd even offered an in-depth one-on-one for her side of the story should she want it. Van had told them no, thank you.

Phoenix spent half her day fielding calls from overeager gossip rags. It had been her idea for Van and Bryant to parade around town together. They'd made a point of going out to dinner most nights and then for drinks at Tessa's. If Van wasn't careful, the tabloids were going to be talking about her alcoholism on top of everything else.

It wasn't like Van didn't like a drink; she could basically swim her way through a vat of whiskey if she wanted to, but she wasn't keen on getting plastered every night, reputation as a party girl or no. More often than not, it was Van easing Bryant into bed at night after he'd had one too many, with a dose of painkillers and a glass of water on his bedside table.

Despite enjoying the opportunity to stay up late and chat with Bryant, and finding out fun things like the bar brawl the day before the tornado hadn't been "a friendly misunderstanding" like he'd told Phoenix, but a fight over a woman—not that Bryant would say who—Van longed for more time to disappear into her room to wallow. She did whenever she could, claiming she needed to keep writing her new album.

Really, Van stared at the wall and scrolled through her social media for hours. There was a perverse pleasure in reading through the torrents of sexist vitriol to find the golden nugget of the one or two people out of thousands who believed her.

There were two main hashtags trending when it came to what the blogosphere had titled The Van Birch Incident. #notBishop hadn't surprised her. Everyone had a reason as to why Van would lie about what had happened, including Bishop, but very few people had been able to come up with why Bishop would lie. He was the victim for so many reasons--not in the least of which was because he didn't have a job anymore. Phoenix had paid him a huge severance, even though the thought of giving him money had actually caused Van to vomit.

A lawsuit had hit her lawyer's office just yesterday; Bishop was suing her for defamation of character. His lawyers claimed that Van's continued insistence that he had assaulted her harmed Bishop's present and future job prospects. She was unsympathetic. Her reply on the conference call with his lawyers had been, "Then he shouldn't have raped me."

That had been her public face. The strong, take no bullshit with a side of silliness she'd always given everyone. Except right now, Van was struggling to pull up the light-hearted side of her personality. The sarcastic quips weren't coming as quickly these days, nor the teasing jests. It was like she was dragging herself through a gray, murky swamp, and it took all her energy to keep moving forward. Wrenching that part of her that had licked Bryant's face on the red carpet wasn't a priority when she was weary to her bones. All she had energy for was laying on her bed and scrolling, trying to dredge up outrage at the way people were talking about her on the internet.

The worst posts were the ones that used the hashtag Phoenix had started. #justice4Van was supposed to have been a response to #notBishop, and while a few diehard fans and some writers Van actually really admired had jumped on the bandwagon, #justice4Van was trending mostly because some men's rights activists had gotten a hold of it and were posting it along with screenshots from *Pop Star* as supposed evidence of what a whore she was. Obviously, the hashtag was attached ironically. Even then, Van could barely muster outrage. What had she expected of people, really?

To be sympathetic? To care that she had put her trust in the wrong person? To sit in on the daily therapy sessions and witness the slow, cold terror creep into her as she realized that Bishop had been manipulating her for a while now? That he'd been isolating her from her friends, from her family. That his desire for her to publicly break up with Bryant and rely on Bishop more than Phoenix had been about Bishop's need to control her and her career. That he'd been slowly taking over every aspect of her life, and she'd been letting him because she'd thought she was falling in love with him.

Did Van expect her fans to realize that she didn't even

know who she was anymore? Itsy Bitsy Vanessa Birch who had taken her guitar with her everywhere growing up? Who had moved to L.A. with nothing but a YouTube channel and a dream? She had always only been meant for one thing. And Van had achieved that, but what did you do when your dream was interrupted? How was she supposed to find herself when everything that she'd ever wanted had happened—at least in part—because of the man who had abused her?

Van's stomach clenched as she remembered thinking Bishop was a dangerous man the first time she'd met him. Maybe she should have listened to her gut, but her gut had been more intrigued than wary. She'd wanted a taste of Bishop's particular brand of danger. He'd reeled her in with it, and he'd almost trapped her with it. What did that say about who Van was a person? Because even knowing what she did now, she was still attracted to that unpredictability.

She'd been weighing her two relationships in her mind.

The kernel of the idea had come up with her therapist that morning. That maybe she'd been having trouble writing because Van hadn't been as happy as she was pretending she'd been. Perhaps, the reason she couldn't settle down to write was that her creative side had gone into protection mode; Van just hadn't slowed down enough to notice.

It made sense, but that led into a conversation about how she had willingly been in a relationship with Bishop, and did that mean that she was complicit in what happened?

As much as everyone around her said no, Van felt like

it was somehow her fault, even when cognitively, she knew it wasn't. Van didn't know how to correct that dissonance. She didn't want to victim-blame herself, but it was difficult when it felt like the entire world, minus a handful, thought she deserved to be raped or worse.

Van had been torturing herself by scrolling through #justice4Van for more than an hour, enduring all the awful posts just to have that little thrill light up in her chest when people defended her. It was well known that Van did all her own tweeting, so each little heart was like a tally in her corner, a weight to remind her that Bishop had been the one to do wrong and that she'd done nothing to bring this on herself. Van replied to as many of her supporters as she could manage, even if it meant putting on that public mask that weighed so heavily on her shoulders right now.

@jessiV Thanks for your support! or *@mariw *fistbump* Thanks for having my back.*

But she had to take breaks, because the simplest thing had her sobbing into her pillow, like *Hugs @VanBmusic Stay strong. #metoo #justice4Van #trustwomen.*

She had yet to emerge from her pillow fortress of solitude when her phone vibrated like crazy on the mattress, receiving a volley of text messages all at once.

This wasn't unusual. Van's phone was usually blowing up from social media, but only a few people had her personal phone number.

Her tears stopped the second she saw Bishop's name on her home screen. She couldn't unlock her phone fast enough.

Van hadn't heard from him at all since she'd snuck out of her own house when she'd been thinking with nothing aside from her survival brain. She didn't remember calling Mills, didn't remember anything but the pounding, and she still wasn't sure if that had been her own heart or Bishop's fist on the bathroom door. She wasn't even sure how she'd gotten to the bathroom. Van didn't remember the ride to Phoenix's house, or even if she'd asked Mills to drive her there or if Mills just knew that's where Van needed to be. Only that Phoenix had been there when Van needed her most.

As much as Van had no interest in actually speaking with Bishop, she was curious what words he thought worth texting her after days of silence. She didn't expect an apology, especially considering the lawsuit, but part of her still hoped he'd show some remorse that he'd hurt her. Strictly speaking, he wasn't supposed to be contacting her at all, but Bishop had never been a rule follower. It was one of the things Van had liked best about him.

God, she had been so into Bishop. Probably more into him than any other guy since she realized her relentless crush on Clay Noble was doomed to live unfulfilled because her dad and Mary Beth kept calling him her brother.

Yeah. They'd made it pretty clear *that* kind of relationship between Van and Clay was totally off limits. And then Clay had gone and taken his older brother duties a little too seriously by dragging Brandon West out of her bedroom by his ear. She had the benefit of still holding on to the bedsheet, but Brandon had been completely nude. Van had been sixteen. Clay had been eighteen and still the high school dream boat: head quarterback, homecoming king. His hair had been redder then, shining almost copper in the sun. And he'd looked at Van like she made him sick.

Van's relationships with men had been shallow ever since. She didn't care if people thought she was easy. If Van had a connection with a guy, great. If not, why waste her time? She just hadn't had any good connections with anyone but Bryant in years—and while she loved Bryant, things between them had never been like that. He was her best friend, her beard, her protector.

But she'd found herself wishing more and more the past few weeks that Bryant and she could have a romantic relationship. It would be so easy if she could drum up something other than brotherly affection for the man who had been her fake boyfriend the past five years. Part of her thought that if they hadn't developed romantic feeling for each other after five years of regular make outs, maybe the never would. But maybe that was because they'd never truly given it a try? If Van could hide away with Bryant, maybe she could get over the fact that Bishop wasn't the man she'd thought he was.

Van had always thought Bishop was a hardworking, fun-loving, take-no-bull-shit surfer who also happened to be a fucking fantastic manager. There was no door, it seemed, that Bishop could not open, because he was charming and charismatic and gorgeous. Goddamnit, he'd even got her to fall in love with him.

Van Birch might be the household name, but he was the one everyone loved. Van had given him a stage on her show, and because Bishop knew how to make the fame machine purr, he also knew how to spin all of that to his advantage now.

And as much as Van hated him for it, she hated herself

even more. Every single piece of this awful situation traced back to Van and her decisions. She'd been the one to hire him. She had put him front and center on her show, which he helped them land.

Van had been the one to finally give in to the sparking sexual tension that had developed between them. She had pushed him into the back of her dressing room door in Denver last year after he'd told off a stagehand for making lewd comments about how she looked in her costume. She'd practically mauled him. He'd flipped her so her back was against the door, and they'd fucked without even taking their clothes off. It had been too urgent. Too inconsequential.

They hadn't even used a condom; they had been that reckless. And it had been fucking phenomenal. It had still given her shivers to remember it, even a year later—until.
. .

Until everything changed.

But Henry Bishop still made Van stupid, because of instead of deleting the texts outright or forwarding them to her lawyer or the detective, she read them.

Van read them over and over and over again until the words didn't mean anything anymore.

I miss you, Ness. Come home.

Come home to me. Let's stop all this and just talk about what happened.

We can figure this out. We're the golden couple. We've got this.

God, Ness, I miss you so much. Please just call me if you can't come home.

I cleaned out the closet, just like we talked about. I'm just waiting for you to fill it with your mounds of black clothes.

Please, Ness. I'm begging. I love you. Come home.

Van checked the time at the top of her phone. Six o'clock in the morning. Her alarm was set to go off in fifteen minutes so she could squeeze in her mandatory three-mile run before the scorching August sun burned her alive. That meant that Bishop was pathetically text-begging her at four in the morning L.A. time. Which meant he was either drunk and hadn't gone to bed yet, or like her, he couldn't sleep.

Jesus. Everything she'd known two weeks ago no longer made any sense. Because Bishop had been trying to convince Van to move in with him. He wanted to take their relationship public. He'd wanted her to break things off with Bryant for good and just be together. Live together. Work together.

Hell, they'd spent every night of the last three months together.

Van had planned to do it too. She was going to tell Bryant she didn't need to hide behind him anymore, because she wanted to pursue her relationship with Bishop, because she thought she'd done it. Van had thought she'd found the love of her life.

And she had never been more wrong.

Van archived the messages so she didn't have to see them, but so they'd still be accessible in case her lawyers needed them.

Reading the words hurt. Knowing that he was admitting to loving her over text—words she'd never actually heard him say to her face. Words that he was only saying so Van would drop the charges against him.

It might be her own fault that he was in her life, but it was Van's choice to have nothing to do with him.

The memories that she was in love with were nothing more than that. Memories. Maybe they were even less. Maybe they only represented a gross misrepresentation of the kind of person Bishop was.

Because now that the blinders had fallen away, Van didn't swoon over a damn thing that was in those text messages. She saw the threat and manipulation in each and every one of them.

And she was so through being played.

The A-List Flocks to Kansas for Elite Gala

A who's who of Hollywood and the music industry is set to descend upon the small Kansas town of Wellville Friday night. Pop star Van Birch is hosting an exclusive fundraiser at a local event space to raise money to rebuild her hometown. Wellville was hit by an F5 tornado late last month, destroying close to 10,000 homes and killing 25 people.

Birch has been working to facilitate a swift rebuilding effort for the last four weeks while being noticeably absent from her home in L.A., despite continuing to pursue her sexual assault allegations against former manager, Henry Bishop.

Bishop, who denies any wrongdoing, is still subject of an ongoing investigation on the part of the LAPD. He has issued two public statements declaring his innocence and his love for Birch, all but confirming rumors of their affair.

Meanwhile, Birch has been photographed getting cozy with long-time boyfriend Bryant Wilder as if nothing has changed between the two. We want to know if Bryant is the most understanding man on a planet or simply a doormat. Either way he seems to be entirely wrapped around Van's little finger. Stay tuned for exclusive photos from Birch's fundraiser, which is also being filmed for her reality show. So everyone will be there, regardless whether they're #notBishop or #justice4Van because as controversial as she may be, you can't deny everything the starlet touches turns to gold.

Noticeably absent from the guest list? A certain hunky surfing music exec. Click here to read the transcript from Bishop's swoon-worthy love letter to Van.

4

Clay hadn't seen Van for a week. He had been purposefully avoiding her, like he usually did when she was in town. It wasn't difficult. He and Bryant had so much work because of the tornado that they were putting in twelve-hour days, even in the 100 degree heat. Then it was easy to miss her at Robin's. He'd been mostly staying at Amber's place for the last three weeks.

Amber had been out of town for her grandparents' anniversary when the tornado hit. Her apartment building was left completely unscathed. He had to stop himself from being bitter that Amber still had all her things and hadn't had to endure the night of terror, but Clay was thankful for the retreat. Staying in the same house as Van had been torture.

He couldn't get the feel of her out of his mind. Even though the night Van had spent in Clay's bed had been completely non-sexual, Clay had been doing nothing but sexualizing it in his head in the month since it had happened. When he closed his eyes, Clay could still smell her hair, still feel her smooth skin under his fingers. The soft, delicate weight of her in his arms had felt natural and right. And when he slept in his own bed, it was all he could do to not to crave her there with him.

Finding reprieve in Amber was dishonest and wrong. They'd been seeing each other for six months, which was the longest commitment he'd ever made to anyone. Perhaps it said something about Clay that he was twenty-seven and had never been in a long-term relationship, but he wasn't the kind of guy to fool himself. He'd ever only been seriously interested in one woman.

Van had been off limits from the moment he met her. First, she was too young, then she was his stepsister, then she was interested in every other guy she met, but never Clay.

There had been that one kiss, just after he'd found out Van and Bryant were dating, just after she'd landed her recording contract. That kiss had fueled Clay for years. Afterward, he'd felt good about it. That it had been the perfect farewell to what might have been, but when he was honest with himself, Clay didn't think he'd ever be able to say goodbye to Van, not with any real resolve. Even if she was in love with his best friend.

Van and Bryant had been spending so much time together now that Van was back in Wellville that Clay practically expected them to announce their engagement any time now.

Sure, Clay was jealous Van had chosen Bryant, but that didn't mean Clay would hold it against him. He loved them both, and if they made each other happy, Clay was glad for them, even if disappointment burned in his chest at his own loss. He would find his way through it eventually.

Clay turned in a circle as he waited for Amber in her cramped living room. He had a contractual appearance to make at Van's fundraiser tonight. Clay had been dreading it since Van's invitation showed up on his pillow at Robin's house, followed closely by a call from *Pop Star*'s assistant producer to make sure he was coming.

Amber had never been more excited, which was ironic considering she hated Van with a passion. She had been a year behind Van in high school and had been beneath Van's radar back then. Clay thought Amber was a little bitter about Van's success, because he didn't know anyone in Wellville, even the guys on his construction crew, who didn't watch her show, who didn't fawn over her. Of course, they liked to make fun of him and Bryant for their part in Van's coordinated dramatics, but each and every one of them got moony eyed over Van when she was around and treated her like royalty.

A smile tugged at Clay's lips as he remembered his part in last year's manufactured storyline. Well, it was partly manufactured. Van actually did have a stalker the year before who broke into her house. She hadn't been home at the time, thank God. For the show, they'd hired an actor to play the stalker. It was one of the rare times Clay had flown out to Los Angeles so he could be "staying with Van" when the fake stalker broke in. The filming had actually been kind of fun. It involved a lot of him and Bryant running around without shirts, holding baseball bats in the middle of the night.

The filming had only been fun because there wasn't

any real danger that night. What hadn't been fun was Van coming home, alone, from a day of work and finding her house ransacked. They'd filmed the show a couple weeks after that. Bishop had been the only one there to support her when the real thing had happened. Clay's gut clenched at the thought, because he knew the twisted motherfucker had manipulated that situation to his own advantage.

The police hadn't done much about the stalker until the show aired. After that, they caught the guy. Go figure.

Robin and Bryant had been on Van to hire a full-time, live-in security detail, but she wouldn't do it. Her condo had security—which was better now than it had been before the break-in—and she had a team for when she was performing or travelling, but she refused to have someone living with her.

It was a mistake in Clay's mind, but Van never listened to him about anything.

Amber finally emerged from her bedroom. She wore a short red dress. Her long brown hair fell in loose waves down her back and she wore tall nude heels. She grinned when she saw him checking her out and showed Clay her back. "What do you think?"

The tight dress revealed most of her supple back and hugged the curves of her ass. It was the sort of thing Van would wear—too tight, too revealing but in a tastefully teasing way. "You look amazing," he said, and her grin widened as she gave her booty a little shake.

Amber was gorgeous. There was no doubt about that, but instead of pulling her into his arms and giving her ass a playful smack, Clay offered her his best crooked grin and tried to shake how much he missed Pebbles.

That was the one drawback about staying with Amber.

Her apartment had a no pets policy. Clay still stopped by Robin's to take Pebbles for walks in the morning and make sure she was stocked up on food, but Clay wasn't around for puppy snuggles or to play fetch in the yard. The few times he'd been by Robin's house in the evening, it had been Van or members of her crew who had been playing with Pebbles. She'd wiggled all over herself with excitement when Clay showed up, but it wasn't the same as falling asleep rubbing her silky ears.

That's when it hit him. Clay would rather sleep next to his dog than Amber.

The realization rocked him so soundly, he didn't realize Amber had spoken to him until she said his name in her exasperated voice. "Clay!"

He shook it off. "Sorry. What was that?"

"When's the car service coming?"

Clay checked his watch. It wasn't his usual heavy-duty digital. This was the watch that had arrived along with Clay's "costume" for the evening. It was huge, with a white and rose gold face and wide brown leather band. Clay didn't even want to know how much it cost. The same went for his light blue suit and light brown shoes. The color on the box had read "fawn." All of it, along with the crisp white shirt, on which he was instructed to leave the top three buttons open, were going right back into their garment bags in the morning. Van usually insisted he keep the clothes they'd bought for the show, but Phoenix had no problem taking them back.

"They should be here any minute," Clay said.

Amber wrapped her arms around his shoulders and played with his shirt collar. "Are you going to have a drink with me tonight?" she purred. "Since you don't have to drive?"

Amber had been laboring under the impression for the entire duration of their relationship that Clay didn't drink. Which wasn't true. Bryant and Clay went out for beers all the time. But cheap beer at The Fox while watching baseball wasn't the same as dancing at Tessa's while throwing back doubles like Amber liked to do.

Clay didn't mind alcohol. He just didn't like getting drunk. Not being in control of his mind or his body made him uncomfortable. Irresponsible things happened when people weren't sober, and Clay never wanted to wake up not knowing where he was or who he'd possibly hurt while he'd been intoxicated.

He pressed a kiss to Amber's throat, more out of habit than anything and said, "Maybe one."

She squealed and bounced against him. Clay wasn't sure why she was so excited for him to drink, but he liked that it made her happy. He was going to try harder to make her happy tonight. She deserved more than Clay wishing she were his dog. And Clay owed it to himself to try to fall in love with someone who wasn't Van Birch.

"Have you given any thought to what we were talking about last night?" She asked against his ear in a husky voice. It was the one she used in bed, but right now it was doing nothing for him, and Clay hated himself.

Clay's insides seized exactly as they had done the night before when Amber had suggested the solution to his homelessness problem was that they move in together. Not her place but a new house. She wanted Clay to sell the lot his house had stood on and buy a place with her.

He was all for giving this relationship its fair shot, but Clay was not ready to make that big a commitment.

His phone chirped in his pocket at the same time a horn sounded from outside. Thank God. "We'll talk about it later," he said and tugged her toward the door.

Van had said they'd send a car for them. Clay had not expected a limo, but there it was, a stretch limo that took up most of the empty space in the parking lot in front of Amber's building. The driver opened the door, and Clay motioned for Amber to climb in first. Her grin lit her face up.

By the time Clay scooted in next to her, that grin had vanished. He had landed in a limo full of people. Robin sat in one corner, Phoenix in another, with Van and Bryant between them. Van was practically sitting on Bryant's lap, they were so squished together.

Van didn't seem to mind. She waved merrily at them. Bryant's hand was resting high on Van's exposed thigh. His thumb traced circles over the smooth skin. Clay swallowed the hard knot in his throat and looked away to see that Amber's frown had turned into an outright scowl as she watched Phoenix pull a bottle of whiskey out of her bag.

"Everyone's taking a shot!" she said as she uncorked the bottle and took a quick pull.

Van swigged from the bottle and passed it to Bryant, who did the same. Bryant passed it Robin who sniffed the bottle.

"Come on, Dad," Van said. "Everyone includes you."

Robin shrugged took a strong pull, to the delight of Phoenix and Van, who cheered. When he finished grimacing, Robin held the bottle out to Amber, who held it like it was a smelly gym sock. "I don't think I can drink this," she said and sniffed the bottle, much like Robin had done.

"It's really good." Van's voice was sweet, nice. Clay recognized it as the voice she used with her fans. Meaning it was her fake voice, but at least she was trying.

"It's an Irish-style whiskey from an woman-run distillery," Phoenix said, like that would change Amber's mind.

She passed the bottle to Clay. "Sorry, I just can't do whiskey."

Clay glanced at the label; not being a drinker, there was no reason for him to recognize the brand. As he tipped it back and let the flavor of fire and caramel flow over his tongue, he heard Van stage whisper "Who doesn't like whiskey?" to Bryant.

Clay wiped his lips and suppressed a cough as the whiskey burned his throat. It wasn't an unpleasant burn, just one he wasn't used to.

Phoenix grabbed the bottle back and grinned at Van. "Another round?"

"Did Michael RSVP?" Van asked.

Phoenix rolled her eyes. "You know he did."

Van blew out a breath. Her bangs fluttered from the force of her sigh. "I'm gonna need a lot more whiskey."

"Michael Astor?" Amber asked. Clay still didn't know who that was.

"Unfortunately," Van groaned and took a long swig before passing the bottle over to a grinning Bryant.

"Who's Michael Astor?" Clay asked.

To his surprise, it was Bryant who answered. "An actor who's been harassing Van."

"Harassing?" Clay asked. His eyebrows knit as Van fidgeted on Bryant's lap—a sure sign she was uncomfortable.

"Michael's harmless," Van said. "But he does like to make it known what a big fan he is."

Amber harrumphed from beside Clay and passed the whiskey. Clay took another long sip from the bottle. There was less fire this time and more sweet caramel flavor, as a soothing warmth settled over his shoulders. Amber glared as he passed the bottle back to Phoenix, who was careful her fingers didn't accidentally brush his.

"What?" he asked Amber.

She only raised her eyebrows and crossed her arms over her chest. Clay didn't understand why she was upset when she'd wanted him to have a drink.

Clay felt eyes on him and knew immediately it was Van. Phoenix was on her phone. Bryant watched Van, and Robin's eyes were on Phoenix. It was only Van who looked at him, then to Amber and back to Clay.

His gaze locked with Van's and awareness pulsed through him. Van cocked her head, and Clay would have given his right arm to know what she was thinking. He couldn't read her, despite her half smile. She nodded at Amber, and Clay realized his girlfriend was glaring at him.

He reached for her hand, but she turned to face the window. Everyone's eyes were on them now, and Clay wasn't sure exactly what he'd done wrong by enjoying a little time with his family, but he was definitely in trouble for it.

It was a short drive to the club, and everyone was silent for the rest of the ride. Bryant's hand never stopped caressing Van's thigh. Bryant might be like a brother to Clay, but he had to clench his fists to keep from batting Bryant's hand off Van's leg and telling him to keep it in his pants until they got home later.

Amber stuck by Clay's side as they got out of the car, posing for the cameras like she was on the red carpet at the Oscars, whereas Clay tried to hurry her inside away from the flashing cameras and babbling reporters. Once they were through Tessa's front doors though, she dropped his arm and put three feet between them

"You really embarrassed me back there," she said.

"I'm sorry," Clay said as he corralled her out of the entryway and to the corner by the door so they were out of the flow of traffic. "I didn't mean to."

She rolled her eyes, but Clay could tell she was more hurt than annoyed. "Could you at least try to keep your eyes in your head when Van's around?"

His heart stuttered. "What do you mean?"

"I'm not stupid, Clay. The whole town knew you had the hots for her when your parents got married. I just didn't realize you still did."

"Van's my sister." It sounded hollow, even to his own ears.

Amber levelled Clay with a disbelieving stare. "She chose Bryant."

"I know."

Amber blanched, and Clay knew it sounded too defensive. "God, I don't even know why you're interested in her. She was a whore in high school, and she's a whore now. Everybody knows she was cheating on Bryant with

83

her manager. I don't know why Bryant's standing by her in all this mess. If you ask me, she's only playing the rape card so she can hop right back into Bryant's bed with zero consequences. I bet—"

Clay's hand was over Amber's mouth before he knew what he was doing. His other hand wrapped around her upper arm as he pulled her in close. Clay was careful to keep his touch light, even though so much rage pulsed in his blood, he could have lifted a car.

"Don't you dare finish that sentence," he said. His voice was dark and icy. "You don't have to like Van, and you don't have to believe me when I tell you there is nothing going on between us, even though it's true. But if you want a future with me you will not spread falsehoods about Van —not about this. I saw the bruises, Amber. I watched her cry. She's not making it up. This shit is as real as it gets."

Amber's eyes bulged, and Clay removed his fingers from her lips. She shrugged off his grip and stepped out of reach. "I'm sorry," she said. But Clay saw fear in her eyes for the first time ever.

Great, now his own girlfriend was afraid of him.

"I'm gonna go get a drink. You want one?" he asked. Clay tried to relax his shoulders and unfist his hands, but he knew the way he was clenching his teeth made him look angry. Even his voice was reluctant.

"I'll be over in a minute. I'm going to find the ladies room first."

Clay nodded, his heart sinking. Had he just messed this whole relationship up just when he'd decided to put more effort into it?

He found Bryant at the bar. His suit was similar in cut

to Clay's, but his was a dusky gray color. He was alone, though the bar was crowded. Van stood a few yards away, enjoying a reunion with the guys from her band. They were all laughing at something she said. Bryant smiled as Clay elbowed an action star out of the way to join him and ordered a drink.

"Van's on an Old Fashioned kick," he explained as the bartender delivered Clay's drink.

"Sounds good, as long as we're sticking to one type of liquor for the night." He took a sip. It wasn't too sweet, and he could tell it was different whiskey than they'd been sipping in the car. "It's good."

Bryant raised his Old Fashioned and took a sip. "Is Amber okay?"

Clay shook his head. "I don't think so."

Bryant clapped him on the shoulder. "Sorry. I know she was excited about tonight."

Clay only shrugged. He couldn't admit to what had just happened. He knocked back the rest of his drink and ordered another. The pleasant tingle-burn of the whiskey settled in his belly, and a relaxed heat radiated up to his shoulders and through his arms. He was ready to admit that alcohol certainly did have its place if he could feel like less of a dick that quickly.

"We'll figure it out," Clay said when his second drink was in his hand, but Bryant's eyes were back on Van. The governor and the action star had joined her little group. The action star had hugged her a little too long but seemed to take the hint when she took an extra step back and kept his hands to himself.

"How is she?" Clay asked.

Bryant shook his head. "You shouldn't have to ask me that."

Clay's back stiffened. Was he in for criticism from his best friend now too? "What's that supposed to mean?"

"It means she's hurting, and she needs all the support she can get, and you're playing house with Amber instead of being there for Van."

"I have a responsibility to Amber."

"And what about your responsibility to Robin and Van?"

"They don't need me."

Bryant shook his head. "You're a fucking idiot if you believe that."

Clay let the comment hang in the air between them, even as Bryant didn't drop his glare. He pushed his glasses up his nose, pinning Clay with his eyes.

"Did she tell you about the night she showed me the bruises?" Clay asked.

Bryant shook his head. "She hasn't said anything."

"It was the day she came back. She came to my room after we all went to bed and broke down. I did my best, but then she showed me the bruises and I couldn't do anything but hold her, even though I wanted blood. I've never wanted to actually murder someone before."

"You and me both." Bryant's hands fisted on the edge of the bar so hard, his knuckles went white. The overwhelming urge to be honest with him overtook Clay, and he remembered why they never talked about Van. Bryant knew exactly how Clay felt about her, and he was too good a guy to rub Clay's face in his relationship with her.

"She slept in my bed that night—" Clay said, his words

coming out too fast. "It was nothing. We just fell asleep. Nothing happened."

Bryant quirked his lips into a grim smile. "You don't have to confess your sins to me."

Clay held his hands up. The ice in his second drink clinked. The glass was already almost empty, as if by magic. "It wasn't like that, I swear."

"You don't have to explain yourself to me."

All Clay could see in his mind was Bryant's hand on her exposed thigh juxtaposed against the way Van and Bishop had been all over each other during Christmas dinner with no interference from Bryant. None of it made sense to Clay. If you were in a relationship with someone, you were *with* them, and Van and Bryant always seemed to be neither here nor there when it came to commitment. Clay remembered a couple years ago when Bryant had been so swept away by some guy, he'd disappeared for almost two months. Clay had never wanted to punch Bryant before; remembering that betrayal, Clay was having trouble mastering the desire. "Are you together or not?"

Bryant sighed, long and heavy. "Technically? Yes. But it's never been what you thought it was."

Clay's eyebrows shot up. "What does that mean?"

"It means that I would do anything to help Van, but I'm not sure being in a relationship with me is the best thing for her anymore."

Clay knew he looked confused, because Bryant chuckled into his drink, but he didn't elaborate on why he was amused.

"I love Van," he said, "But I think I love her more like a sister than you do."

Clay chalked that comment up to the alcohol, because as Van broke away from her group and cozied into Bryant, he placed a kiss to her neck at the same moment that she pinched Bryant's ass. Van giggled, then pressed her generous rear into Bryant's crotch, wiggled, and led him to the dancefloor. Clay watched them laugh together as Bryant tried to keep up with Van's professional dance moves. They looked happy. Familiar. Comfortable. When Van planted a kiss on Bryant as the cameras swung by, Clay decided it was time to find Amber.

Only when he spotted Amber, she was dancing with Michael Astor. A smile was glued over her mouth, so he took a seat at the bar and ordered another Old Fashioned. It was going to be a long night.

Thirty minutes later, Clay had lost track of everyone. Bryant and Van had disappeared, Amber had never joined him at the bar, and he couldn't spot Michael Astor's black hair and chiseled jaw in the bar anywhere either.

Phoenix looked to be in a meeting with the reality show producer, and Clay figured it was almost time for Van to give her speech. Not that Phoenix would help him find Amber. She'd probably knee him in the balls and tell him Amber was better off without him.

Clay drifted through the crowd, searching for a brunette in a red dress with no luck.

When he turned down the corridor toward the bathrooms, he heard voices. They were muffled at first, and he didn't think anything of them until he heard, "Michael. Stop." His first thought that the pretty boy was trying to feel up Clay's girlfriend, since they'd been dancing together, but when he rounded the corner behind the bathrooms, it was Van that Astor had crowded into the wall, not Amber.

He leaned in close and said something too low for Clay to hear, but the way Van's hands pushed against his chest while the rest of her body tried to shrink into the wall made it clear she was trying to escape. Clay's blood pounded in his veins as he approached. Neither Van nor the actor noticed him.

"It's not gonna happen."

"It did once." Astor moved his hands from the wall, closing them around her forearms, and pressed his hips into hers.

Van let out a sound halfway between a growl and whimper as she pushed at him again. "That was a long time ago."

Astor's hand went to her jaw, and the fingers on her face were not the gentle caress of a lover. Clay didn't give a damn how deep Michael Astor's pockets went or if he played the most popular doctor on TV this decade, he was not letting Van suffer on his watch.

Clay's hand closed on Michael's shoulder, and he felt the other man go rigid as he said, "Hey, asshole. She said no."

Michael spun, fists raised. Clay dodged his swing and used his momentum to send Astor sprawling on the floor. Once he was out of the way, Clay didn't look back. His focus was only on Van as she stood propped against the wall. She had one hand on her rapidly rising and falling chest, the other pressed against the wall behind her like her world had just turned sideways.

Clay didn't want to crowd her, but he needed to touch her, to make sure she was all right. He warred with himself as he slowly approached her, trying to shove his needs aside and focus on her. When she didn't flinch away, Clay cupped Van's jaw in his hand and angled her head so that she met his eyes.

"Hey," he said in the most soothing voice he could muster. It was not a tone Clay used often. "Are you okay?"

She shook her head and leaned into his palm. Her chest heaved, and Clay covered the hand she held over her heart with his own. Her heart was pounding scary fast. He thought that maybe Van was having a panic attack. She'd had them a few times when they'd been teenagers.

Clay was vaguely aware of Michael, muttering to himself and getting to his feet, over his shoulder. Van's eyes shot to him, and her breath came even faster. She was going to hyperventilate.

"Don't look at him," Clay said, capturing her gaze again. "Look at me. Good. Now, breathe with me." He stepped in close, putting their hands over his heart. Clay's heartbeat wasn't exactly slow and steady, but it was calmer than hers.

Van closed her eyes and matched the rise and fall of her chest to his. Finally, she relaxed into him, her head rolling onto his shoulder.

"I have to give a speech in a few minutes." Her voice was wavering and muffled by his shirt.

"Take some time. They'll wait for you," Clay said and wrapped his arms more fully around her. He wanted to rail at her, to tell her she needed 24-hour security, but now wasn't the time.

"Thank you," she said. "I—" She balled her fingers into his shirt.

"Shhh."

Clay chanced a glance over his shoulder, and Michael had disappeared. Good riddance, fuckwad.

He tightened his hold on Van and held her until both their heart rates had returned to normal. At some point, they'd started to sway together. His thumb caressed the curve of her waist, and he felt Van's nose graze his neck. A second later, her lips brushed over the hollow of Clay's throat.

Her balled fist flattened against his chest, and he pressed his palm into the small of her back. The swaying stopped, and when she raised her eyes to his, the shift in mood was so swift and fierce, Clay barely registered the decision to kiss her before their lips crashed together.

Van tasted like whiskey but also hot and sweet in a flavor that was something all her own. Her lips were naturally plump and supple, and her tongue was like velvet against Clay's as he delved into her mouth again and again. His mind spun with desire as Van's hands couldn't decide where to stay. They roamed up and down his chest, over his shoulders and into his hair before starting all over.

The brush of her nails at the nape of Clay's neck pulled a groan from his chest. She didn't resist as Clay eased her back against the wall and pressed against as much of her small, soft body as he could. She moaned as he ground against her and kissed his way down her neck.

They'd kissed before. Just the once. It had been intense, but not like this. There had been electricity, but there hadn't been this bald longing like there was now, like maybe Van wanted him as much as he wanted her. Like maybe she always had but was only just now willing to admit it.

"Clay." The word was almost a gasp as her leg wrapped around his, pulling him closer as he ground against her again.

God, he wanted her. He wanted her here, now.

Clay was contemplating wrapping her legs around his waist and hiking her skirt up when he heard voices approaching.

He and Van stilled at the same time. Clay's blood was thrumming inside him, telling him to press on, to pull her closer, to pull down his zipper, brush aside her panties, and finish this. He couldn't make himself step away from her. Not yet. Not when he was so close. He didn't even care that he'd tipped his hand. He'd done that five years ago when he'd kissed her the first time. She knew how he felt, but now she was finally letting him show her just how much he loved her.

Van's breath came fast against his ear, heavy and low as if she was trying to regulate her own desire. The voices were drawing closer, and pulling back just enough to meet her eyes, Clay could see that she didn't want to get caught here, like this, with him.

In a daze, he pulled back so their bodies weren't quite so close.

Their eyes met. Van gave him a shy half smile, and Clay couldn't help himself. He had to taste her one last time. He'd meant to keep it sweet and tame and break away before whoever was there came around the corner, but the moment his lips touched hers again, Clay forgot everything but her touch.

"What the fuck?"

The woman's voice startled him out of his stupor as he and Van jumped apart. Cold dread flooded his veins as he turned to see Amber standing in the dimly lit hall behind them. She was accompanied by Phoenix. Neither woman looked pleased, but it was Amber who had spoken. Phoenix shot ice daggers at Clay with her eyes, as usual.

"What the actual fuck, Clay?" Amber said again.

Shit. He looked over his shoulder at Van, but she'd folded in on herself, her shoulders hunched. Her eyes downcast, and a whole new level of dread filled him. Fuck. Had he just picked up where Astor had left off? Jesus Christ, what kind of man was he? He'd thought everything had been consensual, but he was definitely not thinking clearly. He'd asked before. He should have asked if he could kiss her. Three Old Fashioneds was three too many. This was why Clay didn't drink.

They hadn't spoken a word. He'd just assumed. But Van had been looking for comfort, and Clay had completely taken advantage of her.

Not to mention the fact that she was in a relationship with Clay's best friend.

And Clay had a girlfriend, who had just caught him groping Van..

Phoenix crossed to Van, muttering, "You fucking bastard," as she passed him.

When Clay turned back toward Amber and saw the tears slip down her cheeks, he shared Phoenix sentiments one-hundred percent.

Clay approached his girlfriend but didn't try to hold her. He offered her the only thing he could. "I'm sorry, Amber."

She shook her head, scrubbed the moisture from her face and said, "Take me home."

He nodded and called a cab. Clay had a feeling it was going to be a long night.

@MrHollywood attending @VanBmusic's gala is the same thing as agreeing that you believe the worthless lying slut. We see you rallying around a petty bitch who doesn't care that she's ruined @Bishop's life for her own gain.

Controversy Rises Surrounding Van Birch's Humanitarian Work

Twitter exploded last evening as photos were released from the gala Van Birch put on in Wellville, Kansas to aid the tornado relief effort. Photos of stars on the red carpet were retweeted with captions condemning them for supporting Van's cause while she continues to refuse to drop charges against former manager Henry Bishop. Fans of the music mogul and reality-TV star are protesting that the allegations levelled against Bishop are false and that Van Birch is ruining his life.

When reached for comment, Bishop said that he's still hoping to mend his relationship with the starlet but hasn't called for a social-media ceasefire, saying that people are allowed their opinions.

Van Birch's camp did not return our phone calls, but word is that she left the event tipsy and draped over long-time beau, Bryant Wilder's arm. We think it's safe to say that Van Birch is feeling pretty secure, cozy, and unconcerned in Wellville right now.

5

*V*an woke up with a sharp, pounding headache. The room spun a little bit, even as the sun peeked over the horizon. A glance at her phone showed she'd only been in bed a couple of hours—but it wasn't her bed she was in—it was Bryant's. He was still passed out on the other side of the bed, one arm under his pillow, the other splayed out over his head.

He always slept like that. It was adorable.

She wanted to be able to snuggle up to him and just pretend last night hadn't happened. Instead, she forced herself out of bed and down the stairs in search of water and pain reliever.

Van had somehow made it through the formal part of the evening, though she couldn't guarantee her words weren't slurred while she did it. Whatever. Everyone else was drunk too. Her one drink *before* everything happened didn't do much in the way of excusing her behavior.

Bryant had done his best to shield her from unwanted attention for the last five years. What else was a fake hometown boyfriend for? It was the perfect cover—and an amazing story. Everyone knew she had a serious relationship going on back home. First Bryant had been in the Army, then he was living his dream in Kansas while Van was living hers in California. They made the long-distance thing look romantic in the public eye. And bonus, men who wanted to take advantage of a young, possibly naive pop star were mostly deterred, because her love story with Bryant was the reason she was famous in the first place. No one wanted to mess that up.

It had worked marvelously until it hadn't.

Van and Bryant had kept the truth of their relationship so far under wraps that not even Clay knew it wasn't genuine. There was nothing between Van and Bryant but deep and abiding friendship. They'd never even had sex, despite trying to provide the public with every reason to suspect otherwise. Van had asked Bryant to be her fake boyfriend for a reason. She hadn't wanted a real one at the time, and Bryant had been game, saying he didn't think of Van that way anyway. No surprise, the two of them sought their sexual fulfillment elsewhere. Van'd had her fair share of lovers in the last five years. And Bryant'd had his, but when it came to the public eye, they were solid. Committed. In love.

Until Bishop anyway.

Van had been so stupid in love that it had made her careless, and now creeps like Michael Astor, who she'd had a drunken one-night stand with three years ago, thought they had free rein to assault her in empty corridors.

She still wasn't sure what happened with Clay. One second she was freaking out, the next she wanted to climb him like a tree. She was pretty sure she had kissed him first, and hand to God, in two more seconds, she would have wrapped her legs around his waist and come all over him. At least she hadn't embarrassed herself that much.

He'd already been mortified when he realized what he was doing, and later, Bryant told her how much he'd had to drink, so it's possible he thought Van was Amber. They were about the same size and build. It could happen.

But holy shit did making out with Clay ever ruin Van's plans for the night.

Because she'd had plans for getting down and dirty, but it had been with Bryant, not Clay.

Over the last month, Bryant and Van had been having a lot of late-night discussions. They'd talked about Bishop, about the rebuilding, about filming, and about each of their careers. But more than anything else, they'd talked about them. They'd discussed their pasts and how the platonic relationship they'd always shared had been the path that felt right. But maybe the bond they shared *could* be something more, if they just gave it a chance. Like always, Bryant had been on board for whatever Van wanted to do. And she'd appreciated how their farce had relieved some of the heat from the ongoing debacle with Bishop. Some of the name-calling on Twitter had escalated to threats, but a lot more people had started asking when Van and Bryant were going to get married.

And that got Van thinking.

Weddings were a such a happy topic.

Which was why, when Bryant asked how far Van was willing to take the whole fake relationship thing, she drew up her courage and said, "Maybe it shouldn't be fake?"

Because why not? She and Bryant were good together.

They were comfortable. He was her best friend, and just because they'd never had a sexual relationship didn't mean they couldn't see if that fit too.

He said he was willing to try if she was. So for the past two weeks, they'd been dating for real. It wasn't all that different from how they normally spent time together, except that once or twice they had kissed when there weren't cameras around too.

And last night, after the party, they had planned to take the plunge and finally take each other's clothes off. Van had been looking forward to it. She was ready to be touched. Ready to do something active to wash off the lingering taint she still felt when she was alone.

She and Bryant had been teasing each other all day. There had been a teasing text waiting for her when she'd emerged from her therapy session. She'd sent him a picture of her newly shaven legs after she got out of the shower. When they picked him up from his house, his eyes had roved over her with definite hunger, and Van had to admit, he looked gorgeous in his casual suit and ruffled hair. She'd straightened his glasses and given him a long, lingering kiss. He hadn't been able to keep his hands off her legs, and she had been feeling like maybe they could make this whole thing work.

They could get married and be happy and not be in a fake relationship anymore but in a real, healthy, whole one.

She even thought it could work after Clay had ducked into the car, looking like walking sex. Van even told herself that she wasn't jealous of Amber anymore because Bryant was hers for real. And then she'd attacked Clay like a hungry cheetah the second she was alone with him in a dark hallway.

Suddenly sex with Bryant didn't seem like such an exciting prospect anymore.

Water retrieved, painkillers knocked back, Van climbed back in bed. Bryant hadn't stirred, and she didn't cozy up to him. It felt wrong when she could still feel Clay's hands on her. She squeezed her legs together when she remembered the feel of his tongue against hers, his fingers pressed against the small of her back. His breath in her ear as he muttered soothing words.

If Phoenix hadn't come looking for her, Van probably would have had unprotected sex with her stepbrother in a public, if mostly abandoned, hallway.

And God, Van wasn't even sorry.

Phoenix was pissed as hell, and Van knew there would be a lecture from her today. Van was sorry she'd probably ruined Clay's relationship with Amber. They didn't deserve to become part of the walking disaster better known as Van Birch.

She'd been feeling more and more like an unending tornado lately. All she did was stir up controversy and disaster wherever she went. Now she'd swept in and taken away everything Clay had left. At least she felt guilty for that, even if she couldn't feel guilty for sticking her tongue down a man's throat who was off-limits for a million different reasons.

Instead of concentrating on those reasons, all Van could feel was his body against hers, and it was not doing her any favors in the whole "have hot sex with her kind-of maybe fiancé" category.

She scrubbed her hands over her face. Van was going

to have to talk about all of this with her therapist, wasn't she? That was going to be painful. She'd been seeing Maggie for three years now. She'd had a mini break-down while writing her second album—and by mini break-down, Van meant anxiety so high she drank enough whiskey to drown a freaking horse because she couldn't handle the panic attacks anymore.

With Maggie's help, she'd been keeping the anxiety under control. Plus, her second album had outsold her first, so her imposter syndrome had dialed back a little bit. Van hadn't had a panic attack in more than two years —until the night of The Incident.

She'd been having them every few days since, but it wasn't because she was afraid she wouldn't be able to live up to her own expectations for herself anymore. According to Maggie, it was because she wasn't dealing with what had happened to her. They'd decided a long time ago that avoidance was one of her unhealthier coping mechanisms.

Van thought she'd been doing okay the last few days. Being home with her dad and Bryant and having Phoenix around had helped. And coordinating the relief effort gave her plenty to do. But one confrontation with fucking Michael Astor in a dark hallway had her avoiding so much, she'd almost climbed Clay like a spider monkey. Instead of thinking about why, Van was fantasizing about how it could happen again.

Because those are the thought patterns of a mentally stable human being.

As the painkillers kicked in, her body grew restless, and her thrashing woke Bryant. He stretched and rolled to face her, pulling her up against his chest. His skin was warm and taut over defined muscle, and she should have been into it, but she just . . . wasn't.

"How's your head?" he asked as he pressed a kiss to her neck.

She shrugged. "I was thinking of calling Maggie." Even though she knew that's not what he meant.

Bryant's arms tensed around her.

"Did that bastard text you again?"

Van winced and shook her head, even though Bishop *had* texted her again last night. He'd been texting almost every day. Like the queen of avoidance she was, she'd been ignoring them. No one except Bryant even knew she'd been getting messages from Bishop. The constant influx of begging was not doing her any favors. And neither was everyone calling him names all the time.

"Can you please just say his name?"

"His name should be Moth—"

Van cut him off with a finger over his lips. "Saying shit like that just makes me feel like even more of an idiot."

Bryant sighed and rested his forehead against hers. "I'm sorry. I'll be better."

"Thank you." She allowed herself to settle into his arms and tried to relax into the security of Bryant's friendship.

"He had us all fooled too, you know."

"Yeah?"

Bryant brushed a lock of hair off her cheek. "I was happy for you, V."

"I was happy for me too."

They lay together in silence for a few minutes. The beginning tremors of the panic attack she'd been working herself into slowly receded into a steady thrum of anxiety she could function with.

"Do you wanna talk to me about it?"

Van let out a long, reluctant breath.

"Come on. I can do a good impression of Maggie."

He grabbed his glasses from the side table and slid them up his nose, then frowned while pursing his lips. Considering he'd never met Maggie, it wasn't bad.

"You'd make a ridiculously ugly woman," she said through a laugh.

He stuck his hairy leg out from beneath the sheet. "Come on, V. You know I have the gams for dresses and heels."

She plucked out one of his leg hairs, and Bryant cursed and rubbed his leg. "Remind me to take you along to my next waxing appointment then."

"Christ, that hurt."

"You're such a man-baby."

Bryant pinched her arm, and she socked him in the shoulder.

He winced and narrowed his eyes. Van knew what was coming next and tried to scramble away, but she wasn't fast enough. When Bryant's fingers grazed her ribs, she let out a shriek of a laugh. No matter how hard she tried, she couldn't escape his tickles, and he didn't let up until she was panting and grinning on the bed beside him.

With a superior smirk, Bryant propped himself up on one elbow and loomed over her. "So, ready to talk about what went down last night yet?"

Van stretched her abs, now even more sore from yesterday's core workout.

"Michael Astor propositioned me outside the bathroom and then wouldn't take no for an answer."

Bryant was instantly sitting up, taking the sheet along with him, making Van super conscious that she wasn't wearing pants. All she had on were black cotton boy shorts with her black camisole. Bryant wasn't looking at her body. He was glowering at her something fierce, but she knew it was an expression meant for Michael.

"That slimy son of a bitch. Why the fuck didn't you tell anyone?"

Van reached over and pulled the sheet up to her chin. She loved Bryant's enthusiasm, but his violent reactions only made her feel more vulnerable. "It's fine. I mean, I panicked, like usual. But Clay showed up and saved the day. Plus, I don't think Michael would have actually done anything."

"That's not the point. Jesus, tell me Clay was nice to you at least?"

"Define nice?" Van hedged.

"No comments that could have been misconstrued that you were asking for it somehow. Not just grabbing you by the wrist and depositing you in front of Phoenix so he wouldn't have to look at you."

Van snorted. Based on past performance, it was exactly how Clay might have reacted.

"He helped me get my breathing under control," she said, but Bryant heard the caveat in her voice.

"And?"

She couldn't look him in the eye. "And then we made out like horny teenagers left alone at church."

Of all of the reactions she might have expected out of

Bryant upon hearing of her infidelity—especially when such transgressions were happening with his lifelong best friend— laughter was not one of them. But, boy howdy, was the man cracking up. Knee-slapping, side-holding cackling like Van had just told him the funniest joke on earth.

She waited for him to get himself under control—which took about five minutes longer than it should have. When he finally was only spluttering to himself, she asked, "Care to share what you find so hilarious about your fiancé making out with your best friend?"

Bryant's eyes still shone with laughter-induced tears when he reached for her and squeezed her fingers. "I have been waiting for you and Clay to figure this out for years now."

Van's mind went into full on war room mode. Steel walls crashed down as alarm bells rang. LED-lit maps popped to life along the walls and the Joint Chiefs all rushed in in full uniform as they tried to wrangle her synapses into control. She had never told anyone about her crush on Clay—well, she'd confessed it to Phoenix once a long time ago, but that was part of a bigger story, and she'd made it seemed like a teenaged thing, something she'd left behind instead of just buried deep and tried to ignore.

And she'd never told a soul about that kiss.

"What are you talking about?"

Bryant only narrowed at his eyes at her in a way that said, *Girl, I am not stupid.*

"You're not mad?"

"Why would I be mad?"

Van returned the look he was giving her in a manner

that suggested he was indeed stupid after all. "We were supposed to hump like bunnies last night."

That got another chuckle out of him. "And I was looking forward to doing my best not to make it awkward as hell."

Van would have asked him to explain, but she knew exactly what he meant. They loved each other but not like that.

"When *was* the last time you got laid?" she asked, avoiding the issue of how this whole conversation meant they were back to being in a fake relationship. Because that's right, avoiding is what she did best.

"I don't know. Eighteen months. Two years. Somewhere in there."

Van made a face and Bryant's smile turned pained, though he tried to hide it a with a laugh. "What? It's not easy finding lovers when you're supposedly dating one of the most famous women on the planet. No one wants to be in the tabloids as the person who broke up Van Birch's fairytale romance."

Oh, yeah. Bryant played along, but there was some bitterness under those words. Just a little bit.

A dread settled in her stomach. How selfish was she? Bryant was missing out on his whole life just to offer her a kernel of security.

"Has there been anyone special?" she asked.

"One girl, but she's moved on."

"I'm sorry. I shouldn't ask you to do this for me anymore. It's so ridiculous how much you're giving up for me. I—"

Bryant squeezed her hand and shushed her. "I told you I was here for you as long as you needed it. And I was serious when I said I'd marry you if that's what you needed." His thumb grazed hers for emphasis.

"You should marry someone you're in love with."

Bryant's eyes turned hard. "I love you."

"I love you too, but you know that's not what I mean."

A long sigh and sad granite eyes greeted the truth of her admission. Hey, look at her, *not avoiding*.

"The woman I'm in love with just had a baby with someone else, and I'm not in a hurry to get my heart ripped out of my chest like that again anytime soon."

Van blinked at the outright bitterness in his voice. The Bryant she knew could be a little overly serious sometimes, but that usually meant he was in the middle of really good book. Mostly he was kind and goofy and a little sarcastic if distracted. It was one of the reasons she felt like she sometimes took advantage of his kindness, but they had so much fun devising their shenanigans that she didn't let herself think about it too hard.

Van's mouth opened and shut at least three times before she found her words again. "I didn't know you'd been seeing anyone."

"It's been a while."

"Long enough to have a baby with someone else?"

"Barely, but yeah."

"How did that happen?"

"We met, and she had zero clue who I was. She was young and sweet, and we talked about Andrew Sean Greer. It was the best few weeks of my life, and then she found out about you—about who I'm supposed to be to you, and she hasn't spoken to me since."

"You didn't tell her that it's not real?"

A muscle in Bryant's jaw flexed. "We made a pact. Not even Clay knows."

She averted her eyes and fiddled with the hem of her shirt as she said, "Bishop knew."

His hand landed on her jaw, and he tipped her chin up to meet his eyes. "Of course you told Bishop. You were trying to build a relationship with him. And I was going to tell her, but I waited too long, and now she's moved on."

Van threw her arms around his shoulders. Guilt and sorrow settled into her core. His pain was her fault.

"If I hadn't roped you into this ridic—"

"No. I'm the one that messed things up with Minnie. You don't get to blame yourself for that too, okay?"

Van nodded against his shoulder. He ran his fingers up and down the length of her spine, and she relaxed into his embrace. The soothing motion settled her anxiety, and for a few minutes, she was able to just be. This was why she'd fought so hard to keep Bryant in her life, because there was zero turbulence between them. Everything was always just good.

"So, you made out with Clay, huh?"

Van stiffened and tried to pull away, but Bryant held her close and continued his soothing spine tracing. "I thought we were pretending that didn't happen."

"That's a horrible idea."

"Why?"

"Because you two are perfect for each other."

Van rolled her eyes, but Bryant couldn't see that. And then her phone rang. Because of course Phoenix was already up and working. Someday, Van would teach her how to take a morning off.

Heartbreak in Wellville

*While most celebrities who descended upon Wellville, Kansas,
Van Birch's hometown, just long enough to attend a fundraising
event and put in a day's work volunteering with the clean up,
actor Michael Astor hasn't left yet.*

*By day he's been building houses with the crew, but by night,
our photographers have spotted him out with none other than
nurse, Amber Farmer.*

*Don't fret if you don't recognize Amber, we didn't either until
we checked the red carpet photos from singer Van Birch's
charity gala last week, where she arrived on the arm of Birch's
stepbrother, Clay Noble.*

*Looks like poor Noble can't compete with Hollywood royalty.
But we'd let him cry on our shoulder anytime.*

---

6

*V*an had officially been avoiding him for a week. She was busy—Clay got that—but she'd stayed with Bryant almost every night since the gala, and Clay had a feeling it wasn't only because they were boning every chance they got while they were in town together. She was avoiding *him* —avoiding telling him what had happened in that hallway had been a mistake.

Hell, Clay knew it.

And frankly, he didn't want to run into her either.

It had been awkward enough apologizing to Bryant. Must be nice to be so freaking secure in your relationship that you know even if your girl messes around on you, she's still yours for life. When Clay had talked to Bryant about it the next day, he'd cracked up. Bryant hadn't stopped laughing for five minutes. And it had made Clay want to punch him in the face.

Amber had kicked him to the curb the second they were in the cab, screaming about how could he embarrass her in public like that and how disgusting he was for kissing his sister. Clay put a stop to the tirade when she started insulting Van, which only made Amber cry.

Her parting words, as she tossed what few belongings Clay had left at his head as he stood in the hallway outside her apartment were, "You are so pathetic. She doesn't even see you, Clay. You're just another toy for her to play with until she's bored."

Clay didn't say anything in response. He didn't defend himself. He hadn't said anything at all to Amber other than to apologize for embarrassing her and to reprimand her for calling Van a whore. He deserved all Amber's ire. Amber had been good to him, and he knew she was hurting, but he *couldn't* apologize, because he'd enjoyed the interlude in the hallway. If that was the last taste of Van he ever got, Clay wanted to savor it.

Van was all passion and heat, and Clay's life had been nothing but routine and sorrow for years. Like the land he lived on, it was dry, serene, sunny, but isolated and lonesome and barren.

Moving back into Robin's house hadn't been Clay's first choice, but the alternative was living with Bryant, and at least Clay knew he wouldn't overhear Bryant and Van having sex at Robin's. The house itself wasn't a bad place to be. It was big and airy and well-maintained for such an old place, but the lingering sense of failure at sleeping in his high school bedroom gnawed at Clay. He knew there was nothing he could do about a natural disaster, but maybe if he had planned better, he could at least afford to rent an apartment while he saved enough money to rebuild his house.

Robin's house had quieted now that Van had turned over most of the relief effort to the team she'd assembled. She was supposed to be focused on writing her new album and filming the new season of her show. While the cameras had been around for the last month, Clay hadn't had much to do with the filming so far—but that was about to change. He parked his new truck in front of the little bookstore downtown—one of the only businesses left unscathed by the tornado.

He was happy that the little shop was still standing. The girl who ran it was sweet, and as far as he could tell, her store and her family were just about all she had. At least Clay's business had benefited from the disaster. If she'd lost this little piece of downtown Wellville, Clay wasn't sure she would have had much to start over with.

He buoyed himself with goodwill thoughts toward the cute young owner, as he prepared to face the woman who was perhaps Clay's least favorite person in the world. Phoenix had called him yesterday to set up this meeting. She wanted to talk contracts for his expanded role in this special season of *Pop Star*, since they were focusing on the rebuilding effort. Van was going to be coming around to the building sites, but they were also going to have crews following Clay and Bryant a few days a week—not that there was a lot of drama to find on the jobsite, but the idea was to profile the families they were building for—to make the disaster that much more human—if Clay understood everything right.

He'd only agreed to it for the extra cash. He'd been able to replace his still-missing truck easily enough, but his house was a different story. Becoming a larger part of the Van Birch machine was possibly the most annoying way he could think to bring in more money, but it was also the most immediately profitable.

The door chimed as he opened it. The front half was a cafe and bakery. The back half was a used bookstore. The place had been one of Bryant's favorite haunts when it opened a couple years back. Clay came in and traded out his stack of old paperback westerns every few months, but Bryant read a book every couple of days—books on every subject under the sun.

Bryant had never gone to college, but he should have. He *should* have been a damn professor, but he'd stuck with Clay through the Army and made an astute business partner. Clay had lucked out when it came to how loyal Bryant was.

He half expected to see Bryant sprawled out in the armchair next to the first bookshelf, but he wasn't there. It was mid-morning, and a few customers lingered over lattes and pastries in the cafe part, but Phoenix wasn't one of them.

Clay waved to the proprietor, who stood behind the espresso machine, and she waved back. He could have used a second cup of coffee, but he preferred not give Phoenix any more weapons to use against him, and a hot beverage was just that in her hands.

He wandered through the stacks, his hands skimming the wood on the bookshelves he'd built back before the store had opened. Phoenix had likely set up shop at the large table in the middle of the maze of bookshelves. Sure enough, she'd spread out over the entire eight-person table with papers, files, electronics of every shape and size.

She must carry an office supply store on her back like a turtle. It had done nothing to bow her spine though.

Simply put, Phoenix was stunning. She was tall and lithe, too thin like all the yoga hippies he'd met in California, but she managed to look graceful instead of corpse-like. She had long, naturally red hair that hadn't faded with age the way his mother's had. She also had the most striking blue eyes he'd ever seen. Next to Van, she was the most gorgeous woman Clay ever met. And she was an absolute nightmare—but only to him.

Clay had no idea what he'd done to offend her, but she either insulted him at every opportunity or actively avoided him. Even when she was trying to be civil for Van's and Robin's sake, her words were barbed and pointed, always letting Clay know that she was only not gouging his eyes out because it would upset Van if she did.

She was on the phone and typing when Clay pulled out the chair across from her. She glanced up as he sat, and already he could see the disdain flashing in her blue eyes. He didn't want to let it bother him, but since she'd borne witness to his mistake with Van the other night and he hadn't heard anything about it yet, Clay knew he was going to be in for an earful this morning.

She extracted herself from her phone call within thirty seconds but didn't stop typing until Clay reached a full count of sixty in his head.

His posture didn't invite cordiality either. He'd pulled his chair back away from the dark, elegant table and sat with his legs splayed wide and his arms crossed over his chest. He hoped the expression on his face read more bored than petulant child, but honestly, he felt more like the latter.

Phoenix handed him a file. "Read these, sign, and initial where marked."

"What is it?"

"Just an expanded contract allowing us and the film crew on your job sites like we discussed."

"No hidden strings?"

Phoenix resembled an annoyed librarian the way she raised her eyebrows. All she needed was a pair of reading glasses to look over and she would have mastered the sourpuss expression. "Like what?"

"Like, I'm required to have my shirt off in seventy-five percent of the filming."

Phoenix tapped her stylus on the side of her tablet as she barely contained a sneer. "As much as the women of America seem to enjoy the sight of man chest, believe it or not, we don't need you to take your shirt off to attract viewers."

"You make it sound like you *don't* enjoy a well-sculpted male body, Fe."

Now she sneered, but her voice was serene as she said. "Some of us have taste. And if you use that nickname again, I will tear your balls out through your throat. Understand?"

"Aw. And here I thought we were getting along so well this trip."

Phoenix set her tablet aside and braced her hands on the edge of the table as she rose to loom over him. "Listen to me, you disgusting opportunist, because I am only going to say this once. Keep your filthy, roving hands off Van. She has been through enough without you taking advantage of her vulnerability."

Clay gritted his teeth. "What happened with Van the other night was consensual."

"She was drunk and scared."

He rose, mimicking Phoenix's posture so that we were nose to nose. "She knew exactly what she was doing."

She fisted a piece paper between immaculately manicured red fingernails. "You know the last person who said those words to me was? Bishop. The day after he raped Van. He was trying to get me to let him past the security gate and into my house. I protected her then, and I will protect her now. Stay the hell away from Van."

Her words didn't have the intended effect. Clay was nothing like that bastard.

He leaned in closer. "I would never hurt Van."

"Too late, asshole."

She glared at him, daring him to argue, and Clay opened his mouth to ask what she meant. But he'd been there Saturday night. Even if Van might have been into it, touching her had not ben appropriate in the moment.

Bryant broke through the bookcases before Clay could say anything. His friend's shoulders were hunched, one hand in his pocket, the other clutched around a cup of coffee, his face set in a frown until he noticed Phoenix and Clay standing off. Then he sighed and looked even more defeated as he collapsed into an armchair in the corner and muttered, "Jesus Christ, who left you two alone together?"

Phoenix stood then and handed a folder to Bryant that looked identical to Clay's. "Morning, Bryant," she said in a pleasant voice. She smiled at him, a genuinely fond expression that Clay had trouble reconciling with the hellcat who had, just a moment ago, had her claws at his throat.

"Could you two not tear each other's heads off this morning, please?" Bryant asked as he rubbed his temples. "I don't have the patience to deal with the cleanup right now."

Phoenix shrugged, like she couldn't be bothered to apologize for the hatred that came so naturally to her.

Clay frowned at Bryant. "You okay?"

"Just a headache." He pushed his glasses up his nose and turned his pained eyes toward Phoenix. "Can we get this over with? I have a meeting with our lumber supplier at eleven."

Phoenix gave him a sympathetic smile, which Clay thought was completely unjustified since Bryant was being a dick. Then she pretended not to notice when Bryant pulled a flask out of his pocket and poured a shot of whiskey into his coffee before hiding it away again. She walked them through the contracts as they signed another ten hours of their week away.

Twenty minutes later, Bryant handed over his folder and stalked out of the shop with barely a word. Clay hurried out of Phoenix's makeshift office just after but stopped by the cafe counter for a coffee and sandwich to go.

Clay interrupted an adorable family scene. The gal who owned the place was handing a diaper bag off to a man Clay had always assumed she'd married since she'd opened the place. He'd seen him around town; he was stocky and broad and had the same dark messy hair as the baby Minnie was still bouncing on her hip. The baby wasn't quite a year old yet, and Clay had seen him hanging around the shop with his mom a few times. Minnie kissed the baby on the cheek and handed him over to his dad before coming over to help Clay.

Why couldn't life be that simple and elegant for him?

A job, a partner, a kid. A place to live with them. Love them.

It wasn't too much to ask, was it?

@chad_69xX: @VanBMusic violated? lol. she was giving it to @Bishop for months and fucking enjoyed it. #notBishop

@_Chadtheman_X_69: We are all victims of #fakecases. The feminazis are out to take all men who like pussy to court

7

*P*hoenix was hiding at the coffee shop again.

Van thought she did it to intimidate people, because Phoenix almost never worked in her office—and there was one in the little apartment in the basement Phoenix always stayed in. Apparently, all that space was good for was charging Phoenix's multitude of devices. She didn't even use the office she paid and arm and a leg for in L.A. unless she had to meet with someone super important. Otherwise it was where she stored her filing cabinets.

Today, Van found her taking up a gigantic conference table in the middle of a circle of bookshelves, like they were in a college library and there was going to be a cram session for Reality TV Producing 101.

To be fair, Phoenix could totally teach that class.

Butch, Van's personal security guard, had trailed her into the coffee shop today. Which was a turn. Normally he waited outside or discreetly in the front lobby of whatever building she was in, if she had him with her at all, but today he'd stood in line with her for coffee. She'd tried to get him to eat a scone, but he patted his no-doubt washboard abs and said he wasn't much for sugar. Van had smirked up at him, and he'd given her a wink. She liked Butch. He was a kind, serious, boulder of a man who had been with Van for years. Butch wasn't his real name, that was Martin Weisenhauer, but Van preferred the nickname he'd earned in the Marines. No man who carried around 300 pounds of muscle fit the name "Martin." He stopped at the end of the corridor and did his best impression of a Secret Service agent.

Van had expected Phoenix to be working on three things at once in that way she has that makes you want to suggest she hire another assistant, but you don't dare because Phoenix can cut you with her eyes. Instead, she was leaning back in her chair with nary an electronic screen in her hand as she stared at the big glass globe light fixture over the table.

She had sort of a moony expression on her face. Van had never seen Phoenix moony. Ever.

"Are you coming down with something?" Van asked as she took the seat across from her. "You look funny."

Phoenix startled and glared at her. "You're late."

Van shrugged. She hadn't been sleeping. She'd stayed the night at Bryant's last night, and he'd been acting all twitchy and moody and refused to talk to her. And Van hadn't talked to him—or anyone—about the new messages she'd been receiving, some from Bishop, some from other people, and they'd both tossed and turned all night long.

It had been miserable.

"Well, Clay and Bryant are officially in for the new filming schedule."

"Did Clay ask any questions about why he was frontrunner instead of Bryant?"

Phoenix shook her head. "I don't think he read it that closely. And Bryant put whiskey in his coffee, so I doubt he noticed either."

Van swore. She was going to have to talk to Bryant soon about how much he was drinking.

"He doesn't deserve it, you know," Phoenix said. Van, who had been thinking about Bryant, raised her eyebrows. "Clay," Phoenix said, "does not deserve the effort your putting in to make him famous."

Van shrugged. "You convince him to let me pay to rebuild his house outright then."

Phoenix only made a face and continued with Van's schedule. "You have an interview with some face of some home improvement channel about the progress of the rebuilding effort so far tomorrow, and the lawyers in L.A. are getting the runaround from the detective again."

"What does that mean?" Van asked, not trying to hide the massive yawn that stole over her now that she was sitting. Van had very purposefully not sat all morning. Since she couldn't sleep, she'd gotten up early for a run before the sun was all the way up. Then she had an hour-long virtual session with her trainer that involved so many squats and deadlifts, she thought her ass was going to fall off instead of get bigger. It was a perpetual struggle to keep up with the ideal beauty standards for her naturally petite frame. And then she'd spent the rest of the morning with the volunteer coordinator. They'd had a bunch of press for watching the celebrities get all down and dirty last week, but now they had to make sure they had a steady,long-term team to get solid homes built before the cold weather showed up.

Sure it was one-hundred degrees every day now, and that could last through October, but more likely that would swiftly turn to seventy sometime in September, then it would be freezing by Halloween. You never knew exactly when fall would hit, but when it did, it was a sharp, frosty turn.

"It means that every time we try to figure out how the investigation is going and press for a court date, they tell us they are still collecting evidence."

"What evidence is there left to collect? It's been more than a month."

"That's a fantastic question. Your dad has been talking about flying out there himself to see if he can get some answers."

Van rolled her eyes. Robin Birch, defense attorney and amateur private detective extraordinaire. She was going to have to take away his mystery novels. "He doesn't have a license in California."

"He's been looking into that," Phoenix said in a quiet voice, like she was trying to sound nonchalant.

Van did a double take. "Gross. Did he tell you that?"

She shrugged and picked up her phone like she had a notification even when, for once, she didn't.

"Since when are you two all buddy-buddy?"

Phoenix levelled her ice eyes at Van. "Who else am I supposed to hang out with at night with you hiding at Bryant's all the time?"

"Oh." She had Van there. She had abandoned Phoenix recently. She'd given Van her opinion on what she thought about Van making out with Clay the other night, and it hadn't been nearly as positive as Bryant's strange reaction. She'd been spitting mad and reminded Van— again—how she shouldn't trust Clay. Phoenix was thoroughly convinced that he was no better than Bishop —had been for most of their acquaintance, even though Van had told her a thousand times that Clay wasn't a predator. He'd just been a stupid kid running his mouth.

But Van could see Phoenix's point. Van had made a lot of huge decisions in her life based around those few sentences out of Clay's mouth about how she'd behaved when she was younger. Ones that had hurt like hell at the time.

"I just needed to get out of the house for a little while," Van said.

Phoenix's eyes softened. "Look, I get the need to avoid Clay and avoid being alone at night. And I am not complaining. I like your dad. He has exquisite taste in wine."

There was that. The side of the basement that wasn't Phoenix's apartment was used for storage, but aside from some of her mom's old stuff and the Christmas decorations, her dad didn't hold onto a lot of useless things. No, he mostly used the basement as a wine cellar, because the one thing he did collect had to be *useful*, even if it was a bunch of old dusty bottles of wine, which he barely drank.

Van had noticed more bottles than usual in the recycling lately, but she figured it had been Phoenix's doing, since they were all her favorite brand of Pinot Noir. Now Van would have to investigate her dad's stash. Because she was not sure she was okay with the implications of him suddenly stocking up on Phoenix's favorite wine and then drinking it with her.

Her suspicions were erased however when the barista arrived with Van's almond milk latte and apricot scone. "Oh, bless you," Van said.

The woman glanced at Butch over her shoulder, as if unnerved by his presence. Van didn't blame her. It was totally weird having a huge guy just standing there pretending he wasn't listening to your conversation. It had taken Van ages to get used to. Having just a little bit of privacy was why Van had always refused the live-in security in the first place.

The woman gave Van a watery smile. Van didn't miss that her hands were shaking. She'd gone a bit pale when Van had stepped up to the counter to order, but otherwise was holding it together pretty well. Van's presence tended to have this effect on people. She preferred the quiet nervousness to the shrieking and swooning. Van didn't mind making people a little nervous and self-conscious. It just meant they recognized her but were trying to respect her privacy, even if they were really kind of excited.

Van let them be nervous and tried not to let on too much that she'd noticed that they'd noticed Van was a famous person. It worked out better for everyone. The nervous ones usually remembered more of their experience—or so they told her later on Twitter.

"Minnie, have you met Van yet?"

"Not officially," the barista said. She sidled closer to Phoenix, as if seeking comfort and protection.

Van cocked her head to the side; the name sounded familiar, but Van didn't recognize her.

Phoenix gave the young woman a friendly smile, and

Van looked at her more closely. Phoenix didn't smile at many people that way. Minnie was blonde and small, around Van's height, and thin, but with more natural curves than Van had. Her boobs were huge, and frankly, Van was jealous. Van had told her trainer more than once that she'd never have tits or an ass if he kept making her sweat them off every day. He only laughed at her. The jerk.

"Van, this is Minneapolis Halvarson. She owns the place."

Van raised her eyebrows in surprise. This meek little mouse who didn't look a day over twenty-two owned her own business? Color Van impressed.

"Minneapolis?" she asked. "That's a unique name."

She shifted from one foot to the other and picked at the crocheted hem of her pretty, pink tunic blouse. "My mom had a thing for Jeff Goldblum," she said.

Van smiled and Phoenix squeaked. "Funny. So does Phoenix, but I don't recall a Minneapolis, though."

A smile curved the corner of her mouth as Phoenix sat up like a kid around a campfire who was prepared to hear the best, most scariest story ever.

"It's a little obscure, but there was this episode of Sesame Street way back when. My mom was babysitting my cousin Rocco when she was pregnant with me, and Jeff Goldblum did a guest appearance. His character was an archaeologist named Minneapolis—you know, a riff on Indiana Jones."

Phoenix's eyes had glazed over. "Oh my God, I have to see this. Please tell me you have it."

Minnie shook her head. "We had it on tape once upon a time, but it's gone now."

Phoenix tapped away at her iPad, probably doing a YouTube search for the thing right there. That or emailing her contact at HBO to see if they have access to the archived footage they could send her.

"Do you have a second to join us?" Van asked, pulling out the chair beside her.

Minnie shifted from one foot to the other and glanced toward the front of the store.

"Just for a minute?" Van said.

"Just for a minute," Minnie said and took the chair. Her jitters had increased, and she was blushing, but Van forged ahead anyway.

"Minnie," Van said, recalling where she'd heard the name before. Bryant had mentioned her. The woman who had been special but had moved on. And if she dug deep, she could dredge up a memory from years ago of him mentioning a bookstore owner. Had that been the same person? Van decided to test her hypothesis. "Like Bryant's Minnie?"

She colored at the question and looked away as her eyes grew hard. "I don't know what you mean."

Oh yeah. This was the woman Bryant was in love with for sure. "He told me about you," Van said. And because Van could practically see Minnie breaking, Van took pity on her and tried to put her at ease. It wasn't everyday you were confronted by the girlfriend of the man you'd had an affair with.

"He said you had a baby recently?"

Minnie's shoulders relaxed a little bit as she realized she wasn't about to get grilled. "I haven't seen him in so long; I didn't realize he knew about Malcolm."

Van was about to ask more about Minnie's son, but Phoenix jumped in. "Wait. Malcolm? Like, Ian Malcolm?"

Minnie grinned then, looking sheepish. "Apparently Jeff Goldblum love is genetic."

"Oh my God. You are my new favorite person," Phoenix said. Then turned to Van. "Sorry, Van, I resign. I'm going to move here and promote this coffee shop for nothing. Minneapolis needs me."

Van laughed, and it felt good. "Who am I to stand in the way of true love?"

Minnie's head snapped to the right; and she truly looked at Van for the first time. Her eyes scanned Van from head to toe in the way that women did to one another when they were sizing up the competition. A bold move coming from this meek little thing, but Van let her look, and when Minnie turned away, Van said, "We should put together a movie night. My dad's TV is huge. We can do it up right. Your three favorite Jeff Goldblum movies, pizza, cookies, ice cream, and unlimited M&Ms. What do you say?"

"Do you have time for something like that?" Minnie asked.

Van nodded at Phoenix. "You'd have to ask her what my schedule's like. I just go where she tells me."

Phoenix nodded. "I'll check our calendars and send you a text."

"I don't know," she said blushing. "I don't always have someone to watch Malcolm in the evenings."

"So bring him along. We like babies," Van said.

"You'd be okay with that?" Minnie looked between Van and Phoenix like she thought maybe they were playing a joke on her.

"Of course."

Minnie chewed the inside of her lip like she wasn't sure whether she should accept, so Van played the pity vote. "Phoenix and I don't have any girlfriends in Kansas. It's all dudes all the time between my dad, my stepbrother, and Bryant."

Van did not expect Minnie to flinch, so she tried to smile encouragingly as Minnie asked, "But they won't be around will they?"

Oh, whatever had happened between Bryant and Minnie had to have been just as juicy as it was heart wrenching. Otherwise, Van didn't think Minnie would look skeptical and stricken. "Absolutely not. Girls only."

Minnie twiddled her thumbs in her lap for a minute. "Well, I guess I could use some girl time too," she said. "I haven't had much time to make friends since I moved here. Opening the shop and then getting pregnant with Malcolm hasn't left a lot of time for playing. About all I get is gossiping with the baristas in the morning."

"It's a date," Van said, and the chime on the front door rang.

Minnie stood, "I better get back up front."

Phoenix and Van spent the rest of the morning going over the coming week's schedule and approving scripts for upcoming episodes. The boring stuff.

"How's the album coming?" Phoenix asked just as Van stood to leave.

"We're not talking about the album right now," Van said.

Phoenix ignored her. "The record company just gave us eight weeks, so even if we're not talking about the album, you better be working on the album."

Van felt her scone try to come back up. "Eight weeks?"

"They want it by Halloween."

"Then they'll have it," Van said with more conviction than she felt. She hadn't missed a deadline yet, and she wouldn't miss this one, even if she had zero clue how she was going to make it happen. She'd been working with Maggie. Van had called her every day this past week, but she still felt like a jumbled mess of anxiety that she had to keep tamped down and stuffed in a safe so she could function. There hadn't been time to unpack any of that emotion and just be.

Writing had always been an emotional process, and tapping into her emotions now, when she was barely holding it together? Van felt like she might burn away from the inside out and be nothing more than a pile of ash to be swept away by the wind.

Van Birch Now With Armed Guards

t's well known that Van Birch eschews personal security when she's not traveling, but in the last few days, we've spotted extra people around the Van Birch family home in Wellville, Kansas who have nothing to do but stand outside the house and glare at paparazzi. Could it be that Ms. Van B fears for her safety in the wake of her accusations against her former manager? We hear some people on social media are getting pretty nasty. Are you Team #notBishop or Team #justice4van? Tell us in the comments.

8

Something suspicious had been afoot in the house the last few nights, and Clay hoped to God he was wrong about what it was. Robin's house was nice, spacious, and well-maintained, but it was also old. The stairs creaked and the walls were thin. There wasn't much going on in the house you couldn't hear. Footsteps, doors opening and closing, water running, toilets flushing, moaning, creaking bed frames. With Van spending most of her nights at Bryant's, Clay knew it wasn't them who'd woken him up at two in the morning the past two nights.

Clay had been holding out hope that Robin had been sneaking a secret girlfriend into the house after they'd all gone to bed because the alternative was a reality he didn't want to face. Then he came downstairs to let Pebbles out Sunday morning after a night of blissfully uninterrupted sleep to find Robin and Phoenix emerging from the basement stairwell that led to Phoenix's apartment. Together. Holding hands.

They stopped when they spotted him, and though his gut dropped to his toes, Clay kept his expression as neutral as he could. Well neutral with a side of disgusted accusation.

Phoenix glared, and Robin looked like a kid caught with his hand in the cookie jar. They all said nothing, staring at each other as Pebbles wiggled beside the back door, ready to for her morning zoom around the yard.

Finally, when Pebbles whined with impatience, Clay moved past where they stood at the top of the stairwell and unchained the back door. "If you two are trying to keep this secret, you're doing a hell of a bad job of it."

He didn't wait for them to speak before he headed outside to play with Pebbles. He wished he could erase the sight from his head. Clay might have already been sixteen when Robin married his mom, but he was the closest thing to a father Clay had ever had. But shit, Phoenix was only a year older than Clay. She was only three years older than Van.

Robin wasn't old. He was only fifty-three. He still jogged and played tennis regularly, and Clay supposed he was probably attractive in a silver fox sort of way, but attractive to women his own age. Phoenix was twenty-eight. The age gap was large enough that Clay swore every time he thought about it.

For Van's sake, Clay hoped they were just fucking around. Jesus. And for his own. Phoenix would make one seriously sinister evil stepmother.

It was already topping eighty-five degrees at eight o'clock, and Pebbles was panting heavily when they came back inside. She lapped up an entire bowl of water while Clay got her food ready.

The camera crews had also arrived. They were only allowed in Van's home a few hours a week, and they'd all settled on Sunday family breakfasts for one of those hours. One cameraman filmed Robin whistling as he made pancakes as if he didn't have a gigantic camera crowding him from the left. Another closed in on Clay on the other side of the kitchen as he placed Pebbles's food bowl on the floor.

Sweat dripped into his eye, so he did the responsible thing and whipped off his t-shirt and mopped his brow with it. True to Phoenix's word, there hadn't been any clauses in the new show contract about a certain amount of film hours for Clay to have his pecs out, but there had been a paragraph or two about agreeing to play to the audience that more or less suggested, *take your shirt off at every opportunity because your main role in this show is as man candy*, without saying anything that could be construed as possible sexual harassment.

Clay felt the camera focus in on his stomach as he crossed the kitchen for a glass of juice. Oh well, he probably wouldn't have a six pack forever. Might as well immortalize it now.

Clay couldn't tell if the cameras could pick up on the tension radiating between him and Robin. Obviously, they couldn't discuss Robin's sex life at the moment. Even thinking the words made him cringe, because up until the past few days, Robin had existed in a sex-free zone in Clay's head. It was childish of him, and unfair to Robin, but it was going to take time for Clay to wrap his head around it. And even more time to accept that he was in some sort of relationship with Phoenix of all people.

Clearly, Robin didn't find Phoenix as abrasive as Clay did.

When Robin did speak, his words surprised Clay, "Have you seen Van eat anything over the last couple of days?"

Was this really the conversation he wanted to have on the air?

Clay downed his juice with a raised eyebrow and went for the coffee pot. "I've barely seen her, period."

Robin pursed his lips and nodded, and Clay thought he might genuinely be worried. This was the problem with the stupid reality show. Clay never knew what was scripted and what was actually a problem until they were already in the thick of it.

Maybe Clay wasn't better for much more than ornamentation because he couldn't ever figure what was going on with Van either. All he knew was that he'd seen through Bishop before anyone else. Clay never thought Bishop would physically hurt her—but that didn't matter anymore.

"Keep an eye on her, would you?" was all he said as Van's footsteps sounded down the creaky back staircase.

She breezed in and grabbed a strawberry off the top of the bowl on the island on her way to the coffee pot. That was five calories at least. She was wearing running shorts that barely covered her ass and a strappy tank top that showed off more of her sports bra than covered her torso.

She already had her running shoes on and held her pink Camelbak water bottle in one hand while sipping coffee from the other. "Pancakes smell good, Dad."

She hopped up on her toes and placed a kiss on his

cheek then collapsed onto the floor, mug, water bottle and all, and wrestled with Pebbles.

Clay rescued the coffee from swift death via puppy tail while Van spoke to Pebbles in baby talk and avoided all eye contact with him.

When Robin brought over two plates of pancakes with bacon, she popped up from the floor. She took approximately two bites of pancake before popping a blueberry in her mouth and slipping a slice of bacon to Pebbles.

"Do you mind if I take Pebbles on my run with me?" she asked, her eyes hovering somewhere over Clay's shoulder.

He tried to meet her gaze, but she averted her eyes, and Clay wondered if she was trying to be awkward or if she was really feeling shy about their interlude at Tessa's all these weeks later. For his part, it had been the highlight of Clay's month.

Relenting, he said, "As long as you're not gone too long. It's already pretty hot."

"Just a short one on the books today," Van said. "I'll finish this when I get back."

Van turned to leave, but Robin caught her elbow. "Butch is going with you?"

Van rolled her eyes. "Alvin's got babysitting duty this morning. He's waiting on the porch. I already checked."

"Be careful," Robin said.

"It's just a run," she said, and after one last sip of coffee, Van was gone, Pebbles tripping at her heels.

Clay leaned to the left, noting the guards still stationed around the property, guarding the rope they'd put up as a barrier against the paparazzi. Robin had been grumbling about how they were going to force him to put up a fence to keep them from trampling his lawn. Clay only saw a few photographers at the curb this morning.

Robin watched Van leave out of the far window, ensuring her guard was with her, then took the stool Van had briefly occupied, pushing her plate aside for one of his own. He covered his pancakes with berries and a shake of powdered sugar instead of syrup.

"Is Phoenix joining us for breakfast?" Clay asked.

Robin raised his eyebrows and, completely nonplussed, said, "I doubt it."

Robin and Clay finished their meals in silence. And still the cameras circled. What a cozy family scene. When it aired, perhaps they would cast it as stilted malice or quiet rage. It would not be shown as two men with nothing to say to each other, that was for sure.

After breakfast, Clay met with Bryant at their office—a space Clay rarely visited. Bryant saw to most of the sourcing and organizing the supplies for the jobsites, while Clay usually spent more time with the crews or, formerly, in his garage working on custom carpentry pieces. With the rebuilding, there wasn't time for that. They had crews running seven days a week to keep up with the construction and repair schedule. The two of them barely had time to touch base, so they'd taken to spending Sundays in the office with Marie, just to keep everything on track.

Bryant had been a treat as they'd gone over the budget and the schedule. It wasn't often that something got under his skin, so Clay put up with it, but if he was still in a mood in the morning, Clay was going to say something. He should have today before he left, but he'd been out of patience. Clay couldn't take another day of Bryant treating him like shit just because Van wasn't putting out.

The thought of the Bryant and Van screwing made Clay grind his teeth. As touchy-feely as they were most of the time, there were just some things a guy didn't need to think about; his best friend and the woman he wanted getting it on was one of those things.

An uninvited vision of what it might be like to have Van underneath him stopped Clay in his tracks on his way to the refrigerator for dinner. She would be warm and soft. Her head would be thrown back, exposing her neck. Clay would lean forward and nip and suck the skin beneath her ear as he shifted his hips forward and—Pebbles jumped on him, narrowly missing his semi-hard cock in her clatter for attention. Clay had to shake his head to clear his mind of the useless fantasy, as he guided the puppy's paws to the floor.

The faint strumming of Van's acoustic floated down the stairs. She was playing in that meandering way that told Clay she was figuring out something new. It was a sound he hadn't heard in years, since before he enlisted. But hearing it now, the soft progression of chords, then a pause, then the same progression again before she changed it up, transported Clay right back to high school. Van had carried her guitar with her everywhere then. She had only ever stopped playing if a guy was showing her attention—but the guys never lasted very long before she lost interest and went back to her guitar. Clay had never considered before that maybe that was why she clung to Bryant so hard when she was home. She didn't have any other friends here.

After letting Pebbles out, Clay opened the fridge. He

wasn't really hungry; it was a left-over habit from high school, coming home after work or school and scoping out the food situation. So even though he didn't want to eat, he took stock of what Robin and, he guessed, Van and Phoenix were keeping in the fridge. The food inventory hadn't changed much since the girls moved in. There was a carton of almond milk and a bottle of probiotics, but otherwise, it didn't look the girls had added much. The pancakes that Van was supposed to eat after her run still sat on the plastic-wrap covered plate Robin had put in the fridge twelve hours earlier.

Clay took the plate out of the fridge and popped it in the microwave for a few seconds. He tossed a handful of berries over it, drizzled it with fresh syrup, and because he was feeling generous, he rolled up a few pieces of the nice sliced ham he had been going to use in his lunch the next day and arranged them alongside the pancakes. The plate looked like a little sunburst with the rolled ham slices sticking out of the pancakes. It was one-hundred percent lame, but Clay grabbed two forks anyway and headed up the rickety old back steps.

He hoped Van would hear him coming, but she was still strumming a little aimlessly on her guitar when he knocked on her door. She didn't stop playing but said, "Come in."

When Clay stepped through, she missed half the strings on her downward strum, and her fingers slid over the frets in a squeak and clang that made him wince. So, she hadn't expected to see him at all. She'd probably assumed he was Phoenix—which made sense. Aside from the night in his room and the incident at Tessa's, Van and Clay hadn't interacted one-on-one in years. Robin or

Bryant or Phoenix was always around when she was in town. Usually all three.

"Is everything okay?" she asked, propping the guitar against her bed.

"That's what I was going to ask you," Clay said. He pulled the chair away from the white desk in the corner and hauled it next to Van's bed. He sat in it backwards and set the plate on the bed between them.

"I'm fine," she said. Clay didn't believe her for a second. She sat rigid on her bed, her knees together, her shoulders back, her hands folded in her lap. Her black hair was pulled back in a long curling ponytail, but her side-swept bangs hung over one eye. The other eye was looking anywhere but at Clay. He didn't take his eyes off her face.

"Have you eaten anything today?" Clay asked as he played it casual and speared one of the ham rolls with his fork. She looked up as he bit the end off. Annoyance sparked in her eyes, and Clay mentally raised his arms in victory.

"Of course I've eaten."

"Oh yeah? What?"

"What are you? The food police?"

He shrugged and stuffed the rest of the ham slice into his mouth. "You've barely eaten since you got here."

"I'm small," she said, looking back at her guitar again. "I don't need much food."

"Sure. But you still need to eat at least a thousand calories a day. Preferably two."

Van rolled her eyes and snatched a slice of ham from the plate. "Oh my God, I eat." She took a huge bite and said, "See," with her mouth full.

"Good." He pushed the plate further toward her. "What are you working on?"

"It's nothing." And instead of talking about her song, Van dug into the reheated food in front of her, shoving a huge bite of pancake into her mouth.

Interesting.

The Van he'd grown up with could talk about her music for days, weeks, months without stopping. And then she'd play for you whether you wanted to listen or not.

"Sounded like a little bit of something."

Van blew out a breath and said, "Have you ever been to Revive?"

"The coffee shop?"

"Yeah."

"Bryant and I did the bookshelves there. And they have a fantastic supply of old westerns."

Van's brow creased. "You read westerns?"

"And mysteries. I like the old noir stuff the best."

"I never pictured you as much of a reader."

Clay poked her in the side with the blunt end of his fork. "I'm not Bryant or anything, but I usually get through a couple books a month."

Van picked up her guitar again and strummed along with no particular melody Clay could discern. "And you go to Revive to replenish your supply?"

He didn't like the vulnerability that crept into Van's voice as she asked the question. His hand landed on her knee, and he didn't have the willpower to force himself to remove it. "Sometimes. Why?"

"Do you know Minneapolis?" Clay frowned, and she amended, "Minnie, the little blonde that owns it."

Clay shrugged. "I've seen her around. I think she had a baby a few months ago. Why?"

"I can't stop thinking about her." Van started strumming more intentionally on her guitar. "She's just a block away from where the tornado hit. And she has a baby, and she's rocking the business owner thing. She could have lost absolutely everything, you know."

"You mean like me?"

"You still have your business."

"I have zero personal possessions," Clay said. "I had to wear Bryant's clothes for days until I could get more." Van cringed, but since she wouldn't meet his eye, Clay hit her with more. "I lost my birth certificate. All my mom's old photo albums. I had a half-finished set of cabinets and all of my tools in the garage. My truck still hasn't been found. The neck of my guitar was in three pieces in my driveway with all the strings still attached, and Pebbles's kennel was a twisted heap in the neighbor's yard."

Van's hand covered Clay's where his fingertips squeezed her knee. He recalled the bruises she'd shown him a month ago and let go abruptly. She didn't deserve for him to take his frustration out on her.

Van caught his still-hovering hand, squeezed his fingers, and asked, "Do you still play?"

Clay entwined his fingers with hers for just a moment, recalling their hot kisses as she touched on the only thing they had ever had in common. It had been why Clay noticed her in the first place. Back before he'd even known their parents were dating, Clay had seen Van at the music shop. They'd had lessons back-to-back. Hers were first, and though the rooms were supposed to be soundproof, they definitely weren't. He could hear every note Van played through the thin wooden door, and even then he could tell she was special. He wanted to know her. Wanted to find the kernel of pain that drove her to play with such vigor and emotion and to share it with her.

It was why she was famous now, even when her music was darker, harder than the sweet pop the Taylor Swift and Katy Perry wannabes of the music industry were making. She was soulful, a little bluesy sometimes. And damn, she was little, but she had a mighty voice.

She strummed a few random chords, but Clay held his hand out for the guitar as his answer. He picked out the opening bars of one of her songs, the first single off her second album. It was Clay's favorite song of Van's, and he nodded at her when she met his gaze with surprised eyes. "You sing."

Clay almost didn't think she was going to join him and was prepared to start the progression toward the lyrics again when Van opened her mouth and sang.

He could hear the pain in her voice and wondered if she was remembering that night. Clay tried not to picture what it had been like for her to realize someone she trusted was going to hurt her. Whether Clay thought she should have trusted him was irrelevant. Van *had* trusted Bishop. Maybe the reason she couldn't commit to Bryant was because she'd loved Bishop. As much as it made Clay's stomach turn, he'd known it was a possibility ever since the last season of her reality show aired.

And yeah. Clay watched it, because he was a sucker and wanted to keep up with Van however he could, even if he knew half the content was fabricated. The way Bishop had touched her last season, his hand on the small of the back wherever they went, it was obvious something was going on. Bishop couldn't even sit beside her at a conference table without a possessive hand closing around the nape of her neck.

Clay should have known that something was off. He had told himself Bishop was putting on an act for the cameras to create drama for the show. He and Bryant had even gotten into it on screen, Bryant telling Bishop to back off and leave Van alone. Clay had assumed at the time it was fabricated, but the more he replayed the scene in his mind, and yeah, from the dozen of times he'd looked it up on YouTube, Clay could see that Bryant was legitimately pissed off. And Clay hadn't caught the anger until after Van's confession. He needed to ask Bryant if he had known something Clay didn't.

Clay needed to know exactly where Bryant's relationship stood with Van, but they were always so cagey about the details.

As Van sang, as tears ran down her cheeks, Clay wanted to be the man that made it all better for her. He wanted to be the one that kissed away her tears.

When the song ended, Van wiped away her own tears and offered him a weak smile.

"You've been practicing," she said and held out her hand for her guitar.

@69xxchadsterxx: @VanBMusic I know where you live. Gonna climb in your window later and show you what its really like to have someone "violate you"

9

Clay was a good musician. Better than Van remembered. "How come we've never played together before?" she asked as he handed her guitar back.

Her fingers immediately began picking out a melody that it seemed they knew, but it wasn't something Van had played before. It was like her hands were excited, inspired, so Van let them play.

She repeated the strain twice more before Clay said, "I was on the football team and beneath your notice."

There was truth to that. Van never had much patience for sports.

"Bryant was on the football team too," she said. She pulled up the recording app on her phone and played the melody again before she forgot what it was. The song already had a bluesy sound, and she could already hear a hard bass behind that would get an audience clapping their hands.

"Yeah, but Bryant was also in Chess Club—and band."

Van snorted—the closest thing she'd given to a laugh

in a while. "That's right. He was on drumline. I always forget that."

"You two didn't play together?" Clay's eyebrows were drawn together in disbelief.

She shrugged and played a few chords that would make good backing to the melody she was still working out in her head. "Oh, all the time. We used to pretend we were the White Stripes, but that was so long ago. I forget that he used to perform in front of people, you know?"

Clay nodded and watched her fingers play over the frets for a few minutes.

"Does he still play?" Van asked.

"You're his girlfriend. You tell me." Clay sounded like the words had stabbed him in the throat, and Van rolled her eyes.

"You know that's just a front so that Hollywood smarmbags will leave me alone, right?"

He was quiet for a moment, watching her beneath the hair that fell into his eyes, like he didn't quite believe her. "Does it actually work?"

Van didn't appreciate the skepticism in his voice. Did he not realize how big of a deal this was? Her telling him the truth? He had always been the number one person Van hadn't wanted to know that she wasn't really with Bryant. She'd never been able to articulate why, except that the idea of Clay knowing that she was using Bryant as a shield left her feeling vulnerable in a way she hadn't been comfortable with until this exact moment.

Standing behind Bryant's protection had helped a lot the first couple of years Van had been in L.A.. The very first publicity stunt Van and Phoenix had ever pulled off had been a viral video that made it look like Bryant had surprised Van at one of her street corner performances when he came home for Christmas from being on leave in the Army. He'd been in his uniform, and Van had cried, and they'd kissed in front of a crowd. That video had basically gotten her the record deal. It had been the impetus for her reality show. Bryant had been a part of Van's appeal from the very beginning. Because a girl with a guy back home who she missed and wrote songs for was infinitely more marketable than a quick fuck with a husky voice.

Ending that story? It might possibly have a lasting impact on her career. Van knew Phoenix had some strategies tucked away in her back pocket, but Van knew she would be a gossip-rag headline harlot for months for dumping the most beloved celebrity boyfriend there ever was.

But watching Clay now? Seeing the adorable crinkle over his brow, the slight downturn to his lips as he frowned her, the golden glow of his red-blonde stubble pebbling over his jaw. . . Van wondered if it was better to bail while things were already bad rather than pretend everything was hunky-dory. Because Van wasn't okay. Not even a little bit, and she wanted to stop pretending, even if it was just for a little while.

"Most of the time it did, yeah."

Clay's jaw tightened as he ground his teeth together. He obviously wanted to say something rude and annoying. Van recognized that same look in his eye from when he was a teenager and she'd started going out with a new guy. "Just say it," she said, moving her eyes back to her guitar.

"Then what the hell happened with Bishop?"

Van experimented with a minor chord progression. "He knew the score."

"How many people actually know the truth about you and Bryant?"

She'd never mentioned it to anyone who didn't need to know. It only took one gossiping makeup artist for her cover to be blown. "Dad. Phoenix. Anyone Bryant's told, I suppose. And Bishop knew."

"Because you told him?"

"Yes."

"Why?"

Van stopped playing and looked at the way her feet dangled over the side of her bed, not touching the floor. She'd forgotten. This was why she didn't talk to Clay about stuff. He always made her feel like shit for every decision she'd ever made in her life. He approved of nothing she did, and all Van wanted was for him to smile at her—just once.

"What are you trying to ask, Clay?"

"So you weren't cheating on Bryant with Bishop?" His voice was calm, quiet. Like he knew that Van might lash out at any moment. Maybe she was that volatile. He really didn't know anymore. Maybe she always had been. Or maybe he was just having trouble wrapping his mind around the concept of a whole five-year-long relationship being a sham.

"No." She leaned her guitar against the bed and did her best to look Clay in the eyes and face his disapproval. "And all those times you got pissed at Bryant for hooking up with people behind my back—that wasn't cheating either."

Clay's shoulders rose and fell as he sucked in a deep

breath and let it out slowly, even as a vein stood out on his forehead. Van imagined he was reciting a mantra to himself. *Don't yell at her. Don't yell at her. Don't yell at her. She's broken enough.*

"So, for five years, you've let me think my best friend was a coward," he said after a minute. "Because he made me think he was hiding behind his bisexuality as an excuse not to be faithful to you, and I have wanted to pummel him every single time."

"Yeah. . ." Van hadn't thought very much about how Bryant dealt with his side of the farce, and she felt like even more of a selfish asshole. She'd know Bryant had always wanted to tell Clay about their arrangement. She hadn't realized it had complicated Bryant and Clay's relationship that way. "That was shitty. I'm sorry."

Clay flopped back in his chair and crossed his arms as he looked toward her curtained window. Van could tell he was annoyed, but she needed him to understand. "I couldn't have anyone finding out."

Clay harrumphed, his pecs standing out against his t-shirt with more detail for a tantalizing moment. "You think that I care so little about your safety that I'd leak that to someone? Tabloids aren't exactly after me for interviews."

Van knew that was a lie. He was approached every few months by someone looking for dirt. All her friends and family were. Mary Beth had texted Van in delight each time it had happened. She'd always say, "I never told them anything, of course," and Van would laugh, because Mary Beth had always told them *something*, like how she'd nearly failed Physics, or how Van had gotten kicked out of

Jazz Band because she'd been caught smoking outside a basketball game.

"Did my mom know?" Clay asked. He slumped forward, resting his elbows on his knees, his head ducked.

Van shook her head, and because Clay was looking at her feet, Van said, "I never told her. She seemed to like Bryant and I together so much; I didn't want to break her heart."

A small, sad, but appreciative smile curled one corner of Clay's lips upward. "She basically had your wedding planned. She started every other sentence with, 'When Van and Bryant get married…' I thought I was going to puke every time."

Van hooked her fingers through Clay's the way they'd done earlier, only this time she squeezed their palms together. "I miss her," she said.

Moisture glazed Clay's eyes, but the tears didn't fall. He sniffed as he said, "Me too. There are days I still have to remind myself that she's gone. Something good happens at work, and I want to text her. I walk in the back door here, and I expect to find her sitting at the breakfast bar grading papers."

Van did let her tears fall, because she expected the same exact thing every single time. "I miss raiding her stash of Hershey's Kisses in the back of the pantry after school."

Clay broke into a grin then. His mom had kept a big bowl of Kisses, every variety imaginable all mixed together, that she ate absently as she graded. "I still buy the almond ones sometimes, just because."

They shared watery smiles, then Van had to dash the tears from her cheeks with her free hand. "And I really wish she was here to talk to now." Van gestured toward her body, "You know, about this."

Clay's hand was under her chin, forcing her to look at him. His eyes were hard and the blue-gray sharp as steel. They'd never talked about what had happened to his mom. How Clay had been the product of an assault that had left a teenaged Mary Beth broken and battered, and the older man who'd taken advantage of her had never been held accountable.

"She would have told you it wasn't your fault. She would have told you that you were meant for too much to let that bastard destroy you. That you are so special and so loved—" Clay's voice cracked, and he had to pause to swallow. "She would have told you not to stay quiet or be docile. She would have told you to fight."

Van tried, and failed, to blink back more tears, but she couldn't. She could hear Mary Beth's voice in her son's words. And with Clay's conviction behind them, Van believed for just a moment that it was all true, that she was capable of everything she'd been hiding from the last few weeks, of confronting every frightening thing she had been avoiding. Talking about The Incident in public, finishing her album, testifying, telling her story and facing down the Twitter trolls because she was not going to let them keep her down. But it was all still so terrifying that Van felt frozen. Incapable. Broken. She'd never felt this way in her life, and she had no idea how to make it stop.

His eyes turned softer as a sob shuddered through her body and tears streamed down over his fingers.

"Aw, Van."

Then Clay was beside her on the bed, wrapping his arms around her as she tried to stop crying. But she couldn't, and the way Clay kept saying, "It's okay, let it out," only spurred Van on.

It was crazy. She was in Clay's arms. She'd been so annoyed with him, but now he was warm and comfortable, and they'd been sharing a moment. She'd almost triumphed at her moment of peace with him, but as she cried, Van found herself missing Phoenix.

As much as Van loved Phoenix, they hadn't even really talked about what happened outside of the professional implications. Phoenix boiled over with rage every time it came up, and Van didn't want to have to talk her off the ledge if she didn't have to. It was hard enough for Van to keep her own emotions under control. She thought Phoenix knew she couldn't be the friend Van needed in this instance, so they danced around it. Found work to talk about instead. But that didn't stop Van from wishing Phoenix was there too.

"I miss Phoenix," Van said in a watery voice.

Clay huffed out a dry laugh. "She's probably downstairs. Do you want me to get her?"

Van shook her head and hid her face in the crook of Clay's neck. "I'm sorry. Everything's catching up with me."

Clay's fingers traced smooth lines up and down her spine as he told her not to worry about it.

Van sighed and relaxed further into Clay's arms. She could only remember three other times they'd ever shared more than a perfunctory hug at Christmas time. The good luck kiss he'd given her before her first performance as a signed artist in California, the night they'd slept curled up together just after the tornado, and the night they'd groped each other in a dark hallway, which, so far, they'd both pretended hadn't happened.

As Clay's fingers twined with the end of her ponytail and she breathed in his fresh-cut wood scent, Van wondered why they were pretending it hadn't happened. Touching him, kissing him had felt so good she almost groaned out loud as she remembered the electricity.

Van took a deep breath, inhaling the comforting scent of him before she gave Clay the whole truth. "I saw a future with him, you know. For the first time, I actually saw someone I could build a life with."

Clay stiffened beneath her, but she kept talking. "I was considering breaking up with Bryant—publicly. Making things with Bishop official. Bishop and I had never actually had a discussion about it. But he made comments about it all the time, like how long was I going to let things with Bryant go on? How long I was going to keep up the farce? When was I going to move into his house? Stuff like that."

"Sounds like a fucking bastard," Clay said, his voice not as harsh as his words.

He'd turned from comfortable and stable beneath her touch to brittle, like if Van pressed too hard, he would crumble like old plaster beneath her fingertips. She wondered how often anybody really listened to what Clay needed anymore. He was always so busy taking care of everyone else, maybe he didn't get close enough to anybody to share.

"He didn't really want to be with you," Clay asked. "He wanted to possess you, like a fucking trophy."

"I see that now. Before, I didn't understand why I was so frustrated. Now," Van traced the line of stitching along the collar of Clay's t-shirt. "I still can't write, but at least I know why."

Clay squeezed her, then asked, "Why didn't you break it off with Bryant?" She could feel Clay's heartbeat tick up beneath her cheek, and she wondered what about that question in particular made him nervous.

"I think I was waiting for him to fall in love with a local, for him to have someone to confide in once we didn't have an excuse to hang out all the time anymore, but I should have known better than that."

"What does that mean?"

Van smiled at the defensiveness in Clay's tone, and she loved how much he wanted to understand all of this. Understand *her*.

"Just that Bryant is so loyal, he'd never be the one to end our relationship. He'd protect me until the end, even if he lived the rest of his life lonely and celibate."

Clay snorted, and the bitterness rose the hairs on the back of Van's neck. "He'd be having sex with you at least."

Van jolted back, and Clay's hands slid from around her shoulders to grasp the dip in her waist. "Did he tell you he was sleeping with me?" She could feel the heat of the anger welling inside her showing on her face.

Clay's face flushed as well, and Van couldn't tell if he was blushing or responding to the obvious wrath twisting Van's lips and hardening her eyes.

"Bryant's never given me any details about your relationship. I just assumed you'd been together fives years—and even if it was mostly a farce, you still sleep over at his house most of the time." He paused, his hands squeezing Van's waist as he flexed his forearms. His shoulders rolled under Van's palms, and she realized she was basically straddling him on her bed. Her face turned redder, and she tried to keep her eyes focused in anger instead of feeling his muscled legs beneath her thighs. "I thought, maybe sometimes…"

"You thought that I just used my best friend for sex whenever I felt like it. Because why else would he keep pretending to be my boyfriend for so long?" Van moved to shove off of him, but he caught her with one hand at her shoulders, the other catching her beneath her thigh and pulling her close so that she *was* straddling him.

"No. I think that Bryant's so in love with you that he'll do whatever you ask him to."

Van flinched. She knew she flinched hard and that Clay watched her do it. "You really think I'm that mean?" She tried to squirm away.

Clay tightened his hands on her, holding her against his chest. "I don't think you mean to be. I just think Bryant doesn't know how to tell you no, and you're beautiful and funny and a little mean, sure, but I can see why he can't quite quit you."

"Quit me?"

His hand stroked over Van's bare thigh, and she watched him swallow as he tried to figure out how to get himself out of this muddy little ditch he'd just dug himself into.

"You know what I mean."

"You mean that you think your friend has so little self-respect that he'll do whatever I ask for a little action?"

Clay didn't answer. His hand was tracing small circles over her thigh, and his breath caressed her neck as he said, "It sounds crude when you put it that way. I don't think you are malicious about it, and I don't think Bryant is pathetic—just in love. We do things we shouldn't when we're in love."

Like make out in dark hallways.

Van shook her head and squirmed against the motion his hand was making. Her skin prickled at the heat his fingerprints ignited, and she didn't know what to do with it. Any other time she'd been in an attractive man's lap and he was touching her like this, the course of action had always been clear. Kiss him and see how far he was willing to push it. But with Clay? Van shouldn't even be sitting on him like this.

What they were doing was dangerous, but Van couldn't bring herself to shift off his legs. A deep-seated instinct had her wanting to writhe against him, just to find out if this was affecting his body.

"Bryant's not in love with me," Van said. "And as much as I'd like to claim a magical pussy, I can't."

Clay's arms tightened around her on the word pussy, and she felt his hips buck against hers. Van tried to ignore the way her body hummed. She wanted to arch her back so her hips ground back into him while offering her breasts to him like a sacrifice.

God, Van hadn't felt desire in so long. It had only been a few weeks, but it had also been a lifetime ago. The woman that had wanted Bishop was a different person— and that was enough to bring back the memory of Bishop's hands too tight against her hips, of his heavy body over her as she begged him to stop.

Van slid to the side, off Clay's lap and pulled a pillow into her lap, clinging to it like maybe holding something tight would help the memory, the hurt, the betrayal, the devastation go away.

In an effort to hide her pain, to save face in front of Clay, Van said, "And even if I did. Bryant wouldn't know."

Clay was confused. One hand was hanging in the air, paused from reaching for Van to pull her back into his lap. His body was still stuck in the intimate embrace they'd just stolen, and his mind catching up to what Van had just said.

"What?"

"I've never had sex with Bryant, Clay."

His brows pulled into a frown, but he said, "I'd assumed—I'm sorry."

"Yeah, well, once a whore always a whore, right?"

It wasn't fair. To throw something he'd said in high school in his face. He hadn't even meant it when he said it. He'd just tossed Justin Spencer out of her room after he'd walked in on them having sex. It wasn't the first time he'd caught Van with a guy in her room either, and as much as Van had raged at him to have some respect and knock, he'd yelled right back that people were going to start calling her a whore if she kept sleeping around.

He'd been angry. And worried about her, and he really hadn't liked Justin Spencer, but the sentiment had stuck with Van for a long time. It had been part of the reason why she'd asked Bryant to be her pretend boyfriend in public. You were a lot less likely to be labeled a slut when you were in a long-term, committed relationship.

A hand landed on her knee. "Van, you know—"

She shoved him away. "You should go."

There was a rustle of fabric as Clay stood, then the clink of metal against porcelain as he set the plate full of food down in front of her. "Try to eat something, please."

Then he left Van alone, and she was even angrier than she had been before.

Bishop Still Fighting Charges

The photo above shows Bishop coming out of the coffee shop in Santa Monica where he met Van Birch in 2014, just after she moved to California. Birch was playing on the corner in front of the cafe, and Bishop watched her grow as an artist for months before eventually brokering her a record deal. When asked why he was there, Bishop told reporters that he liked the coffee and that he misses Van, who he called, "Ness." A pet name. Our hearts are melting.

Van Birch has not dropped the charges against her former manager, despite his claims that it was all a misunderstanding.

10

*C*lay collapsed back onto his childhood bed, cursing himself. He couldn't have made that encounter more confusing if he'd tried. Comfort. Insult. Indulgence. Clay couldn't just pick one when it came to Van; he had to work all three into every encounter.

His mind was still spinning from learning the truth about Van and Bryant. He felt like an idiot. His closest friend hadn't been able to confide in Clay for five years. A different man might have been pissed off, but Clay understood. Bryant had always known how Clay felt about Van and been sensitive to it. Clay would have been angrier about the relationship being fake at the beginning. More betrayed. And it would have been Clay's own fault, because he'd never been able to admit his feelings for Van out loud. But tonight he'd longed to tell her. He'd wanted to just say, *I'm worried about you. Please eat. Please talk to me. Let me take care of you. Let me love you.*

But he'd screwed that up too.

Clay groaned and covered his eyes with his palms as

he rolled onto his stomach to bury his burning face in his pillows. He didn't always like himself very much for loving Van. He hated it right now, after holding her, after hearing that she had actually been in love with that motherfucker—or thought she had been. Clay's stomach turned as he imagined how small she would look in Bishop arms.

Bishop was huge. Six feet tall with the lean, well-muscled physique most surfers had. And he had the added bonus of designer clothes, a man bun that didn't look ridiculous, and one of those over-groomed beards. He looked like he'd walked out of the pages of a men's fashion magazine, and Clay understood how Van could have been taken in by the facade, but it was obvious that all of that was a clever trap. The man was an ambitious bastard, and he'd latched himself onto Van as soon as she signed her first record deal. All she was to him was dollar signs. And what better way to prove it than to do what he did.

Clay's imagined Bishop's hands digging into Van's hips where the bruises had been.

Rage so sharp exploded inside him that he was off his bed and stomping down the hall before he knew where he was going. He must have sounded like thunder on the stairs because when he landed in the kitchen, Phoenix and Robin were blinking at him from the breakfast bar where they were sharing a bottle of wine.

"Where do I find him?" Clay asked Phoenix.

She wrinkled her brow. "Who?"

"Bishop. Where is he?"

She shook her head. "I don't know. And I don't want to."

"Did you know they were dating?" Clay asked her.

Phoenix set her wine down. "Of course I knew they were dating. But I'd want to rip his balls off even if they hadn't been."

He rushed the breakfast bar, leaning over it, scowling into her face as he said, "Then why haven't you?"

Phoenix stood, getting right back in his face. "Because it would only make things worse for Van, you prick."

"Fe," Robin said in a soothing tone, his hand landing on the curve of her hip. An intimate gesture Clay didn't have time to process as she slapped Robin's hand away and shook a finger in Clay's face.

"Don't you dare make this harder on her than it already is. You put on your protective big brother pants whenever it suits you, but the rest of the time, you treat Van like dirt. I don't care how much she loves you, I will squash you like the little roach of a man you are if you hurt her again."

Again?

Clay schooled his shock. When had he ever hurt Van? And what had he ever done to get on Phoenix's bad side? As far as Clay was concerned there wasn't a problem outside of this current situation. "What I want to know is why you aren't crushing Henry Bishop?"

Phoenix slapped her phone on the counter, glared at Clay, then pulled up a series of text messages and shoved them in his face.

"That's why."

Clay had to read the exchange three times before the meaning set in.

"He has a fucking sex tape?"

Phoenix inhaled slowly through her nose. "I'm not taking the chance that he's bluffing. Not right now."

Clay cut his glance to Robin. He was frowning, but he didn't look nearly as shocked or as angry as Clay would expect a man to be who just found out his daughter had a sex tape with the man who had also raped her.

"You knew about this?" Clay asked.

"Phoenix mentioned it," he nodded. "I think it's best to play on the side of caution until the legal system bows out completely."

Clay held out Phoenix's phone to her before he smashed it into the tiled floor. He. Wanted. Blood.

"What does Van say?"

Phoenix squared her shoulders. "I haven't told her about his threats yet. I'm not certain she even knows about the tape."

The butt of Clay's fist hit the granite countertop, and the impact shook the silverware in the drawer below. "She doesn't know about it?"

"I'm not sure," Phoenix said, poking him in the chest. "And if you fucking say anything, I'll have your balls in a vice for sure. So don't go mouthing off about it before I have all the details."

"He can't get away with this," Clay said, forcing all of the menace he felt into his voice.

"It's a waiting game," Robin said. "We can't do anything unless he makes a move, and he won't while he's still under investigation. We've informed the police, but we can't even get a restraining order right now, not unless we have proof of violent intent." Clay had always loved how steadfast and logical Robin was, but right now, he wanted Robin to rage with him. To demand justice. He was a goddamn attorney, and he was doing nothing to help his daughter.

Clay wanted to rave about the ever-increasing security around the house. About the cameras, about the armed guards, about the death threats on social media, the rape threats that came in daily. The tens of thousands of people who told Van she'd deserved it. What about any of that didn't imply violent intent? But Clay settled on, "The police are idiots. She showed me the bruises. There is no way—no way that was consensual."

Phoenix looked like he'd slapped her. "She showed you the bruises? When?"

Clay's hands clenched down on the edge of the counter so hard, his knuckles hurt. He wished he was strong enough to break the slab of stone. It would give all of this feeling some outlet at least.

"The first night she was back. She needed to talk, so," Clay shrugged, "I listened."

"Oh," was all Phoenix said, and she looked just as devastated as Van had the night she'd come to his room. Because Van had been hurting? Or because Van hadn't confided in her? Clay looked to Robin, but he only had eyes for Phoenix, concern pursing the corners of his lips.

"Does anybody else know about his threats?" Clay asked, his mind firing all the different things they could do to protect Van from Bishop.

"We've talked to the lawyers in L.A.," Robin said. "They're ready with a lawsuit if he releases the tape."

"And we have a P.I. sniffing around in case there's a reason why they won't prosecute," Phoenix said.

"You mean like Bishop bribing the DA?"

"Yes." Robin and Phoenix said at the same time.

Clay looked between the two of them, noting the easy way they sat so close together at the breakfast bar. The open bottle of wine between them. They looked comfortable, like this wasn't the first time they'd shared a late-night drink. Were they merely strategizing for Van's sake? Maybe, but as Clay switched his gaze from Phoenix's face to Robin's and back again, Phoenix raised her chin and Robin stroked two fingers over the salt and pepper beard at the corner of his mouth.

For a lawyer, he really should have been a better liar.

There was a lot more to this affair than just crawling into each other's beds at night.

"Does Van know?" Clay asked.

"About the P.I.? She knows we're looking into things. The private investigator was implied." Phoenix said, hiding behind business, but Robin gave a minute shake of his head.

"Jesus," Clay said and rubbed his hands over his face. Twice. Then looked at Robin. "You need to tell her. The sooner the better." Then he shot a glare at Phoenix too. "And you need to tell her about the tape. She deserves to know. About everything."

Then Clay grabbed his keys, whistled for Pebbles, and took her for a long walk. It would have been better had the stupid photographers not followed him for the first two miles before they realized he wasn't doing anything interesting. All Clay wanted was some fucking privacy.

He had to fight his way back through the camp of them outside the security barriers around the house on his way back inside, and they were shouting questions at him like, "What's it like living with your stepdad? Is it true Van's going to rebuild your house? How do you feel about your ex-girlfriend dating Michael Astor?" Clay didn't answer any of them. Each one was just as inane as the last.

When he finally collapsed into bed, he didn't think he would sleep; his mind was so filled with outrage and anger and confusion. But he must have drifted off about the time he started wondering what he'd done in the past to hurt Van, because the next thing he knew Van herself was shaking him awake.

Both her hands were on his shoulders, shoving feebly as she spoke, "Wake up, Man-whore. The cameras are here," were the first words Clay made out clearly.

"Man-whore?" His voice was gravelly and hoarse, like he'd been screaming all night instead of walking.

"That's my new nickname for you," she said. "Isn't it cute?"

Clay wanted to argue with her, but after making sure he had a new girlfriend each time Van came home and then feeling her up in public, maybe the nickname was warranted.

All thought shut down when she straddled him, jeans and combat boots and all, her palms still against his shoulders.

"Listen up, Man-whore. We have a big-deal reporter coming today; it's going to be just like when all the celebrities were here except we'll actually get work done. We're going to be filmed looking at plans, and then you are going to show me the neighborhood you're working on. We'll meet some of the families. They'll be grateful. You'll be humble and smile and play up the dimples and the midwestern accent just a little bit. And I will hammer something inconsequential, and you will do none of the looking at me with pity or puppy dog eyes. And you will pretend we get along. Do you hear me?"

"Good morning, Van. Sleep well?"

Clay ran his hands up her thighs and over her hips until his secured his fingers around her waist. He could feel how thin she was through her tank top, and he wanted to ask her if she'd eaten breakfast but knew better.

"Do you hear me?" she asked again, her eyes narrowing as he worked his fingertips under the hem of her shirt until he found the bare skin above the waistline of her jeans.

"I can play nice," Clay said.

She glared down at him, frozen in her dislike. Possibly in disgust. But Clay had a feeling that was only a front.

"What are you thinking, Van?" Clay asked.

"That you shouldn't be touching me like that." But she didn't move.

And because Clay didn't want to be on that list of people that kept things from her, he traced his fingers higher up her ribs in slow, methodical circles. Her eyes fluttered, and Clay grinned, even though he knew it tipped his hand. "Why shouldn't I touch you?"

"Because you're my stepbrother," she said, her breath coming shorter than it had a minute ago.

"My mother and your father were married for eight years. We lived in the same house for three before I enlisted, but I have never, will never, think of myself as your brother."

Clay's fingertips hit the lace edge of her bra. He was tempted to slip beneath the silky fabric, that or flip her beneath him just for a taste of what it would finally,

finally feel like to hover over her—but if she didn't want it, he couldn't do that to her. He had probably gone too far already.

All of Clay's bravado and confidence fled as he pulled his hands from underneath her shirt. Guilt set in. He had no right to touch her like that. Even if he saw her as a woman rather than a sister, that didn't mean she felt the same way about him. Clay understood how pushing that line, especially after what had happened with Bishop, would be going too far.

Clay smoothed her shirt back down over her hips and tucked his hands behind his head, attempting to keep up the appearance of the stupid macho arrogance that he'd been riding a moment before. "But I can play a brother on TV if that's what you need."

Van narrowed her eyes and pursed her lips. "Get dressed. We need to leave in twenty minutes."

Then she left, slamming the door behind her.

Phoenix was waiting in the foyer with Van when Clay descended the stairs. Clay couldn't remember the last time he'd used the front door to Robin's house, but that was the way it went with the cameras around. Ducking out the side door behind the kitchen that was closest to the driveway wasn't as visually pleasing as walking on the wide front porch surrounded with zinnias.

Clay would never get used to having the cameras around and to how life seemed just a little bit less authentic when you weren't ever able to just be yourself. But they were already filming as he stooped to pull on his work boots and used the few seconds it took to tie his laces to school his features into brotherly contractor mode.

Phoenix ran through the schedule for the day, and Clay was glad for the time Bryant and he had taken yesterday to run over the logistics of actually building, because it didn't sound like he'd have much time for anything practical since he was playing the role of Van's babysitter. Who knew how many times they would make them reshoot walking through the empty streets where houses used to stand?

Clay wanted to ask why Bryant wasn't doing this with Van. Bryant had just as much at stake in this business as Clay did, and really, Clay was better suited at organizing the crews while Bryant played host to Van and looked serious and lovesick for the cameras. There was no way Clay was going to say any of that while they were filming. But if he could get Van alone, he might ask her what her game was.

"The paparazzi have landed, folks," Phoenix said as Clay stood tall, willing himself not to touch Van even though she stood so close he could feel her body heat pricking the hairs on his arm. The one or two photographers that had been at the barrier seemed to have alerted their counterparts, because there had to be at least twenty flashing pictures of them standing on the porch.

"Be careful out there. Don't give them anything to sell to the gossip rags. Be professional and aloof." The stare Phoenix levelled at Clay left nothing to the imagination, and he could see the camera guys zeroing in on her reaction and on his.

Clay nodded for the cameras and reminded himself he only had to put up with this intrusion for a couple of months. Soon they would all move on. Wellville would be on its way to recovery, and Van would be back in L.A., and everything would return to normal. The idea left a gnawing pit in the bottom of his stomach, and while he knew it was because he didn't want Van to leave, he also knew that there was nothing he could do to change the fact that she would go eventually.

Trouble in Paradise?

There have been rumors over the years that Van Birch and long-time beau Bryant Wilder haven't been one-hundred percent faithful to each other. With Van's affair with former manager Henry Bishop come to light, it seems like we finally have evidence that Bryant Wilder has had an indiscretion or two. Below are photos of Bryant at hometown haunt, Tessa's, in the arms of another woman. No word on who the buxom blonde is in these grainy photos, but there's no doubt about where Bryant's hands or his lips are for that matter. Which begs the question, was Van's affair with Bishop retribution for this little indiscretion, or is the famous couple way freakier than we thought?

11

*V*an followed Clay to his new truck, the replacement for the one the tornado kidnapped. The old one had been red and old and a little bit of a clunker. This one was newer, silver, and huge. There was mud splatter all over it. Van loved it. She loved it even more when Clay opened the door for her and helped her up into the giant monstrosity of a vehicle. She loved it most when Clay's hand lingered at the small of her back as she climbed into her seat, a move she knew the cameras wouldn't miss.

There would probably be a still of it on the internet by noon with as many paps as there were camped outside the house today. Thanks, guys. Now all the bloggers were going to think she was having an affair with her stepbrother.

Van watched Clay jog around to the driver's side door, admiring the way his t-shirt showed off his biceps, and wondered if maybe she *was* having an affair with Clay—or starting one at least. The way he kept touching her at every opportunity, Van just about believed that was exactly what he wanted. Clay couldn't keep his hands off her bare skin. And this morning? In his bed? He had most definitely been naked under that sheet. It had used all Van's willpower to keep from gyrating all over him and licking his gorgeous pecs.

That wasn't normal. Was it?

Van wasn't sure. She'd had the longest, most persistent crush on Clay all throughout high school. She sometimes even pretended she was kissing him when she had to kiss Bryant in public. Did she mind all his under the shirt touches this morning? Absolutely not. Did they make Van feel things she wasn't sure she should feel? That was a hell yes, and it was damn confusing. Just like everything else in her life.

The paparazzi were pooled at the end of the driveway, nearly blocking the street, even as Butch's security team cleared the way for the caravan of trucks that were leaving the house. Security, urged by Phoenix and Robin, had grown so tight over the last couple of weeks that Van was no longer going anywhere, not even to Clay's construction site, without two guards at all times. So not only was the *Pop Star* crew van following them but so were Butch and Alvin, in their big armored SUV.

For now, they were all idling in the driveway, waiting for Clay to pull out, but he reached behind his seat into the tiny space there and pulled up a silver hard hat with two big pink stars on either side.

"I got you something," he said, not meeting Van's eye as he handed the hard hat over.Van traced the stars with her fingertip, a smile playing on her lips. On both her albums, her name had been bracketed by two pink stars, just like this. "You got me a pretty hard hat. And it's even on brand. Phoenix is going to be so pleased."

"I don't give a damn what Phoenix thinks," he said. "But I know you like pretty things, and hard hats are ugly, and I know you don't like that old yellow one you've been wearing, so..." he trailed off and started the car.

Van beamed and plopped the hat on her head. "Everyone is going to be so jealous now. Your whole crew is gonna want pink hard hats, just you wait."

"We can get them for the whole team." Clay said as he shifted into reverse. "Your own army of construction workers." Van watched him, his body twisted to make sure he backed out of the driveway without running anybody over. The photographers swarmed the truck, knocking at the windows and shouting questions through the glass about Amber and Bishop and Michael Astor and Twitter trolls.

Clay switched on the radio, and Van's own voice blared from the speakers, drowning out all the other voices.

Van swiveled her head to Clay so fast, she nearly lost her hard hat. "You listen to my music?" she shouted.

Clay gave her a wide, unapologetic grin, which showed off the dimples she'd told him to use to his advantage earlier, and winked. Clay *winked* at her. Van slumped back against her seat and covered her face with the hard hat to hide the cherry-red color. A chuckle came from Clay's direction as they inched through the photographers and made their way down the street.

When they were well away from the house, Clay turned the volume down and his hand landed on Van's knee, squeezing it briefly between shifting gears, and she peeked out from behind her hat. She fanned herself, hoping her color would return to normal before they got to the site.

"Why are you so embarrassed?" he asked, cutting his gaze to her for just a moment.

Van motioned toward the console. "I didn't think this was your kind of thing." They were listening to her first album; the song had been her second single and a particularly poppy departure from her usual soulful sound, but a song she was proud of none-the-less—and not just because she'd made oodles of money from it. "I remember you being a country purist back in the day."

"I still listen to country on occasion," he said. "But I've been broadening my horizons."

"Like Van Birch?"

"Like Van Birch." he nodded.

They shared a sweet smile, and her heart settled into a contented rhythm as they drove along a smooth, newly paved street. There were only a few houses on either side of the road. Some lots were entirely empty except for a concrete pad while others had basements covered with tarps. It was late August, so the grass was already mostly dead from the heat and the sun, but the yards were less sod, more turned-up dirt and dried-out tracks from the large trucks that had come to pull away the debris.

The sight broke Van's heart every time. She knew, though, that within a few months, this neighborhood would be rebuilt and full of happy families and running, smiling children again. It calmed a little of the anxiety roiling inside her. Van took as much comfort as she could that she was helping to make that happen, because she felt like the tornado had picked up off the ground in Wellville and dived right between her ribs, where it had churned for more than a month now.

"Your house was near here, right?" she asked.

Van had never actually seen Clay's house. He'd only finished building it last year, and though she'd been home to visit her dad, Clay's visits had been sparse. He'd made a couple of cameos on the show, and there had been that short segment last season with him and Bryant hanging out at Tessa's while Phoenix and Van danced, but that was about as much as they'd seen each other in the last two years, despite fans of the show begging for more footage with Van's hunky blonde brother.

She examined Clay's hair. It had been redder as a teenager, but he could pass for blonde these days. Van picked at the end of her braid. She had naturally chestnut hair but had kept it mostly black since high school. The quality of the hair dye she used had improved but still. Blonde hair was obviously nowhere in her genetics. So it was clear that Clay wasn't her biological brother, right?

"I was a couple blocks to the east," he said. "Nothing left but the basement." His voice was quiet, strained. It had to be hard for him to think about, all his hard work disappearing in a moment.

"Can we stop by later?" Van asked. "I've never seen your house."

"There's nothing left to see, Van. It's all gone."

"But you're rebuilding, right?" She had to make sure he didn't give up on the idea to rebuild, not with all the strings she'd been pulling to get him the money to pay for it.

"Eventually." He shrugged and pulled to a stop in front of a mostly vacant lot. There was a trailer set up on the side of the street, and a few men were already setting up sawhorses in the yard, while a few others were pulling the tarp from the top of the basement. Some paparazzi milled about across the street and started snapping photos as they parked.

The next couple of days were crammed with training sessions and filming and greeting people who were so grateful for the work Van had been doing.

But they were also filled with notifications. #notBishop and #justice4Van were still trending six weeks after The Incident.

And things had gotten even more heated in that time.

Phoenix was fielding phone calls every day from reporters and bloggers wanting to know Van's take on the story, wanting interviews and soundbites for their latest videos. She shut them all down. If they weren't calling about Van's next album or about the rebuilding effort, Phoenix didn't talk to them. It had been the bloggers who had started with the snide remarks first. Van had watched their videos in her room at night before bed, curious to see how public opinion was developing as she continued to make national headlines for the work she was doing in Wellville—but she knew it was the gossip rags and social media that told the truth about what the people actually believed.

The bloggers sniped about Van's refusal to comment, like she was hiding something instead of just not wanting to relive the worst night of her life over and over and over again for other people's entertainment. Then the talk show hosts, and the tabloids, picked up on the sentiment.

The pictures of Van on the front covers had changed from shots of her and Bishop to shots of Van around

Wellville, accompanied by articles critiquing her weight, her pallor, questioning whether or not she was on drugs or drinking too much or whether she was hiding because she was ashamed of her false allegations against such a powerful man like Bishop.

There were shots of Bishop too. He looked sad, haggard, like he wasn't trimming his beard and had been letting the saltwater dry into his hair after he went surfing. He looked raw and vulnerable and harassed, and it only brought out more of his inherent sex appeal— whereas Van had been photoshopped to look like she weighed eighty pounds.

Both her therapist and Phoenix had told her to stay away from social media, to not think about what other people were saying, but she needed to know how vicious things were getting. She needed to see how the men's rights activists had evolved from suggesting she didn't know what a good fuck was to outright offering to rape her so she could see what it was really like to be at some guy's mercy.

Following one of their conversations led her to Reddit, where there was talk of organizing a trip to Wellville to see if one of them could corner her and do just that.

She'd called Butch then, and he'd tightened her security even more, so much so that she was doing her daily run on a goddamn treadmill, which she despised.

And then of course there was Michael Astor spouting off his mouth to any reporter who would listen, per usual.

Van had slept with Michael once a couple of years ago after an awards show. It had been entirely alcohol fueled, and she didn't remember much about it. Michael had texted her whenever they were in the same city, looking for a hookup. You'd think after years of "No thanks, I'm in a relationship. That night was a mistake," the guy would get the picture, but apparently it had only made him bitter.

Not only was he telling everyone it was routine for Van to cheat on Bryant, he'd apparently gotten the inside scoop from Amber that Van and Clay had been having an off-again, on-again affair since their parents got married. The gossip sites were having a field day with that. Shots of Clay and Van together were appearing all over the internet now. They were almost always at a job site with Bryant in them too, but no one seemed to care about that part. It was all about how much time Clay and Van were spending together.

Except Van wasn't about to complain about how much time she was getting to spend with Clay recently. Turned out, he was halfway pleasant when he let his guard down. And that crush Van thought she'd smashed into smithereens a few years ago slowly started to piece its way back together. She lived for the brush of his fingers over her forearm as he passed behind her at work. His grins. His dimples. The gentle way he spoke to her when no one else was listening, like every word was secret meant just for her.

It was a good thing Clay headed for the garage when they got home from work that day. Van didn't think the butterflies in her tummy could take much more of his presence. She left him to tinker with his woodworking project while she made a break for the backdoor. There would be zero pictures of them doing anything but being practical. That was safe. Van would keep it that way if she was smart. She had too much else going on to be distracted by dimples and pecs. And another text from Bishop as Butch unlocked the back door for her didn't help.

The sound of piano music greeted her when she entered the house. She followed the sounds into the formal living room to find her dad sitting at the old baby grand. Though Van preferred the guitar, she could play the piano. She'd started her musical education on this beautiful, ancient instrument.

She slid onto the bench next to her dad. He smiled down at her. "Hey, Bitsy," he said, leaning over to kiss the top of her head without ever missing a note. Okay, so kisses from her dad were permissible. Hugs too. With him at least, the lines defining their relationship were clear. Father, daughter. In it together. Always sticking together since they'd lost her mom.

He'd been playing Mozart, but he switched into a quieter Bach piece that Van recognized but couldn't name. "You wanna talk about it?" he asked.

Van hadn't realized she'd been scowling until then. She quirked her lips to the side to attempt to change the dour expression. She didn't know where to start, so she placed her cellphone on the music holder in front of her dad. The text messages from Bishop on the screen. The most recent one on top. Until this afternoon all of Bishop's texts had been apologetic attempts at reconciliation. They'd been coming more frequently over the last couple of weeks. Him entreating Van to call him, talk to him, work things out. This text had chilled her to the bone.

It simply read, "Love that you matched your shirt to your hard hat, babe. You're adorable."

Her dad's fingers stilled over the keys, then his eyes cut to her shirt—a dusty black t-shirt with hot pink stars all over it. He frowned, then picked up her phone and read everything on the screen.

"How long has this been going on?" he asked.

"Since the beginning."

He scrolled up, and Van cringed inwardly. There were some messages a little ways up that were definitely not something a girl wanted her dad to read, but he handed back her phone after a second, and Van saw his inner lawyer kick in.

"Have you had any other contact with him?"

Van shook her head. "I haven't responded, just like you told me not to. No emails. Phone calls. Nothing. Zero contact since The Incident."

The Incident. Van was starting to hate that euphemism, but as she watched her dad's breath catch in his throat for a second before he regained his composure, she was glad she had it. Van couldn't talk baldly about what happened with her father. It was too hard knowing how helpless he felt about it all. Knowing that she'd been hurt and he couldn't do anything about it but try be a solid foundation for her now. And her dad couldn't be solid when he let go of that inner rage she'd seen so few times in her life.

"Good," he said. "Keep it that way. We'll call your team in L.A. and let them know about the texts. That last one qualifies as a threat."

Van's blood ran cold. "Do you think he's here?" she asked. "I mean, I've been wearing that hard hat for days. He's bound to have seen it in the photos online. And there were paparazzi around all day too, so it's possible that he just saw a photo from today on some gossip site right? He's not here stalking me or anything."

"I don't know, Bitsy. I think it's best if we let Butch and Phoenix in on this."

She blew out an exasperated breath and rested her head against her dad's shoulder. He wrapped an arm around her and squeezed. Yes. Dad hugs were definitely on the list of approved touches.

But Van wasn't sure how much more "security" she could take. She was pretty sure Phoenix and her Dad were about to conspire with Butch to hide her away in a bunker and make her record her album underground.

"Why can't things go back to normal?" Van asked.

Her dad squeezed her side, then placed his hands back on the keys in front of them. "This is one of those times where we have to find a new normal, I think."

He played a few random chords. "Like after Mom?"

"Like after Mom," he said.

There had been other times they'd had to find a new normal. Van hadn't been happy when he'd announced he was marrying Clay's mom. She'd had no real problem with Mary Beth, but she was a teenager and hadn't wanted to share her dad with anyone. Let alone have a stranger *and* the hottest guy in school move into her house and cramp her style. She'd gotten used to Clay and learned to love Mary Beth. And then after Mary Beth had passed . . . even though Van hadn't lived in Kansas anymore, it had still shocked her to come home and not have her stepmother's sweet smile and warm hugs.

Van's dad played a few chords, tapping out a melody that made her grin. It was a song they'd played together a lot growing up, just him and her on the piano. Her voice, his fingers, no need for fiery electric guitars.

Van sang "Carry on My Wayward Son" by Kansas without prompting, and Robin joined her on the chorus. It was their song. He even improvised the guitar solo on the piano, and it cracked Van up every time, because it was the silliest thing she'd ever seen him do the first time he did it. Her serious, lawyer dad, emulating electric guitars on his ancient piano. He had been trying to convince Van that pianos were cooler than guitars. It hadn't stuck, but maybe that was why Van had always preferred acoustic instruments.

When they finished the song, Van felt lighter. Fortified. Whatever came next, she'd get through it. And she wouldn't be alone.

Her dad launched into one of Van's songs, and her heart warmed. It never ceased to amaze her that her dad took the time to learn her songs, even the ones that didn't have piano parts. Because she knew this house was the safest place in the world for her heart, Van sat up straight and let her voice echo throughout the old house.

@MrBigChad: #justice4Van would be a hard fucking by every guy she's wronged in her quest for fame.
Reply to @MrBigChad: Put her Feminazi pussy on a pike when you're done

_____

When Clay had started his shower, Robin had been playing one of his favorite classical songs. When he'd stepped out a few minutes later, Robin and Van were laughing at his attempts to manufacture the guitar riff from that Kansas song on the piano. They were having fun. Clay couldn't remember the last time he'd heard Van laugh like that. A smile split his own lips as Clay listened to them crooning.

The song changed as he pulled on his jeans. It was the song Clay and Van had played together the other night. The first single from her second album. A lot of people thought it was a fuck you to her critics, but Clay had always thought it had to be more than that, like there was someone she was singing it to specifically. It started out a little poppy and upbeat but grew intense and angry. The song always left him feeling heavy but grounded. It was the kind of song that told him Van knew her own strength. He tossed a t-shirt over his head, anxious not to miss the performance. Van started singing just as he reached the bottom of the stairs.

I woke up today
    And you tried to define me
    Told me how to be
    But I'm more than this
    More than you

Take it easy
    Hold me close
    Tell me to take it slow
    Or not at all
    You want me
    But you'll let me take the fall

Maybe someday I'll grow up
    Step up
    Make something of myself
    And prove to you that I'm
    More than this
    More than you

Take it easy
    Hold me close
    Tell me to take it slow
    Or not at all

You want me
But you'll let me take the fall

You think you have it all
That I'm yours for the taking
You think I'll let you in my room
Ooo, but I'm already escaping

Take it easy
Hold me close
Tell me to take it slow
Or not at all
You want me
But you'll let me take the fall

Phoenix had appeared in the doorway next to Clay halfway through the song. He tried to smile at her, to see if she was appreciating the father-daughter moment, but she had apparently not forgiven him for the other night, because all he got was a flat stare.

When they'd finished, Clay expected them to start again, but Robin said, "I've been thinking about that song a lot lately."

Van plinked through a series of notes near the middle of the keyboard. "Almost seems appropriate, huh?"

Clay hated the wry sadness in her voice.

"I remember when you wrote it."

"You do?" Her head jerked up to meet her father's eyes.

"I do. It's one of the first songs you truly finished. You played it over and over and over again. Day and night. Right before Clay left too."

She snorted. "Yeah, well, it's about Clay. It was my way of wishing him a fond farewell and fuck you too, I suppose."

Clay stiffened at the mention of his name.

Robin nodded. "Do you mind if I ask what happened between you two?" When Van cringed, he added, "You used to adore him."

"Well, that was before he spouted off to his buddies that I'd fuck anything with a dick, and all he'd have to do to get with me would be to sneak into my room in the dark."

Clay's stomach dropped out as Robin's shoulders and back tensed. "He never—"

"No," Van said, almost too quickly. "It was just stupid immature posturing—but it still hurt."

Clay scrubbed his hands over his face as shame nearly drowned him. He had said that. He remembered the incident, because Bryant had socked him in the jaw for it. They'd already started working out, getting ready for bootcamp, and it had hurt. The bruise had only just faded by the time he shipped out a few weeks later.

It had been stupid. Bryant, another high school friend, Race, and Clay had been crowded around the breakfast bar, devouring some junk food after a workout, and Race had been asking if Van was around, hinting that he wanted to make a move there. As a bullshit way of marking his territory, Clay had told him he didn't want to go there—exaggerated about the number of guys he'd tossed out of Van's room, and then capped it off with that little gem.

Blowing breath out from between his lips, Clay shook his head. He hadn't realized Van had witnessed that event. He looked up to find Phoenix in his face. She jabbed him in the chest with a sharp, red fingernail and whispered, "You wanted to know what you did to her. And now you know why you make me sick." She stomped on his foot as she stalked off, and she was wearing heels.

Van's and Robin's murmuring voices had given way to more notes, the two of them playing another of her songs together. A sad duet she'd done with an R&B artist.

Clay grabbed Pebbles, and limping slightly, took her for a long walk, deciding it'd be for the best to make himself scarce for the rest of the night.

He'd walked Pebbles down to the little taco shop a few blocks away, bought himself dinner, then let her run around the bark park while he ate. The photographers must have been bored taking picture of Clay walking his dog, because none of them followed him.

It was almost eight when he refilled Pebbles's water bowl in the kitchen sink. He thought he might make it to his room without intruding on any one else's privacy when he heard creaking floorboards, then soft footsteps as hardwood gave way to tile. Clay straightened from setting the water bowl on the floor in the corner to find Robin behind him, leaning against the refrigerator, arms crossed over his chest.

He didn't say anything for a long time, just stared at Clay with assessing, calculating eyes.

Clay didn't let himself look away as the shame and horror at something he'd said years ago welled inside him again. Clay hated himself for it now, even if he hadn't meant it. He'd never believed anything like that about Van, but he'd been a frustrated kid with a soul-consuming forbidden crush and no idea what to do about it but ship himself off so he'd be forced to move on.

"You overhead this afternoon."

It wasn't a question. Clay said, "Yes, sir" anyway.

"What Van told me disappoints me."

Clay wanted to hang his head, but he held Robin's gaze, ready to take whatever he wanted to give.

"I trusted you with her, you know."

"Yes, sir. I'm sorry."

"You need to apologize to her. What you said hurt *her*."

Clay nodded. "I will. Is she in her room?"

Robin shook his head. "She's staying at Bryant's tonight."

Clay dipped his head, and Robin gave him a break; as he passed him on his way to the living room, Robin clapped Clay on the shoulder. "I trust you to make this right," he said.

Those few words felt so heavy, like Robin had looped an iron chain around Clay's neck with a giant padlock that hung right over his heart. The weight was a responsibility, an obligation to repair the years-long hurt he'd started with Van—and perhaps repair the gulf hearing what Clay had said had opened up between Robin and himself as well.

Clay had watched it happen, as Robin stiffened his

shoulders, as he wondered if he'd been wrong about Clay all this time, if he'd unwittingly invited a predator into his home. If maybe the thing with Bishop wasn't the first time something like that had happened to Van. And that Robin could doubt Clay like that, even for a second, was entirely Clay's fault.

Hot or Not?

Van and Bryant went out for what looks like a cozy, romantic dinner in Wellville last night. What do you think, does the couple look on fire or is the flame fizzling out?

---

13

*B*ryant picked Van up for dinner not long after she'd finished her jam session with her dad. They'd only played together the once since Christmas, and even then it had been an eggnog-induced Christmas carol silly-fest with Bryant and Bryant's mom and Bishop and Phoenix all getting along for once. The only person who hadn't been there was Clay. He'd been volunteering somewhere with disadvantaged kids, Van remembered—with the girlfriend *before* Amber. While the volunteering was nice, Van still wished Clay had been there. Robin and Van had been at the piano, the other three crowded behind them. Bishop's hand had been on Van's shoulder the whole time, and it had felt like home.

Everything had been right in the moment. The warmth and the merriment had felt like the family Van hadn't experienced since her mother died. Having Mary Beth and Clay around had helped in high school, but Mary Beth had also been her freshman English teacher.

Van had trouble not calling her Ms. Noble at home for the first couple of years.

It was only after Van left for California that she appreciated everything Mary Beth had done for her dad and for her family. But did she make the house feel more like a home? NoIn high school, having a stepmother had just been another obstacle to Van living her life. As a teenager, there was nothing she couldn't do, nothing she didn't want to do just so she knew what it was like. That included drinking, drugs, boys but also learning how to skateboard with the stoner guys, playing the lead in the musical at school, driving too fast, and going with Bryant and his mom to the Universalist church.

But last Christmas? With Bishop there, Van thought she'd finally found her true family. Phoenix was more like a sister than anything, and Bryant had always been the best brother in the world. Then Bishop, her lover, her friend. That had been the moment when Van had started picturing a future with Bishop. And it still ripped Van's heart in two to compare the two images of Bishop in her mind. One wearing a stupid green and red sweater singing "Silent Night" and harmonizing with her, his voice a beautiful, smooth baritone. The other, the bathroom door rattling on its hinges with Bishop's voice, dangerous and intoxicated, boomed from the other side

She found herself unconsciously rubbing her right hip, where the most painful of the bruises had been, wondering if he'd been manipulating her from the start. That she wasn't sure made Van feel insane, like she couldn't trust her own mind.

"I wish I could erase him from your mind, *Eternal Sunshine* style," Bryant said, waving his fork in the air as he talked, like it was a magic wand that could vanish Bishop from all their lives.

"I was thinking about Christmas," Van said and pushed her noodles around on her plate. Pad Thai was one of her favorite dishes, but she'd only managed a few bites before her stomach cramped down on itself again and refused any more food.

"Do you remember when we were all singing carols together?"

Bryant nodded.

"I really thought Bishop was it after that, you know?"

Bryant gave a reluctant shrug, but nodded again, even though he frowned. "It was a good night," he said. "Though I don't think there would have been near as much peace without all the eggnog."

"I was just happy that you and Bishop weren't snarling at each other."

"I wished I'd snarled at him," Bryant took a big bite of his curry. "I wish Clay and I had ganged up on him and scared him off."

Van rolled her eyes. "Never would have worked."

"I still wish I'd been there for you."

She nodded into her noodles, then twisted them into a ball around her chopsticks. She was sick of talking about Bishop. Phoenix and Clay were the only ones who talked to her about anything else these days. Phoenix was all business, all the time. Clay had shown her how to actually hit a nail on its head without killing herself with a hammer. His gentle, calloused fingers guiding her arm as he held the nail in place, sacrificing his own hand so that Van's guitar playing wouldn't be at risk. The memory made Van want to sigh and stare at the ceiling and replay it over and over again, the way she'd done when she was sixteen and would catch Clay making the quick trip from the bathroom to his bedroom in only a towel.

Instead, she said, "So Minnie's super cute. And she's terrified of me. I think you owe me that tea."

Bryant didn't say anything, but his cheeks tinged pink, ever so slightly. "I've told you about her."

Van shook her head. "You told me you were interested in the girl who owns the bookstore a couple years ago, and then you told me you haven't been with anyone since her."

He shrugged, glancing over his shoulder like he was looking for a way out of the conversation.

"The Bryant I've known and loved hasn't been celibate for more than two weeks at a time since he was eighteen, so what gives?"

Bryant shrugged again. "It's not always easy finding partners when everyone thinks you're dating the most famous woman in the world."

Van raised her eyebrows at him. "That never stopped you before."

"Yeah, well. I've slept with all the guys around here that I care to."

"And the women?" Van asked. It was a stupid, mean question, but Van wanted to push him, and if annoying the crap out of him or maybe even pushing him into anger was what she had to do to get him to open up to her, that's what Van would do.

He glared at her over his glasses.

"What?" she asked, feigning ignorance. "You're bi. I thought that meant you liked men and women."

It was mean because Van knew that while Bryant liked

both men and women, seven out of ten times, Bryant would choose a man for a lover. Which made his pining after Minnie even more interesting to Van.

Bryant pushed away from the table and leaned back in his chair, slouching as if he were two seconds away from slithering to the floor and throwing a tantrum like a toddler. "I don't want a relationship with any of the women around here either."

Van's eyebrows knit together, and she knew he registered her confusion when his head dropped backward so he was staring at the ceiling. He took in a deep breath, rubbed the bridge of his nose with his forefingers, then readjusted his glasses and pinned her with an annoyed stare, like he resented having to explain himself. "I like to fuck men. But when it comes to long-term relationships, I've always pictured myself with a woman."

"Oh," Van said, assimilating this new truth about her best friend "I didn't realize—"

"Yeah, well, I don't usually feel like spelling out my sexuality to people who don't understand—especially when I've only started to understand it myself in the last few years."

"I'm not asking for explanations," Van said. "I just want you to be happy, whoever you end up with."

Bryant gave her a wan smile. "That's all I want for both of us."

"And Minnie—"

"Got knocked up by another guy about two seconds after she saw us together on the front of a tabloid for the first time."

"I'm sorry," Van said, reaching for his hand across the

table. He looked so miserable as he twined his fingers with hers. "I can talk to her if you like. Phoenix is fairly certain she's not with Rocco anymore. Maybe—"

Bryant squeezed her hand a little too hard. "No."

"But, maybe—"

"No, Van."

"But you love her, and—"

"And it's over, and there's nothing you can do about it."

"I just want you to be happy," Van said.

Bryant reached for her hand across the table so they both sat with their elbows braced on the table as they stared into each other's eyes. If a pap shot a picture through the window they were sitting in front of—which they were probably doing, though Van refused to look— they would look like a couple sharing an intimate moment. And they were, just not the way everyone would assume.

"I do think it's time we call it quits," he said. "Professionally speaking."

Van nodded. "I've been thinking that for a while now. Purely for selfish reasons before, but now I'm feeling really guilty for how unfair all this has been to you."

He gave her a shy half grin and ran his hands over her knuckles. "Don't. I would do anything for you, V. Remember that."

"Does that mean we can still have sleepovers?" she asked.

Bryant laughed. "If Clay doesn't mind sharing you every once in a while."

"Why would Clay have any opinion on where I sleep?" Van was not proud of how breathless her voice came out.

"Please," Bryant said. "The footage they're picking up of you two at the job sites is nothing short of nauseating."

Heat rose to Van's cheeks. "Don't be ridiculous."

"Fine," Bryant shrugged. "Pretend you two don't want to jump each other's bones and make tons of babies for as long as you want. It's none of my business."

"You suck."

"I only want to see the two of you happy," Bryant said, parroting Van's earlier words with a sly smile.

"That's it," she disengaged her hand from his. "I'm totally breaking up with you."

"Good." Bryant pushed back his chair and stood. "What do you say we hit up Tessa's and celebrate?"

"Fuck, yes. I need a night out."

Van grabbed Bryant's hand and hurried to the corner where Butch watched the dining room. "Better buckle up, Butch. We're headed to Tessa's."

The security guard grumbled under his breath and pulled out his phone, making Van giggle. She'd agreed to remain guarded, but she'd never promised she'd was going to make it easy for them.

Charges Dropped!

L.A. County has dropped all charges against music mogul Henry Bishop due to lack of evidence. Sorry, Van B. Looks like this publicity ploy bombed. Better luck next time!

he house was quiet for the next week. Robin had a big trial about to start and worked late most nights. Phoenix disappeared down into her apartment with a growl after monopolizing Van all day for interviews. Van sequestered herself in her room with her guitar every evening, but Clay could tell she wasn't making any real progress. She played the same three chords over and over again with no real direction.

Clay wanted to get Van alone, to apologize, because he hadn't done that yet. He also just missed her. Clay wanted to talk to her. He thought maybe they could come to a truce. Try to be friends. Clay's stupid teenage crush had given her enough trouble—and every touch he'd stolen in the weeks since she'd been back weighed on him. He should apologize for that too.

It was Friday afternoon before Clay had a moment with her. She'd stopped by the job site over lunch when the family they were building the house for could be there.

They'd filmed a few progress shots, but then Van took off again without any chance for them to talk off-camera. But when Clay got home, Van and Phoenix were just getting home from yoga. They bounced out of Butch's armored SUV wearing tight leggings and skimpy tops. Phoenix wore only a pink sports bra, and Van ripped her tiny shirt off as she bounced into the kitchen and grabbed two bottles of water out of the fridge, so she was clad in a black strappy thing that looked more like a sexy bikini top than anything.

Clay had been helping himself to a second chicken sandwich, since the one he'd packed for his lunch hadn't cut it, and he wasn't due at The Fox for pizza and the baseball game for another two hours. He'd frozen at the sight of Van without her shirt on. He had to shake his head and remind himself not to stare as the girls took seats across from him at the breakfast bar.

"Hot yoga," Van said, and Clay realized he'd been staring again, not at her boobs this time, but at the sheen of sweat across her collar bone.

"I didn't realize we had that around here," he said and forced himself to look away.

Clay could practically hear Phoenix roll her eyes as he replaced the mayo and mustard into the fridge.

By the time he'd finished, they'd moved on to discussing what movies they were going to watch that night, and Clay remembered why he was going out to watch baseball with Bryant. The Rockies *were* playing, and he liked baseball, but it wasn't a thing Clay and Bryant made a point of doing together. No, it was because they were having Minnie over for a girls-only night and were apparently starting their night off with *Jurassic Park*. Of all the movies in the world, that was not the chick flick he'd been expecting.

Phoenix's ever-present phone lay on the counter, but instead of typing on it, she only spun it in a circle as if she were waiting for it to ring. Van noticed Clay watching Phoenix and caught his eye. When he asked her with his eyes if Phoenix was alright, Van pulled an expression that was somewhere between a wince and a grin, which meant no, Phoenix was not okay, but Van didn't know what the problem was.

Phoenix stood abruptly. "I'm going to go shower," she said, tucking her phone in her legging pocket. "I'll order the pizza when I'm done."

"Thanks for clearing out tonight," Van said. "Given Minnie's and Bryant's past, I think it's best if it's just us ladies, you know?"

"What past?" Clay asked, unaware of any past between his best friend and the owner of Revival.

"They had a thing a couple years ago," Van said. "He never told you?"

"Bryant knows better than to talk to me about his conquests."

Van grinned. "Because you would call me and tell me that he was cheating on me. Again. But now you know he was just being human."

"You deserved better," Clay said, his voice coming out a growl.

The idea still made Clay grumpy. That his best friend had lied to him for years. Had let Clay think he was total bastard who didn't love Van enough. But he was working on it.

Van's smile turned sad, and Clay's gut said now was the time to apologize to her. Only he couldn't force himself to say the words. Instead he said, "Is Minnie bringing the baby?"

"Minnie found a sitter for Malcolm. No boys allowed, remember?"

"Wow, you guys are strict," Clay said, trying to sound like everything was perfectly fine between them, like he wasn't having a hard time keeping his body from reacting to hers.

"Man, that was hard shit. I can barely move my arms. No wonder Phoenix sat out most of it," she said. Van's arms were splayed limply on the counter.

Thinking she probably hadn't eaten enough, Clay held out half the sandwich he hadn't taken a bite out of yet. He expected her to wave him off. Instead, she snatched it out of his hand and took a giant bite, moaning a little bit as she did. "This is the best sandwich ever," her mouth was full as she spoke, and Clay didn't even care. The desire to hear her moan his name clanged through him, rooting him to the spot as she swallowed and sighed. "Seriously, that's like sandwich magic. Thanks."

"Don't mention it." He almost choked on the words, his throat was so hoarse. Had he been going to propose they just be friends? Clay didn't think there was any being just friends with Van. Not when lust could blindside him like this in her presence.

She smirked at him, and Clay wondered if she was trying to get a reaction out of him. "I'm going to shower. Do you mind waiting?"

Because they were currently sharing a bathroom.

"Go ahead."

"Thanks." She shoved the rest of her half sandwich in her mouth and retreated up the stairs. Clay had to brace himself on the counter to get his mind and body back under control. To keep himself preoccupied while he waited for the shower, Clay closed himself in his room and picked up his old guitar, playing a little bit louder than he normally would, because he needed some way to let the tension out. After a few minutes, he was absorbed. He hadn't realized how much he'd missed playing. He'd bought that new guitar, but he'd barely touched the thing.

It had been a long time since he'd gotten lost in his music, but when Van asked, "What song is that?" from his doorway, thirty minutes had passed. She was clean, wearing a pair of black jeans and loose gray t-shirt that hung off one shoulder, revealing her black bra strap. Her hair was dry, and Clay hadn't even noticed the sound of the hair dryer.

"It's nothing," he said, as he flipped the pick between his fingers.

"No," she said, letting herself in. "That was something. Something I've never heard before."

Clay only shrugged and made to put his guitar away, but she covered his hand with her own thin, long-fingered one.

"Play it for me?"

"It's nothing, Van."

"Please?" She guided his guitar back onto his lap and knelt in front of him on the rug, so her face was level with the strings.

She watched Clay's fingers as he played, hers tapping out the beat against his leg.

And then she began to sing a melody. No lyrics yet, just a wordless pattern.

Her voice blended with the chords Clay played as if the song were already written, and they just needed to keep going to discover what it sounded like whole. When Clay neared the end of the chorus, Van twirled her fingers in the air, so he played it again as she repeated the chorus melody, then launched into a bridge that Clay improvised his way through.

When the song came to an end, they stared at each other. Van's eyes were wide, and her breath came quick, like they'd just finished something far more intimate than playing music. He set the guitar aside and slid to his knees in front of Van.

He needed to touch her. To hold her. To feel closer to the mind—the soul—that he'd just had a glimpse into through her voice. Apparently, she felt the same way, because she wrapped her arms around his neck at the same time Clay's hands landed on her waist.

"Did we just write a song together?" He asked, his voice barely a rasp.

She nodded as she said, "I think we did."

The intensity hadn't left her eyes, and with her lips so close to his, with the tips of her breasts brushing his chest with every breath, Clay couldn't help himself any longer. "I'm going to kiss you now," he said.

Van's "About time" was on an exhale, and Clay's lips were on hers the next second. She was still warm from her shower, and her lips were soft and a little sticky from

MARLA HOLT

whatever gloss she'd put on. She tasted like mint as her
tongue lapped against his lower lip.

Clay's arms wrapped all the way around her back,
holding her as close as he could. When he swept his
tongue against hers, they both groaned. Clay's hands
snaked up into her hair, angling her head back so he could
devour her. He'd never been so hungry for the taste of a
woman before. He needed her like he needed air, and he
couldn't let her go.

Her fingernails scraped lightly across his back through
his dusty t-shirt. He had the fleeting thought that he'd get
her clothes dirty, but then she looped her arms
underneath his and her fingernails grazed the skin above
his belt, beneath his shirt, and Clay stopped thinking as
his heart thudded in his chest.

He was kissing Van. With her permission. And she'd
just dipped her fingers beneath his waistband. Holy shit,
this was going to happen.

Clay broke off the kiss as gently as he could and kissed
the edge of her jaw, laying little pecks down her neck,
brushing his tongue across a spot on the top of her
shoulder that made her squirm in his arms. Was she
ticklish? He tried again with the same result and grinned
against her skin.

Van tugged up on his shirt, and her intention was
clear. She wanted it off. Clay disentangled himself from
her long enough to yank his shirt over his head by the
neck.

Her hands were instantly on his chest. A little sigh
escaped her lips as she traced the dip between his abs with
her fingernail. When she spied his cock twitch through
his jeans, a wicked gleam shone in her eyes.

Clay cupped Van's chin with both hands and kissed her softly, rolling his tongue against her lips but not penetrating. She let out a whimper and ran her hands up and down his sides, her fingernails teasing and scratching almost hard enough to hurt. She was getting impatient, but Clay had to know—to be clear beyond any doubt— that she wanted this.

He pulled back just far enough to meet her eyes again. "Is this what you want, Van? With me? Now?"

She scratched her nails down his back. "I swear to God if you keep teasing me like this, I'm going to kill you in your sleep."

Clay winced from the pain of her scratch, but his body surged, his hips rocking into where he held her against him. "Yes or no, Van." His words were hardly better than a growl.

She rubbed little circles over the angry skin on his back and kissed the tip of his chin where a light stubble had filled in over the course of the day. "Yes, you idiot."

That was all he needed. Without warning, Clay scooped her up and laid her out on his bed. God, his high school bed, where he'd fantasized endlessly about what it would be like to sink deep into her. His fantasies about Van had always been the most illicit, made even more so by the fact that giving in to them was such a taboo. He had gotten off a million times just imagining the woman who was supposed to be his sister beneath him. And here she was, finally.

He settled over her, kneeling with his legs on either side of her hips. A sliver of her stomach was exposed from where her shirt had ridden up, and Clay caressed that slice of skin.

"You're so soft," He said before flattening his palm over her abdomen. Not defined, but slim and flat. His hand covered the entire space between her belly button and the bottom of her ribs. "And so delicate."

"Moon later," she said. "I need you now."

So Clay obliged her and dipped his tongue into her belly button and licked his way up, pressing her shirt up and off as he went. She wore a black bra. The combination of that and her hair had her skin looking even paler and creamier than usual. He appreciated that she didn't use tanning beds like she had as a teenager—that she was more comfortable in her own skin all around.

Clay continued licking his way up her chest, between her breasts, then over the curve of each, and she writhed beneath him, seeking the friction he was denying her.

"Hurry, Clay," she breathed.

While the sound of his name on her lips spurred Clay's own desire, he said, "I've been waiting for this for ten years. I'm not rushing it now."

She bucked again as he ran his tongue along her collarbone and back down between her breasts, and he stretched himself out over her. Their hips rocked into each other, and even with their clothes on, Clay was nearing climax.

"Please tell me you have condoms," she groaned as she arched her back so he could unclasp her bra.

"I'm covered," He breathed against her skin.

Clay almost didn't hear her say, "Not yet you aren't," as he slid her bra to the floor and her breasts were bared to him for the first time. They weren't large, but her nipples were a bright, inviting pink color.

"God, you're gorgeous," he said. He cupped a breast in each hand and rolled her nipples between his fingers just hard enough to make her breath catch.

"Clay," she gasped as he licked a circle around one pert nipple, then sucked it between his lips at the same time he rocked his hips into hers. Clay could feel how tightly she was wound, and he was going to take his time pushing her higher and higher until she unraveled completely.

Van's hips undulated in time with the movements of his tongue and lips on her breast. Clay wanted to know how wet she was. He wanted to push his fingers inside her and make her come with his mouth still worshipping her tits. He opened his mouth to say as much, to see how she responded to a little dirty talk, when a sharp swift knock sounded at his door.

They froze in each other's arms.

Phoenix's voice sounded on the other side, "Get your ass downstairs, Van. Minnie's here, and she brought *Buckaroo Bonzai.* Girls night starts now!"

Clay positioned his body to shield Van should Phoenix decide to let herself in, but as they heard Phoenix footsteps retreat down the hall, their eyes met, and Van bit her bottom to lip to stifle a laugh.

"Damn," Van said, "Cock blocked by Jeff Goldblum again."

Clay kissed her neck and sat back. "Jeff's interfered with your bedroom exploits before, has he?"

"Once," Van said. The little knowing smile she gave him had Clay wondering if maybe she meant that literally.

Clay hadn't realized he'd been staring—mooning, as she'd put it earlier—until she stroked a gentle hand down his arm. "I should probably get down there."

"Right." He backed off the bed and handed over her bra, then found both their shirts.

"I'll come by later, and we'll work on that song, okay?" she said as she pulled her t-shirt over her head.

"You better."

Van gave him that knowing grin again and slipped out of the bedroom.

@xXAlphaChadxX: It's not like it's a secret where @VanBmusic lives. Hundreds of us could be in Wellville within three days. They wouldn't be able to do anything if we stormed the bitch's house. #justice4van

15

*V*an found Phoenix and Minnie at the kitchen island, each with a glass of wine. Phoenix poured one for her as she joined them.

"Productive jam session with Clay?" From the disapproving tone of her voice and the hard glint in her eye, Van knew she'd heard more than music through the door. Whatever. Phoenix could approve or not. It wasn't a secret that Van had had a crush on Clay. If the two of them wanted to work out some of the sexual tension between them, that was their thing. Phoenix had nothing to do with it.

Van took a casual sip of her wine, trying to cover up how giddy she felt. Van wanted to giggle and squeal like it was first time she'd gotten to second base, but from the dour look on Phoenix's face, she would not join Van in the jumping and the screaming. And Van didn't think Minnie, who still thought Van and Bryant were together, was quite ready to hear about how Van's stepbrother had finally—FINALLY!—touched her boobs.

Instead, she focused on the wine. It was a nice Pinot Noir, one of Phoenix's favorite brands, the one that Van had noticed her father suddenly had a store of down in his wine cellar. At least Van was fairly certain Phoenix hadn't been responsible for the two cases down there. Phoenix paid attention to detail, but she had never learned the value of buying in bulk. Sam's Club was a midwestern marvel as far as she was concerned.

"We wrote a song," Van said. "Or started one anyway," she amended when Phoenix raised her eyebrows.

Van could tell Phoenix wanted to drill her about it—how was it that Van could write a song with Clay in twenty minutes when she hadn't finished a song in the last two months? Plus, Van was pretty sure Phoenix had heard a lot more than guitar music when she'd been outside Clay's door. No, Phoenix had definitely heard Van whimper as Clay had been so deliciously teasing her nipples. She had to suppress a shudder at the memory, but Van could still feel his lips and tongue on her breasts. As she shifted in her seat, Van cursed the slickness he'd left between her thighs. She wanted to cry in frustration. She'd needed that release, and the way Clay had been teasing her, it had been going to be a good one.

Good Lord, what horrible timing.

Van didn't care how late it was when Minnie left, her plan was to sneak straight back up to Clay's room and pick up where they had left off. There was no way she was letting this fester and get awkward.

"You write songs with your brother?" Minnie asked, her head cocked to the side. The way her gaze swept up and down Van's full form, taking in her rumpled t-shirt, and undoubtedly tangled hair, Van could tell Minnie was still unsure about her. It was also possible that Minnie had heard Van and Clay moaning when she'd come in. The front door was at the bottom of the stairs just below Clay's room.

God, Van wished she was still moaning beneath him.

She gave Minnie her sweetest smile, hoping to put her at ease. "First of all, Clay isn't really my brother. Our parents didn't get married until we were teenagers. And second," she switched her grin from sweet to mischievous, "I'd write a song with the devil himself right now if it helped me get my album done on time."

Phoenix huffed a laugh and said, "Same difference really," and even Minnie cracked a hesitant smile.

"I thought maybe you'd already struck a deal with the devil," Minnie said. When Phoenix and Van both turned wide eyes on her, she said shyly, "You know, because you're so successful at such a young age."

It was Van's turn to huff a laugh, and Phoenix let out a reluctant chuckle. Something behind her eyes failed to look amused as she said, "Van makes it look easy, but she's worked her ass off since she was eighteen to get where she is."

"And Phoenix is still working her butt off to keep it going," Van said. "I mostly coast along these days."

Phoenix rolled her eyes and kicked at Van's ankles from the stool next to her. "Only when it comes to songwriting. Everything else is still a grind."

Van shrugged. She supposed it was true. She was putting songwriting last right now. It wasn't like she hadn't been trying. It was just so much pressure when all she wanted was to be left alone for a while. Which reminded her.

"Did you have any trouble getting through the crowd?" she asked Minnie.

"You mean the paparazzi outside?" She shook her head. "They didn't bother me at all, but that's probably because they didn't recognize me."

Van heard the unspoken, "Yet," in Minnie's words, and wondered if there was a reason why Minnie might be recognized.

"Minnie's dad is Jonas Halvarson," Phoenix said.

Van looked at her blankly. "I know the name sounds familiar…"

Minnie winced, and Phoenix's eyes flashed fire. "He's the bastard developer whose donation to the relief effort came with a million strings attached like we're some sort of endowment."

"He's been trying to buy his way into downtown for years," Minnie said. "He doesn't believe me that people who work at the flour mill can't afford luxury lofts, but he still thinks that he can draw people here simply because it's your—" Minnie nodded at Van— "hometown. When I tell him that doesn't create jobs, he doesn't listen. I'm afraid he's causing trouble for Robin and everyone else on the historic preservation board."

Van raised her eyebrows, looking between Minnie and Phoenix. That was the most Van had ever heard Minnie speak, and she'd been going to Revival almost daily since Phoenix had basically moved in there. Van also hadn't realized that Minnie and her father, of all people, were on a first name basis.

"Your dad comes in almost every day for lunch," Minnie said with a grin.

Phoenix rolled her eyes, and said, "That's the hazard of

hanging out with us though. Just because they don't recognize you now doesn't mean they won't dig. Things you don't want unearthed *could* go public."

Minnie shrugged. "It's nothing I didn't deal with in New York."

Now Van was super curious about this woman. Not only was Bryant *still* in love with her, she was not the meek shopkeeper Van had assumed her to be. And what had she done to be gossip fodder in New York? And why hadn't Van heard about her? She was definitely googling Minnie later on tonight—or tomorrow morning. After she jumped Clay's bones. The latter was currently more important.

Van took another too-casual sip of her wine. She'd had no clue this woman was so savvy. Van supposed she shouldn't underestimate Minnie; she had captured Bryant's unwavering attention, which was difficult to do.

"Minnie went to Columbia," Phoenix said. "She has a degree in English with a minor in Business."

"Wow. Congratulations." Van was impressed. She'd barely made it through three semesters at Wellville State. "Phoenix and I are both college drop-outs. We couldn't hack regular educations, but you made it through the Ivy League."

"Hey, I was at Berkeley," Phoenix said, then added, "for one and half semesters before I got the hell out."

"Well, a degree and a small-town coffee shop are hardly the same thing as the empire you've built," Minnie said, and Van couldn't help a self-satisfied smile as she drained her wine. Minnie was right; Van had built a fucking empire. She wasn't quite to Oprah levels of imperial domination yet, but she was doing pretty well for herself. And she'd started it all with her mom's guitar and a father who believed in her. That plus endless ambition and a good dose of restlessness had been the perfect recipe. And meeting Phoenix at just the right time. She wouldn't think about Bishop's role. He didn't get credit anymore.

Her phone buzzed in her pocket, but she ignored it. The last thing she needed right now was more negative feedback from Twitter about what a whore she was. She'd never apologized for her sex life, and nothing—not Bishop, not Minnie, and especially not internet trolls— were going to keep her from making plans for all the things she was going to do with Clay come bedtime.

"We could show you how to scale up if you wanted," Phoenix said. "It's not hard if you know who to ask for help."

Wasn't that the truth? It was all about not being afraid to ask.

But Minnie shook her head. "I'm happy with where I am," she said. "And with Malcolm, I don't know that I have the time or energy to do more."

"The offer doesn't expire," Van said. "If you ever want a boost in business, all it takes is a tweet on my end."

"Oh oh oh," Phoenix said. "We should set up a photo shoot there. We would have social media material for days." Her hand landed on Van's shoulder, and she almost winced. Phoenix might look willowy, but she had the strength of a bodybuilder. That girl knew how to work the gym. "You and Clay in the stacks with your guitars. People would eat that shit up so hard."

"If he'll agree to it, sure."

"Viewers love Clay," Phoenix said to Minnie. "Next to

Bryant, he's our number one most-requested character."

Minnie's lips twitched, and Van had to bite her tongue to keep from asking her if she'd give Bryant a second chance.

"If that's okay with Minnie," Van said.

Minnie offered a tentative smile into her wine. "That would be great—but I didn't—"

Phoenix didn't even let her finish her sentence. "Shush. We know. But when you're friends with Van, you get publicity. And we'll compensate you for lost sales while we're taking over. It's better if we control the conversation early, you know?"

The doorbell rang, and Phoenix jumped up to answer it. "Pizza. Finally." Phoenix sounded normal when she spoke; she was even doing a passable job at looking like she normally did, but Van couldn't shake the feeling that something was off with her friend. Van just couldn't put her finger on what. Was it just the Clay thing? Or was there more going on? It was possible.Van had been so wrapped up in her own head lately that she couldn't say for sure what Phoenix had been up to in the last few weeks. Maybe her friend wasn't as content as Van had assumed she was?

Left alone with Minnie, Van said, "I'm sorry if this is all a little overwhelming. I know you only signed up for a movie night."

"It's okay," Minnie said. She took tiny, quick sips of her wine and watched the living room for Phoenix to reemerge. Oh yeah, Van made her nervous as hell. "It's interesting to see how fame affects almost everything you guys do."

"It's not so bad here. Just a few paps. In L.A., or when

I'm touring, it's way worse." Van motioned toward the direction of the street. "This is like a vacation, really."

"Why even go back to L.A.?" she asked.

Van hesitated, refilling her glass to buy time.

"I'm sorry. Is that too personal a question?" Minnie bit her lip, and Van had to admit, she was cute with her blonde curls, big curves, and unassuming demeanor. "I just have always wondered why you live there when it seems like your life is really here?"

Van frowned. "Are you talking about Bryant?" She asked, not sure what else she could mean by "your life." Because everything Van did was based out of L.A. for a reason. Work, networking, the publicity machine all originated out of California.

"And your Dad. I guess, if money wasn't an issue, I would probably live here and just fly out to the coast when I needed to."

"That would take a lot more flying than it looks like on the surface," Van said as Phoenix returned.

"Doesn't it make it hard, though? Being away from him all the time?"

Van shrugged as Phoenix dropped the pizza on the breakfast bar between Minnie and her.

"Van and Bryant have a really special connection," she smiled sweetly at Minnie. "Distance doesn't really matter in the long term."

"So, is he going to move to L.A. if you guys get married, or are you still going to live apart?"

Van's voice didn't really know how to respond to that question. She'd been away from heavy scrutiny about her relationship because of everything else that was going on, and she had already forgotten that the rest of the world thought Bryant and she were probably going to end up married. No one knew he and Van were going to end their fake relationship. Not even Phoenix. She'd been so busy the last few days, they hadn't even talked about what Bryant and Van had discussed at dinner last week—which was unusual. Normally they talked about everything all the time.

Van grabbed a slice of pizza and said vaguely, "We're still figuring it out."

Phoenix was way ahead of her and had a distraction all ready to go. "I have a special treat before we get this party started," she said. Then herded them into the living room where she forced them to watch the *Sesame Street* sketch that had been the inspiration for Minnie's name.

"Man, why did they do that to him?" Phoenix asked as it finished, outrage coloring her voice.

Van couldn't help giggling. "I know, right? Who knew he couldn't sing?"

Minnie's face was bright red, like the whole thing somehow reflected badly on her, but when Van followed the quick cut of her eyes, she found that they had an audience.

Bryant and Clay stood in the foyer, watching them as they gathered around the TV. Clay leaned against the threshold, his arms crossed casually over her chest, but Bryant just stared and stared and stared at Minnie.

Van looked between the two of them. Minnie pretended she didn't know they were there as she asked Phoenix if they could move straight onto *Buckaroo Bonzai*. Phoenix, to her credit, didn't seem bothered by the guys, but Van knew she knew they were there.

Van watched Minnie ignore Bryant, then cut her

glance back to her friend, and it was like he didn't even see Van at all. His fists clenched, open and closed as he stared at Minnie. Van cut her eyes to Clay, who looked concerned and curious now that he was seeing Bryant and Minnie in the same place for the first time since Van had spilled the beans about their past.

But the way Bryant was frozen in his tracks. . .

Van hadn't realized Bryant would be this upset just seeing Minnie. Van wanted to put him out of his misery and approached him, smoothing her hands over his shoulders like she was used to doing in public.

"You okay, Bry?"

"What's she doing here?" he asked.

"Movie night," Van said and squeezed his shoulders. "We met a few weeks ago. Does it bother you?"

Bryant shook his head and scrubbed his face, pushing his glasses up onto his forehead so he could rub his eyes. "It's okay. You need friends. *She* needs friends. I just—" he stopped and listened for a moment, but the only sound was the movie in the background. "—She didn't bring the baby?"

Van shook her head. "She left Malcolm at home."

Bryant blanched, and Van wondered if he hadn't known the baby's name. She wouldn't blame him for not wanting to.

"You gonna be okay?" she asked. "You want me to tell her the truth?"

Bryant pulled her into a hug that rivaled his hand-squeezing abilities. "You're the best," he said and kissed the top of her head. "But no. It won't change the fact that she chose somebody else."

"Are you sure? Because I can probably have that other

guy killed or something. What's the point of having all this money if I can't use it for good every now and then, you know?"

A hoarse laugh tore through Bryant's chest like he hadn't wanted to let it go. Good. That was better.

"I'm pretty sure—" Van had been going to reiterate that she thought Minnie was currently single, but Phoenix cut her off.

"Hey! No boys allowed!"

"That's my cue to leave," Bryant said.

"You gonna be okay?" Van asked.

He nodded and placed a quick, dry kiss on her lips. As he backed away, Van noticed Clay watching them from the foyer for the first time. He wasn't smirking anymore.

Right. That didn't bode well for Van's plans to ride Clay like a rodeo queen later. They'd have to have a serious conversation about jealousy and fake boyfriends later.

Van's phone buzzed in her pocket as she watched Clay and Bryant load up into Clay's truck. Out of habit, she unlocked her phone before she remembered she wasn't checking messages tonight. She was about to slip it back into her pocket when she saw the two newest notifications were from Bishop.

The first was a link to a news story. Van couldn't see the whole headline, but the words "charges dropped" were enough for her to know what it was. Law enforcement were dropping the case. Van wondered if her dad knew yet.

Anxiety and fear welled in the pit of her stomach, especially when she pulled up the second message and it was a picture of the Welcome to Wellville sign.

Bar Brawl in Wellville

With charges dropped, Henry Bishop is free to travel once more. The first spot on his itinerary? Wellville, Kansas, of course, to win back his lady love. Only before Bishop could meet up with Van Birch, he ran into her boyfriend, Bryant Wilder, and brother, Clay Noble, at a dive bar when he stopped for a drink. Wilder and Noble were less than welcoming. Rumors are that Bishop came away with a broken nose, while Wilder and Noble are facing assault and battery charges. Check out the video below for a play-by-play of the attack.

lay followed Bryant out of the house, and it took all of his will not to slam Bryant up against the side of his truck and ask him what he was playing at with Van. Despite Clay's long, cold shower, he was still revved up from what they'd been up to in his bedroom earlier— and apparently Clay was feeling territorial.

But Bryant scooped a loose piece of cement up from a crack in the driveway and hurled it against the huge sycamore tree in the front yard, and Clay remembered what had happened before Bryant had kissed Van in front of him.

"You wanna head to The Fox?" Clay asked.

Bryant shoved his hands in his pockets and nodded. Good. Clay needed a drink too.

They were silent on the drive to the sports bar. The little dive lacked the decorative appeal that drew Van to Tessa's. The Fox's walls had had the same wood paneling since the dawn of time, and the floor was grungy. The stale tang of old cigarettes still hung in the air, even though it had been more than ten years since it had been legal to smoke inside. It was kind of a shit hole, but the beer was cheap and cold, they played all the local teams, and nobody usually bothered them there.

Clay ordered them a pitcher of PBR and a pizza. It wouldn't be nearly as tasty as the one the girls were eating. The Fox's cheese was always rubbery, the crust soggy, but after smelling theirs, Clay needed pepperoni.

Bryant had stomped across the bar and slumped down into a chair at their normal table. He looked like he could crush stone with his bare hands, and Clay was reluctant to hand him his glass of beer for fear of Bryant crushing the glass into dust the second it was in his first. But the glass held beneath Bryant's grip as he downed the beer in one go.

"You wanna fill me in?" Clay asked as Bryant started in on his second glass. The pitcher was already half gone, and Clay had barely even taken a sip.

Bryant's empty glass hit the table with a thunk. "Have you ever had a woman tear your heart out and then just completely destroy it?"

Clay frowned. There was no way Bryant could know what had gone on between Clay and Van earlier that evening already. And guilt hit Clay. Van had said Bryant had a thing for Minnie, but Clay had just watched Bryant kiss Van in front of everyone, so maybe Van was mistaken. "Van?" Clay asked and downed half his glass.

Bryant snorted. "Van's just a friend, Clay. That's all it's ever been. And I know she's told you that."

"You don't have to—"

But he didn't let Clay finish. "I know how you feel about her. I've *always* known."

"We're not talking about me," Clay said, even as he wanted to demand why Bryant had never said anything. Why he'd persisted with the illusion of their fake relationship for the last five years. Why he'd let Clay believe Van had chosen Bryant all this time. He understood they weren't really together, but the way they acted? The way they behaved was so familiar, so based on that farce, it made Clay's hackles rise, even though he didn't have any right to claim Van as his—not yet.

Bryant stared at his empty glass, swished the last couple drops of beer back and forth before he said, "Minnie and I had a thing a couple of years ago."

"How did that happen?" Clay asked.

He sighed. "You remember how I installed the bookcases before the shop opened?"

Clay nodded. He'd built the bookcases, given them to Bryant to worry about, and forgotten about them. "Well, Minnie stuck around while I was doing the work and we talked, and one thing led to another, and—"

"You slept with her," Clay finished after Bryant trailed off.

"Every chance I got for about six weeks."

"And then?"

Bryant filled his glass to the brim. He took a long sip, then said, "She found out about Van."

"And you didn't correct her."

Bryant's shoulders rose and fell with resignation. "I promised Van I wouldn't tell anyone the truth. That included Minnie—so I let her think I was a cheating bastard."

The whole situation rolled through Clay's head like the tornado had Wellville. "Do you love her?"

"Minnie? Till the day I die."

"Then you should tell her the truth."

A server dropped the pizza off at the table without a word, not even with the offer to fill their now-empty pitcher. Ah, The Fox. Such stellar service.

Bryant shook his head. "She found another man in less than a month. She had his baby. There's no coming back from that."

Clay hadn't been going to mention that. Minnie brought the baby to work with her a lot, and Clay had seen her handing the little guy off to a burly, dark haired guy who looked like he played rugby. Clay had always assumed he was the father, but he hadn't wanted to pry. And Minnie was too sweet for people to gossip much.

He wondered if Bryant's mom would know the details. She didn't live anywhere in particular but traveled most of the year. She was the only fifty-year-old travel blogger Clay knew. She'd been a journalist her entire life and always knew exactly what was going on in Wellville the day after she got back to town. Maybe Clay would ask her when she came back for a visit. She always stayed with Bryant, so it shouldn't be difficult to find her alone and tell her to spill.

"But you're still not over her."

Bryant grabbed a slice of pizza and took a gigantic bite, then washed it down with the rest of the beer. "Grab us another pitcher?" he asked.

Clay hadn't even finished his first beer. "Sure."

Clay grabbed a slice of pizza as he stood, afraid Bryant would eat the whole damn thing in the couple of minutes it would take Clay to get another pitcher. Nobody cared that Clay munched at the bar as he waited. The bartender's attention was more on the baseball game than on his customers, so Clay was contemplating heading back to the table for a second of slice of pizza when the front door banged open and a flurry of people rushed in, accompanied by flashing cameras and shouting voices. They stopped halfway between the door and the bar.

As he craned his neck to see what the hubbub was about, one photographer turned and flashed his camera right in Clay's face. By the time he shoved past the photographer and blinked the spots away, Clay was too late to stop Bryant from hopping over a table and tackling Henry Bishop to the floor.

"You mother-fucking bastard!" He landed a punch right in the fucker's eye. Part of Clay knew he should pull Bryant off. A bigger part of him wanted Bryant to beat Bishop to a bloody pulp. But the biggest part of Clay was pissed that Bryant had landed the first punch.

No one moved as Bryant landed a second punch. The photographers snapped photos, and Bishop squirmed beneath Bryant's weight. They were a near match in size and stature, but Bryant had Bishop's arms pinned under his knees. If the fucker had any training, he'd know how to throw Bryant off with a kick and roll of his hips, but Bishop was panicking.

Finally, common sense kicked in, and Clay forced his way through the crowd of photographers and yanked Bryant to his feet. Bishop came up swinging and cursing, but Clay's training kicked in and had him locking Bishop's hands behind his back and pinning his front against the wall in a second. Blood from where Bryant had broken Bishop's nose smeared on an old Rockies' lineup photo. Bishop tried to spit at Clay over his shoulder, "You're both going to pri—" but Clay put more pressure on his arm and Bishop cut off with a whimper. It would be so easy to break his arm right now.

"You're lucky I didn't let him kill you," Clay said. He pulled harder on Bishop's arm, and he groaned but didn't beg. Clay leaned in and said in his ear, "You'll be even luckier if I don't, you motherfucker."

A pathetic, labored snort came from Bishop's broken nose. "Was that a threat, Noble?"

Sirens sounded in the distance, and Clay knew his time was almost up.

He didn't feel the need to answer Bishop's question. Of course it was a threat. It was taking all of Clay's self-control not to bash Bishop's skull against the wall. The only thing stopping him was that he knew how flimsy The Fox was. He'd probably do more damage to the building than he would to Bishop. "She trusted you, and you violated her, you piece of shit."

"You're just jealous that I got a piece of what you've always wanted." Clay put more pressure on Bishop's arm again, but by now, he knew Clay wouldn't break it. He breathed through the pain and said, "What kind of sick fuck wants to screw his sister anyway?"

Clay knew Bishop was baiting him, even as he heard the sirens turn into the parking lot, but Clay didn't care. He swung Bishop around to face him and landed a hard punch straight into his already broken nose. Bishop's head jerked back and dented the drywall behind him, but he was still on his feet, if slumped against the wall. He was still breathing. Clay pulled his fist back with the intention of knocking Bishop out, but Bryant's hand on Clay's bicep stopped him right as the cops stepped through the ring of photographers.

"Stand down, men," the deputy said. It was Race Carter, the douche Clay had warned off hitting on Van in the worst way possible.

A woman paramedic broke through the crowd and knelt at Bishop's side where he'd finally slid to the floor.

Photographers were still flashing away as two more officers tried to clear them out.

"You two getting in the squad car willingly, or do I have to cuff you?" Race asked.

"We're coming," Bryant said and tugged on Clay's arm.

Clay couldn't take his eyes off Bishop. His face was a bloody mess. His brown beard was stained red, his black shirt dark with it. Clay hoped his nose was smashed beyond repair. Clay wished he had broken Bishop's arm— and a few ribs. He wanted Bishop to hurt more than Van did. Clay wanted to break Bishop for what he'd done to her. He didn't deserve the medical attention he was getting.

"Clay." Race's voice was stern.

Clay finally tore his eyes away from Bishop and nodded at Race. "I'm coming."

*@femnisist_columnist: on a night of men behaving badly, I
believe @VanBmusic. Coming forward takes such courage, and
that she continues to be harassed, not only by @Bishop, but by
the media and by social media at large only proves my point.
Misogyny is alive and well. We heart you Van. #justice4Van
#fuckthepatriarchy*

17

---

*T*hey were at the part in *Jurassic Park* where the raptors corner the kids in the kitchen when Van's dad rapped on the living room door frame from next to the front stairwell.

All three of them jumped.

"Sorry, ladies," he said as Phoenix paused the movie. "But I'm heading to the police station, and I thought you might want to come."

Fear dropped over Van like curtain closing unexpectedly over the stage. Her father making after-hours trips to the police station was nothing new. He was the best lawyer in town, but usually, he didn't offer to bring her with him.

Phoenix, always quick to react, jumped to her feet. "What happened? Who's in trouble?"

Robin scratched his beard, a sign that Van had been programmed since childhood to know meant that he'd rather not say anything. In a quiet, even tone he said,

234

"There was an altercation at The Fox. Both Bryant and Clay have been arrested."

Van shot to her feet, fearing the worst as she heard Minnie gasp. She'd seen the way Clay was scowling at Bryant after he'd kissed her earlier. Van wanted to explain to Clay that Bryant's kisses were harmless. They were more of a friendly habit by now. A peck from Bryant was nothing like the explosive nipple action Clay had been rocking earlier—and obviously they wouldn't have a chance to finish tonight. Damn Clay and his temper.

"Did they get into a fight?" Van asked lamely.

But at the back of her mind, other possibilities were swirling. She'd shown her dad the text from Bishop. He'd been in his office ever since, talking to the lawyers in L.A., talking to the DA to see if he could figure out why the charges had been dropped and why they hadn't been notified. Van had also had a quick meeting with Butch, who advised Van to find someplace more secure to stay. She knew he meant someplace less easy to find than a huge white Victorian house on the edge of town, but Van refused. She was not going to hide in some empty apartment. She told him to bring on as many people as he thought he needed to adequately protect her. She wasn't leaving.

Phoenix had already pulled out her phone, her thumbs flying over the screen. She mumbled something to herself about trying to take one night off and the whole world going to hell. She held her phone up so Van could see the screen. A gossip site already had a photo of the dingy interior of The Fox with Clay's fist connecting with Bishop's face.

Cold seeped in through Van's skin, despite the sticky,

hot August heat. She'd rather Clay and Bryant fought each other. At least she knew they wouldn't press charges in the end, but she knew from the blood already seeping down Bishop's chin in the picture that he wouldn't let this go easily. He had probably walked into the bar knowing they were there, hoping to incite an incident. Proving it would be next to impossible, but, "God-fucking-dammit," Van said aloud. "What the fuck is he even doing here?"

"That's what we still need to find out." Her dad was using what Van liked to call his courtroom voice. When her dad used his courtroom voice, shit was about to get real. He was either gonna destroy you or rock your world. Right then, Van was hoping he was getting ready to destroy Bishop, because what the fuck was he doing in her town? "Get your things," her dad said. "We're leaving in five minutes."

Phoenix had already disappeared down the stairs as Van shot up to her bedroom to grab her purse and a pair of flip flops. Her dad was waiting by the door, his briefcase in hand. Minnie stood awkwardly nearby, as if not sure if she should stay or go, but she'd gone pale and thin lipped and looked even younger than usual.

"I should probably get home," she said, as Van landed in the foyer.

"Yeah. I'm sorry we didn't get to finish movie night."

"Don't be. It's fine. I need to check on Malcolm anyway. I've never been away from him at night."

Van gave her a sad smile. It was all she could muster at the moment. Not only was Van panicking because Clay and Bryant were in trouble but also because Bishop was in town, and Van might freaking lose it if she ran into him on the street. That fear threatened to cripple her.

Phoenix emerged from the basement, having traded her cut offs and oversized t-shirt for a sleek peacock-blue sheath dress and heels and her laptop bag slung over one shoulder, an overnight bag over the other.

Van didn't even care how she looked when she grabbed her dad's hand and inhaled slowly. "Let's go."

The number of paparazzi outside the house had tripled since earlier, and it was a fight to get all three cars—one for her and Phoenix, one for Robin, and another for Butch and company— down the driveway. There were even more at the police station. They were all slinging awful questions about Bishop and about Bryant and how it felt to have three men brawl over her.

Van ignored them, burrowing into her dad's side as he wrapped his arm around her shoulders. Phoenix held Van's free hand. They entered the police station a united front, even though they were immediately separated. Her dad was taken back to speak with Clay and Bryant as their counsel. Phoenix and Van were left to deal with the press nightmare in the waiting room.

Notifications had started blowing up her phone on the drive to the police station. The photos of Bryant and Bishop, and Clay and Bishop, brawling in the bar had hit Twitter already, and all the major gossip sites were picking them up. All her dad knew was that Bishop had shown up at The Fox with an entourage, and Bryant and Clay had come out swinging.

While Van was theoretically flattered that they were both attempting to protect and avenge her, she didn't want them to get in trouble on her account. Because even if she was able to bail them out tonight, Bishop would not drop the charges. And from the look of the pictures, they beat the shit out of him.

As much as she wanted Bishop to be held accountable for what he'd done to her, Van derived no satisfaction from seeing him injured. She sat beside Phoenix as she fielded phone call after phone call from what seemed like every reporter on earth. While Phoenix told them Van wasn't involved in the altercation and that Van had not invited Bishop to Wellville, Van watched every piece of footage she could from the fight.

One of the people with Bishop had been filming as they walked in the door. Van could hear someone comment that "This is gonna be great," just before Bishop stepped into the bar like he was a king and it was his castle.

The light dimmed, then brightened as the party came to a stop inside the bar. The camera scanned the sparsely populated sports bar, then came to rest on Clay, standing by the bar. Van saw the moment he recognized Bishop. He went from leaning against the bar to standing at his full height with fists and jaw clenched. Then there was yelling off-screen, and the camera whipped around just in time to see a red-faced Bryant knock Bishop to the ground.

Van sometimes forgot that Bryant had been in the Army right alongside Clay. She knew he'd enlisted with Clay. Knew they'd served together. Had missed him while he was gone, but Bryant was so gentle with her, Van forgot he knew how to use his body as a weapon. Bishop crumpled under Bryant's weight. He didn't have a chance to put up a fight as Bryant punched him once, twice. Then Clay pulled Bryant off. When Bishop took a swing at Bryant, Clay smashed Bishop into the wall.

Words were exchanged, but Van couldn't hear what they were saying until the person filming stepped in closer, just in time to hear Bishop say, "What kind of sick fuck wants to screw his sister, anyway?"

And then Clay nearly sent Bishop's head through the wall.

The video cut off there. There was another that showed Clay and Bryant climbing, uncuffed, into the back of a police car. And another of Bishop limping out of The Fox with the support of a paramedic. Van rolled her eyes and darkened her phone screen. The asshole was such a faker. There was absolutely nothing wrong with his legs, but she also knew he'd win this one.

If he wanted to press charges, Clay and Bryant would be in real trouble.

He'd made sure there was plenty of evidence so that neither of them could claim self-defense, even though Van knew they wouldn't. Clay and Bryant had more integrity in one rock hard pec than Bishop had in his whole body.

She flipped her phone back on and scrolled through the texts Bishop had been sending her. Not one of them had been threatening. They'd all been in the tone of the jilted boyfriend. A wronged party. And though they'd strategized in the car about how they were going to defend Clay and Bryant, Twitter was already villainizing them as brutes. The most sympathetic defense so far was that "they think Van was raped, of course they beat his ass." Implying of course, that she'd duped those closest to her into believing a lie. Making Van, once again, the vicious bitch who was trying to take down Henry Bishop for no good reason.

She wanted to feel angry. Van wanted to be outraged.

But she was so tired of being upset all the time. She was tired of being afraid of Bishop, and she was tired of hiding away and not dealing with anything. Van was tired of having Phoenix and her dad, and now Clay and Bryant, fight her battles for her. It was time for Van to say something. To *do* something about this mess.

Van grabbed Phoenix's hand and disconnected whatever call she was on. "Call Butch and let him know we're going to L.A.. We need to take control of this narrative, now." Phoenix met Van's eyes with a question, but a slow grin spread over her lips as she noticed Van's bright smile. In that moment, whatever had been off-balance inside her since The Incident had clicked back into place. Van had never let fear stop her before, and this time wasn't going to be any different.

Video of Noble and Wilder in Action

Fans self Did you see that blatant display of raw masculinity last night? If not, check out the video below. We've got to hand it to Van Birch, not only does her long-time boyfriend Bryant Wilder defend her honor, but she somehow has swayed her stepbrother Clay Noble to her cause too. We sometimes forget that both Noble and Wilder are former military, but this video is a pleasant reminder. *swoon*

18

*I*t was nine o'clock the next morning before Bryant and Clay were free on bail—thanks to Van. Clay had been anxious to see her. He needed make sure she was all right with Bishop in town. Clay had been prowling his cell most of the night, going back and forth between being angry with himself for landing in the slammer and feeling satisfied as hell for socking Henry Bishop in the goddamn face.

The asshole deserved worse.

But Clay's number one priority was getting to Van and making sure she was okay. He knew Robin, who'd acted as their counsel, would be waiting for them, but when he caught a glimpse of Van's black hair through a crack in the door ahead, Clay had to actively avoid stepping on the officer's heels.

When they were finally through, Van was the only thing he saw when they exited the long hallway into the lobby. Her hair was tangled and her t-shirt was wrinkled under her leather jacket, but there she stood, petite and mighty and with a teasing smile on her face as she met Clay's eyes. He knew he looked like hell, that his hair was greasy and his clothes grungy. He was pretty sure his deodorant had stopped working a couple hours ago, but none of that was going to stop him from scooping Van into his arms in another two seconds.

He'd fantasized about how she'd wrap her arms around his shoulders and with only a nimble hop, her legs would close around his hips. Clay would angle her head with a hand on the back of her neck, and he'd kiss her in front of everybody. Clay didn't give a fuck who knew he loved Van anymore. He'd loved her for the last ten years, and he wasn't going to let her get hurt ever again.

He'd taken two steps toward her when a cameraman moved in behind her, and Clay realized all the people in the lobby weren't just regular folks taking care of business but Van's entire reality show crew. All three cameras, the producer and her assistant, a couple guys with mics. They formed a circle around the Van and Phoenix who stood with Robin in the middle of the room. Clay halted as Van ran to Bryant, not to Clay, and threw her arms around *his* shoulders.

Bryant pressed a quick kiss to her neck, as a camera swooped in beside them to capture the sweet gesture.

Clay could practically hear the bones in his hands creak as he clenched his fists. There was no doubt one of the cameras was trained on him, and he couldn't let his frustration and jealousy show without setting off a slew of rumors and gossip rag speculations. He didn't doubt that with the bullshit Bishop had spouted right before Clay had made sure his nose stayed broken, there was already plenty of talk.

As much as Clay didn't give two shits about what other people thought, he didn't want to hurt Van.

So he kept his distance and let her hug Bryant and ask him how he was as Robin clapped Clay on the shoulder and suggested breakfast.

"We need to get to work." Clay shrugged off Robin's hand.

"It's okay," Phoenix said, sliding in between Clay and Robin. He knew she wanted to be next to Robin, but she couldn't be too close on camera without an excuse, otherwise their secret wouldn't be a secret anymore. "I spoke with Marie, and she called all the foremen. They have you covered for the morning."

Clay's teeth ground audibly as he zeroed in on Phoenix. Her eyes flashed like a blue flame as she met his glare, daring him to challenge her. Clay wanted to scold her for trying to manage his crew, but he only said, "I could have handled that."

Phoenix rolled her eyes. "No, you couldn't have, because you let an asshole bait you into getting arrested."

Robin laid a hand on Phoenix's shoulder in warning, but she didn't back down as Clay stepped into her space. "At least I've always seen that motherfucker for what he was. If you'd have listened to me last Christmas when I told you that man was bad news, none of this would have happened."

Phoenix's sharp red fingernail dug into Clay's shoulder as she stepped right up into his face, a sneer curling her lips. "Don't you dare put this on me. Bishop's actions are on him and him alone." Phoenix poked Clay over and over as she spoke, emphasizing her words with sharp jabs. "And you are no better than he is, so stay. Away. From. Van."

Clay swatted her hand aside. "What does that mean?"

"You think I don't know what was going on last night? While you and Van were in your room 'writing a song?'"

"That's none of your business."

Phoenix snarled—actually snarled. "I will never let Van fall victim to another predator. Never. So you can take your teenage need to prove how manly you are and shove it up your ass."

"Phoenix," Robin said, both hands on her shoulders now. "Clay isn't a threat to Van."

She shot Robin the same scathing look she'd had trained on Clay and ducked out of his hold. "You didn't see it then either." She straightened her neat navy blazer. "I'll be waiting in the car. In case you've forgotten, we have an appointment." Then she stalked off with heels clicking against the cheap linoleum tiles.

It wasn't until Clay turned around after Phoenix had left that he noticed Van and Bryant—and all of the cameras—had crowded in behind him. Bryant's arm was still locked around Van's shoulders, and she had one arm stretched across his back. Van's teeth worried at her bottom lip, as she met Clay's eyes, but she was in Bryant's arms. Not Clay's. The two of them looked every inch the long-term romance they pretended to be in.

It made Clay's stomach turn. He'd spent all night planning how he was going to take care of Van, and it couldn't be more obvious that Clay wasn't wanted or needed. He didn't care if Bryant was in love with another woman—if Bryant's and Van's relationship wasn't sexual.

They were still *in* a relationship, and Clay was done pretending otherwise.

"I'm going home to shower," Clay said to Robin, who still looked as if Phoenix had slapped him across the face. "Can I have your keys?"

Robin sighed and pulled a jumble of keys from his pocket. "I drove your truck over." He plucked Clay's keyring out of the mess and held it out.

Clay's only response was a nod.

Van didn't even look over her shoulder to watch him go. Clay had gone to jail for her, and he didn't even warrant a second look.

Clay didn't drive back to Robin's. For the first time since the tornado, he didn't want to be around family—what pathetic excuse of it he had left anyway. As he pulled up to the tarp-covered hole where his house used to be, Clay admitted to himself what he'd been denying since his mom died. He was alone. There was no one he could count on. Not even Robin.

Clay did a quick walk of the lot. Some trash, candy bar wrappers, and crushed beer cans had blown in on the wind, but otherwise nothing was out of place. His old truck still hadn't been located, not that he expected it to be at this point—the damn thing was probably in Oz—but his front stoop was right where it had been, leading up to a small porch that had been ripped clean away in the storm. Beyond that was the devastating blue sea of tarp that protected his basement.

That basement had saved Clay's life. And Pebbles's life too.

He wished he'd thought to go pick her up. She at least would sit next to him—even if she'd been sleeping in

Van's room lately. Clay didn't blame her. He would too if Van would let him.

The awful words he'd said about Van when he was twenty came back to him, and he buried his head in his hands. Would he never live that down? Yes, he still needed to apologize to Van, but he had just been posturing, young, and stupid. He would never actually touch her uninvited.

Shame washed over him as he remembered the last couple of weeks, the way he'd pushed the line whenever he and Van were alone. She hadn't objected, but she hadn't been welcoming either. Van hadn't moved into Clay's touch before last night. Maybe he was just as bad as Bishop, taking what he wanted regardless of how it affected anyone else.

Clay didn't know how long he sat there, replaying how they'd been together in his room, trying to recall how he'd wound up on top of Van with his shirt off. He was trying to forget how turned on he'd been when she'd whimpered and begged him to hurry.

A giant black SUV pulled to a stop across the street from Clay's house. The passenger door opened, and Van stepped out. He blinked into the sun, not sure if she was a mirage or if he'd summoned her there with his raunchy imagination. She crossed the street as the SUV pulled down the street a few lots. Still in view but with enough space to give them privacy.

She stopped a foot in front of him. He was aware that all of his loneliness, all of his shame, all of his anguish showed on his face as she ran one of her thin, long-fingered hands through his hair. "Oh, Clay," she said and dipped her head down to capture his lips.

MARLA HOLT

Van's kiss was absolution, and Clay wanted to get lost in the sweet relief of her touch. He would never hurt this woman. He brushed her jacket out of the way to close one hand over her waist. The other he wound through the tangled hair at the base of her neck and angled her head so that he could have better access to her lips.

Van melted into him. Clay helped her ease her knees onto the concrete on either side of his hips as he pulled her in like he'd imagined doing all night. Van's hands met behind his neck, the fingernails on her strumming hand scratching along his hairline and up next to his ear. Clay broke the kiss to lean back into the soothing touch.

"I never knew you liked being scratched behind the ears like a dog," she said. She was so close, Clay could feel her breath flutter across his throat as she spoke.

The hand that had been on her waist now rested at the small of her back, and he pressed her in closer so he could smell her hair. She mostly smelled like leather and the police station lobby, but Clay could detect the faint whiff of her floral shampoo beneath it all. He'd never realized before that Van's scent was the one he associated with home.

"You've never cared what I liked before," he said. He hadn't meant anything by it, just that she'd never touched him before, but she stiffened and pulled back.

"That's not true, Clay, and you know it."

"I don't know it," he said, and when she tried to step out of his embrace completely, he let her. "But I want to know everything."

Van cocked her head as she peered at him beneath scrunched eyebrows. Clay couldn't tell what she was thinking, but she sat down beside him, close enough that

248

their thighs touched, and asked, "Do you miss living on your own?" Which was not what he expected to hear.

He glanced over her shoulder at the void of where his house used to stand. That house, as simple and small as it had been, had been Clay's favorite creation to date. It had been bright and airy with a lot of windows for sunlight and airflow in the milder months. There had been a fireplace for extra coziness in the winter. He'd custom-built the kitchen from scratch—not that he cooked much —but a well-loved kitchen was part of what made a house a home. He'd been proud of the house. It was one of the focal points of his business portfolio, but did he miss living there by himself? No. It's why he'd adopted Pebbles.

"It's lonely, coming home by yourself every night."

Van bumped her shoulder against his. "Is that why you're still at my dad's house?"

He shrugged. "It's nice to have dinner with Robin every now and then—and with you and Phoenix around —" He stopped himself from going any further as he remembered the fire in Phoenix's eyes, the loathing on her tongue, as she warned him off Van.

"It's nothing personal, what's going on with Phoenix," Van said.

"Right," he snorted. "Seemed like it to me."

Van rested her head on his shoulder. "She's going through something. She hasn't even told me about it yet. And," Van paused and sunk further into him, "Phoenix had a stepbrother too."

Clay couldn't help himself and kissed the top of Van's head. Then he threw his arm over her shoulders so his hand came to rest on her hip. "I didn't know that."

Van's voice was soft and gentle, and Clay knew whatever she was going to say next wouldn't be pleasant or easy to hear. "He was older by four or five years. He was in high school while she was in middle school, and he used to sneak into her room at night."

That was all Clay needed to hear for his heart to break. Shame washed over him anew as he remembered the words he'd once said. Then, as he listened to Van recount how she'd overheard what he'd said back then, Clay wanted to castrate himself as much as he wanted to put Henry Bishop in the ground.

"So, Phoenix has barely tolerated you since I told her that story, even though I told her it was just stupid posturing," Van finished.

"That doesn't excuse it." His voice came out strained, and Clay had to pause to clear his throat. "For what I said, what I implied, I am so sorry, Van. I was a jealous kid with a crush on a girl I could never have, but I would never—"

"I know," she cut him off. "At first, I thought you thought I wasn't worth the time and attention you paid to the other girls you dated, that you thought I really would sleep with any guy who came into my room. But after some time and distance, after I moved away, I realized that while you were being a prick about it, you were also trying to protect me from Race Carter's wandering hands."

"He's still a playboy," Clay said.

"Noted." She nudged him in the side with her elbow until he met her eyes. "But you aren't, Clay. And you're not Bishop, and you're not Phoenix's stepbrother either."

"I shouldn't have said what I said."

"No, you shouldn't have," Van agreed.

"And I shouldn't have touched you without your permission. I'm sorry."

Van flinched away and frowned. "When did you touch me without my permission?"

"Since you've been home, whenever we've been alone, I've found ways to—"

Van laughed. "Drive me absolutely fucking crazy is what you've been doing."

"I'm sorry."

"Stop being so pathetic and apologizing for everything. I want you to touch me. The only reason I'm not riding you right here on this stoop is because there are still a few houses in this neighborhood, and I don't want to scar any kids for life."

The idea of Van straddling him on his porch steps, of sliding inside her while she was still mostly clothed, had Clay going hard. She would close her eyes and bite her lip as he filled her. And when he rocked inside her she would moan through her teeth and try to stifle her cries, but she'd fail.

"You're thinking about it, aren't you?" her breath whispered against his ear.

"Of course I'm thinking about it. I've been thinking about it since I was sixteen."

Van's tongue slid from the base of Clay's throat to his chin. His entire body stiffened with want. "If only we had some place to go. Maybe we should rent you an apartment."

All Clay's desire fled at her words. He knew Van was flirting, that she didn't even mean what she said, but Van had more money than she knew what to do with, and Clay had barely been getting by before the storm.

He pushed her away and scooted to the other side of the stoop. "I can't afford to rebuild if I have to pay rent too. I'll have to live at Robin's for a year before I have enough to start as it is."

Van nodded solemnly. "I've been thinking about that, and I think I can help," Van said.

"I'm not taking your money."

"I'm not offering you any." Her tone of voice had changed. Instead of her breathy teasing, she sounded a lot like Phoenix. Confident, calm, one-hundred percent no bull shit. "I could probably get you an early pay-out from *Pop Star* this year. I know you'll be in at least three episodes. And I've had another offer I've been meaning to talk to you about."

It took a lot of effort not to scowl at her. He was not asking for an advance from the stupid reality show. But that didn't mean the second thing wouldn't have merit.

"What kind of offer?" he asked, assuming it would mean he'd have to take part of one of her elaborate made-up plot lines for her reality show so he could be on more episodes.

When she said, "One of the cable home improvement networks wants to do a show centered around us rebuilding your house. They'd pay for everything."

Clay was pretty sure his heart stopped beating. "What?"

She smirked at him. "If you agree to have me hanging around for a couple more months, we can rebuild your house, together, for the low, low price of you agreeing to become a celebrity contractor."

"You want me to sign on for my own reality show?"

"Well, I'd be the co-star, but yeah. America thinks

you're studly. And I'm pretty sure they want me to be your annoying kid sister, but I was thinking on selling them on the insider scoop to a budding romance. And after that you could probably go on to develop your own furniture and home decor line for Target or something."

Clay laughed, ignoring the budding romance part for now. "And if I don't want to sell home decor?"

"Do the show, build your house, and forget about it."

"You make it sound like there's no reason not to do it."

"Basically."

"Aside from the fact that I'd have to put up with even more cameras and have sponsors tell me where to buy my building supplies and what brand of appliances I can have."

"Some of that would be negotiable."

"Right."

Van's fingers skimmed down his arm. "Just think about it. It could be a good thing."

Clay took the opportunity to tangle his fingers in her hair and pull her close. "So far, you're the only good sounding part of it."

Having her pressed against him felt right. He felt complete, and for the moment, Clay let himself forget Bishop and Bryant and Phoenix. He forgot about reality shows and music contracts. He forgot that Van lived in L.A. and would be going back in a few weeks. He forgot everything but the feel of her lips against his.

Clay was so lost in the sounds of her sighs, the feel of her skin and hair beneath his hands, how soft her tongue was against his, that he had forgotten where they were or how long they'd been sitting on his lonely front stoop until a car door slammed a few lots down.

They startled apart, and Van giggled as she stroked her thumb over his cheek, then stood. "Come on. While you're figuring out if you want to star in your own reality show, you're scheduled for filming for mine this afternoon."

Clay groaned but followed her to the truck even so. He wasn't prepared to watch Van prance around a construction site in her pink hard hat all afternoon. He was already going to combust if he didn't get her alone soon; watching her flirt with the guys on the crew wouldn't help.

But as he helped her into his truck, he knew he'd do anything for her. Perform for cameras, say yes to the reality show, wait as long as he needed to for her. He already had, so what was the pointing in fighting it?

Perfect Timing

Van Birch has perfect timing as always. Sources say that she and conjoined business partner Phoenix Lambert landed in L.A. this morning. Perfect timing for putting distance between herself and stepbrother Clay Noble after photographs of them kissing and cuddling on Noble's front porch surfaced late last night. We're not sure if we're turned on or grossed out. Tell us which one you are in the poll below these exclusive snapshots.

19

*A*s soon as they got home from work, Van's dad whisked Clay and Bryant into his office so they could talk legal stuff about Bishop and the arrest. Van spent most of the evening with Phoenix in the little office she'd set up in the basement. There wasn't much to the place, a little kitchenette in one corner, a tiny living space, a bathroom, and a bedroom, but it was dry and had hardwood floors and white walls, which almost made you forget you were in a basement.

Phoenix had been adding her own cozy touches over the last couple of years. She'd replaced the country art Van's mom had hung on the walls with more contemporary prints. She'd added gold vases and fake succulents. She'd replaced the linens on the bed with white sheets and a dove-gray comforter accented with peacock blue and green pillows.

When Van plopped down on the sofa Phoenix had recovered with a soft indigo fabric, she felt like she was in a miniature version of Phoenix's Malibu cottage. Phoenix had been pissy for days but wouldn't say what was wrong, so Van had stopped asking. She had been hoping Phoenix was over it by now, but when she nearly spiked her tablet onto the cushion next to Van, it was clear she was still ticked—probably at Clay still or Van. Possibly both of them.

"I know we had pizza last night, but Stark's all the way in L.A.. There's no way he's going to know if we have pizza two nights in a row," Van said, as Phoenix pulled a bottle of sparkling water out of her tiny fridge. Only one, Van noticed—nothing for her. Thanks, Fe. It was good to know her friend had her back. Van was only about to have a panic attack. She didn't need any water.

"I already ordered sushi."

Van perked up, shifting onto her knees with her elbows on the back of the sofa so she could face Phoenix where she was leaned against her oven. "Even better." Van smiled to hide her disappointment. Sushi was technically trainer approved, but the quality of it here in good old landlocked Kansas wasn't nearly the same as by-the-sea Los Angeles. Van would have much preferred pizza, but Phoenix had strict, non-trainer-induced rules about how much junk food she'd allow herself to eat. And Phoenix had been drinking so much wine with Van's dad in the evenings, Van was a little surprised she'd actually eaten a slice of pizza last night.

Van was so busy thinking about the wounded look on her father's face that morning when Phoenix had snapped at him at the police station that she barely noticed when Phoenix joined her on the sofa. She was aiming her tablet in Van's direction, blinding her with the brightness of a stark white email before Van focused her attention on Phoenix.

"Did you ever make a sex tape with Bishop?"

Van must have stumbled through a portal and wandered into an alternate universe where that might have been a possibility. She blinked slowly once then shook her head. "What?"

Phoenix repeated herself slowly, enunciating the vowels in slow motion, but Van covered Phoenix's lips with her fingers before she could say "sex tape" again.

"I heard you the first time, you freak. And ew. No. I've never made a sex tape, ever."

Phoenix tapped the tablet. "Well Bishop says he has one, and he's threatening to release it to the public if you don't drop your accusations."

Van read the email three times, trying to make sense of how different the words on the screen were from the promises of love and reunion he'd been texting to her.

"But there isn't a sex tape," Van said.

"How do you know? Is it possible he filmed you without your knowledge?"

"Bishop wouldn't . . ." Van started to say but stopped herself. Six weeks ago, she'd thought there were a lot of things Bishop wouldn't do—including rape her—but that's what he had done. Coldness seeped into Van's bones as she realized that she had no fucking clue what Bishop was capable of. Maybe he had taped them together. She didn't know. Every time with him had been so frantic, so full of need, of immediate release, that she would have never noticed a camera on the bookshelf or a phone propped up just so.

Her relationship with Bishop had consumed her. It

had started on her last tour, though they'd flirted with the idea for years; one thing or another had always kept them from taking that last step. But after that first show, a sold-out stadium, he'd appeared at her dressing room door.

They'd both known what he'd come for, and Van had wanted him. He'd been by her side since she signed with the label. He'd been a producer on both her albums. He'd been in charge of booking her tours, had worked with Phoenix on booking interviews and promotions. Bishop had been an integral part of Van's team, and she had admired him for years before they'd slept together. After that, Van had been obsessed.

The sex had been phenomenal. Explosive. Every encounter had left her satisfied, while simultaneously yearning for more and more and more. He was like a drug she didn't want to give up, and he showered her with what she'd taken for affection—love, even.

He'd sent Van flowers and wine and guitar picks. He'd surprised her with dinner and theater tickets and set her up with couture designers. He'd argued with her. He pushed her so hard sometimes, she'd hated him.

Sitting on the lumpy old couch in her dad's basement, looking at the email from Bishop to Phoenix—one that he'd sent weeks ago—Van had never felt more foolish. He could have filmed them having sex. It was still a shock to think of him as someone she couldn't or shouldn't trust sometimes. Just as she'd felt like she'd gotten her feet back under her, the world shifted again, and Van was left staggering. Her stomach rolled, and she must have gone pale because Phoenix set aside her tablet and pushed Van's hair over her shoulder in that startling motherly way Phoenix had.

"I'm sorry." Her thin fingers squeezed Van's shoulder. "I'm so sorry."

"It's not your fault." They'd had this conversation a million times since Phoenix had sneaked Van into the hospital, but it had never gone any further. No deeper than, "It's not your fault."

"Did your dad tell you he hired a private investigator?"

Van jerked out of her grasp. "What? No."

Phoenix bit her lip and met Van's eyes beneath lowered lashes. "He wants to know why L.A. County didn't investigate your case more thoroughly. It's high profile, and with the photos and the rape kit, he thinks it was irresponsible of them to drop the charges."

"So, what, he's trying to dig up dirt on Bishop? That'll somehow get them to reopen the case?"

"It isn't closed, per se," Phoenix readjusted on her seat, pulling up another window on her tablet and reading it before continuing. "It's just sort of languishing."

"But the articles. My lawyers in L.A. told me it was dropped, and there was nothing I could do."

"They said the same thing to me, and when I asked Robin about it, he said it wasn't good enough, so we decided to push."

Van examined the determined set of Phoenix's jaw, the hard glint in her vibrant blue eyes. Dread filled Van as their conversation from the night before registered. Van had said she wanted to change the conversation. That she wanted to take control. To push Bishop back the same way he'd was pushing her by toying with Clay and Bryant.

"You want him to release the sex tape, don't you?"

Phoenix grinned, wide and evil, like a satisfied dragon

with sad eyes ready to devour her prey with one sharp snap of her teeth. "You said you were ready to fight. I think that if we're going to win, we're going to fight dirty."

Van perked up at that. She could fight dirty. She wanted to bite and scratch and knee Bishop in the balls. That knockout punch after would feel so satisfying. So empowering. "What do you want to do?" Van asked.

"I want to call his bluff. If there's a tape, so what? We'll deal with it."

"So what?" Van's whole body flushed with heat and anger. "It's not your exposed hoo-ha on the line."

"I know it's a big risk. If the tape exists, especially if it was filmed without your permission, we can shift the conversation away from how fantastic Bishop is and how the poor guy had his nose broken by your hunky boyfriend and over-protective stepbrother, and over to how he is a manipulative, selfish predator."

"Yes. Let's do that, but I'd rather do it without allowing the whole world to see my O-face?"

"Because right now we look like the bad guys."

"And people aren't gonna be sympathetic when they see the tape. They're just gonna keep saying, 'Look, she had sex with him willingly and cheated on her hunky boyfriend over and over again. What a bitch.'"

"They won't say that."

"They already fucking are."

"Okay, some people will keep saying that, but we can release the blackmail claims. We can do interviews about how the video was filmed without your consent. And when we do, we have tangible evidence that might not help with the assault charges but should help sway public opinion enough for more people to switch from *hashtag notBishop* to *hashtag justiceforVan*."

"I haven't seen a lot of positive uses of that hashtag."

"But you will."

Van wasn't convinced, but when Phoenix showed her the email from an entertainment show wanting an interview with Van the next day about the incident at The Fox and explained how they could use it to push Bishop over the edge, Van agreed to do it.

Phoenix, the cocky witch, already had already arranged for a plane to pick them up from the nearest airport first thing in the morning. They practiced with the interview questions. The sushi was delivered. They ate and worked until after ten, when Van stole Phoenix's tablet and pushed it under the sofa.

"Goddamnit, Van. There's spiders under there."

"Maybe some beetles too. Roly-polies if you're lucky."

Phoenix blew a strand of her red hair out of her face but made no move to retrieve her device. Finally. Van hadn't been able to get her to stop working since they'd landed in Kansas.

"Have you heard from Minnie today?" Van asked. When she'd left the night before, her skin had taken on a greenish tinge, as if she was just as sick at the news that Bishop was in town as Van was. But Van knew it was because it affected Bryant. She might have moved on with whoever the father of her baby was, but Van wondered if she didn't still have feelings for Bryant too.

Van had longed to pull her aside and tell her there was nothing to worry about. Bryant was Minnie's for the taking if she wanted him, but Van knew she wouldn't. Not when she hadn't figured out how to break things off with

Bryant publicly yet. Despite their mutual decision to end the charade, there had been so much else going on that Van hadn't gotten around to telling Phoenix about it. She knew now would be an opportune time, but she knew Phoenix would be pissed, and things had been so weird between them the last couple of weeks. Tonight was almost normal. Van wasn't ready to change that.

"She texted to say thanks for last night and to see if the guys were okay. I told her they were brutes, and a night in jail was probably good for them."

Van snorted, remembering how Clay had been agitated and impatient that morning, where Bryant had just looked exhausted with a side of pissed. "Did you know she and Bryant used to be a thing?"

Phoenix, who had collapsed into the sofa cushions, raised her head. "Not officially, but I've had my suspicions."

"He all but confirmed it last night with his awkwardness."

"Was it recent? Is that why he's been all moody recently?"

Van shook her head. "Before the baby."

"Hmmm," Phoenix's eyes went blank as her mind no doubt whirred. "I never did believe her story about her roommate being the father."

Van's heart stopped. "Wait. What?"

"Check this out," Phoenix said, and in a minute had a photo of Minnie and her baby and a Latinx man Phoenix called "Rocco, AKA, the roommate." The photo had been from Jonas Halvarson's Fourth of July party in Denver. Phoenix was right; she didn't see much resemblance between father and son, but then again, the baby didn't look a lot like Minnie either, and she was definitely Malcolm's mother. But Phoenix said, "Van, look at the eyes. The shape of the forehead."

"Oh my god," Van said.

"I couldn't figure out why Minnie was lying about Rocco, but now it makes so much sense."

"Holy shit," Van said again.

Phoenix sat back, looking stunned and numb. "Just put a pair of stupid black glasses and a raggedy leather jacket on him, and you've got a mini Bryant."

Van took the tablet from a limp Phoenix's hands. She didn't know whether to be shocked or excited or angry or just in awe. "I can't believe Bryant has a kid. Do you think he knows? He doesn't know right? He can't know. There's no way he'd choose not to have contact with his own kid."

Phoenix's eyes grew wide and misty, and she shook her head.

"Hey," Van said, a hand squeezing Phoenix's forearm. "Are you okay?"

"Yeah," she said, though the shaky voice and thumb at the corner of her eye said otherwise. "It's just been a long day and Bryant has a kid and Bishop is still harassing you. And the social media douchebags and all the extra security. I'm tired, I'm worried, and I need a break."

Van didn't quite believe that that was all, but if Phoenix wasn't ready to talk about it, Van wasn't going to press. She'd appreciated Phoenix not pressing her. And when Phoenix was ready to talk about what was going on with her, Van would be there. "We should plan that trip to Paris."

"If we ever have time, I'm in." Phoenix yawned and

discretely wiped at her eyes. "We should head to bed. We need to leave here at four."

Van groaned but stood and stretched, enjoying a loud yawn of her own. "When we fly to Paris, can you book a flight for noon, please?"

Phoenix flipped her off as Van pulled herself up the stairs.

The rest of the house was quiet and dark. None of them had managed much sleep the night before, so it didn't surprise Van that her dad was in bed, but she'd hoped Clay might have waited up for her. After brushing her teeth, Van peeked into his room, but it was empty. She hadn't heard from him. The only texts she'd received all day had been from Bishop again. Hooray. But Clay wasn't obligated to tell her when he was going out. She could understand if he and Bryant would want to have a drink, let off some steam.

Still, she fought disappointment as she pushed open her own bedroom door—only to smile at what she found. Her bedside lamp was on. Clay lay sprawled over her comforter, his guitar next to him on the bed, like he'd been waiting for her so they could finish writing their song.

The lightness, the warmth Van felt whenever Clay was around bloomed in her chest, calming the churning in her stomach that dealing with Bishop and his bullshit dredged up. Clay's touch was at once comforting and arousing. At once familiar and forbidden. Van had nursed her crush on him since way before their parents had gotten together. She'd watched him at school, on the football field, and she'd watched for him every week after guitar lessons. But then, it turned out she hadn't been the only one appreciating the scenery at guitar lessons, because that's how her dad had met Mary Beth. And the more Clay was around, the more Van had wanted him to be around—but it was too taboo to even go near. They were supposed to be siblings—or at the very least tolerate one another for the sake of their parents. But the awful thing was, Van had wanted him to wait for her in her room like this all through high school—but he'd never looked twice.

That wasn't right. Because he'd admitted as much yesterday. When he'd told her he'd had a crush on her that whole time too, Van had almost squealed like a fourteen-year-old girl at a boy band concert. She didn't want to count her chickens where Clay was concerned, but she thought maybe whatever was happening could be a good thing. Different than any relationship she'd had before, but good.

She propped Clay's guitar next to her own and grabbed the quilt she kept folded over her armchair and snapped it open. Clay didn't stir until she swatted his side and said, "Make room, Man-whore. You're hogging the bed."

He said something unintelligible and rolled onto his side but in a jerky way that told Van he wasn't really awake. She snuggled into him and spread the quilt over them. Clay's arm wrapped around her waist and Van sighed.

This was going to be so good.

@_Chadtheman_X_69: We are all victims of #fakecases. The feminazis are out to take all men who like pussy to court

20

*V*an wrote Clay a note and sneaked out of the house with Phoenix before dawn. They arrived at the studio just in time to film the interview. Van had two more texts from Bishop while they were traveling, asking if he could stop by the house. For the first time since The Incident, Van texted him back, telling him she wasn't in Wellville anymore, and no, he couldn't come to her house in L.A. either.

Van wasn't planning to stay at her condo on this trip— or maybe ever again. She just couldn't anymore. If she was going to move on, a physical move seemed like a good idea. She had no idea where she wanted to go, but since she was planning to stay in Kansas through October anyway, finding a new place didn't seem like a huge priority. She'd have Phoenix call a realtor Monday morning and start the process of getting her house on the market.

The interview was awful. They played the video from The Fox before they introduced Van, which already had

Van cranky. While the reporter, and Van used that term loosely since it was totally a gossip show, smiled and nodded at everything Van said, Van answered her questions about how she was doing honestly, saying it hurt being betrayed by someone she trusted but that she was working hard on other things. The celebrity gossip reporter followed up with, "How does Bryant feel about your relationship with Bishop?"

"Considering the footage you all played before came on, I think it's safe to say we both feel betrayed by Bishop more than anything."

"So you're admitting that you did have a relationship with Bishop outside your relationship with Bryant?"

Van took a deep breath as nerves jangled to life inside and glanced off-camera to where Phoenix gave her a double thumbs up. This was it. This is where they blew everyone's minds. "Bryant and I actually haven't been anything more than good friends for more than a year now. We still love each other very much but went separate ways romantically some time ago."

The reporters smile turned as fake as her blonde hair. The juicy exclusive just turned into a different story entirely, and she didn't know what to do with it.

Van continued. "Bryant and Bishop didn't always get along, but Bryant supported the relationship initially. Obviously, we've all changed our minds."

Footage of the altercation at the Fox played on the screen behind Van's head, and she tried not to notice.

"Your brother didn't hesitate to come to your defense either," the reporter said as Clay bashed Bishop's head into the wall

And Van couldn't help it, it just slipped out. "Clay's not my brother."

The reporter just smiled like Van had played right into her trap instead of the other way around. The footage behind Van's head changed to a photo of Van and Clay making out on his front stoop the day before. The photo had gone live that morning, and Phoenix had shown it to Van on their way to the airport. Butch swore he hadn't seen anyone else in the area from where he'd been keeping watch from his SUV. It was taken from above, looking down from across the street. It wasn't great quality, but it was just good enough to tell that Van was on Clay's lap, and that they were wrapped together like twist ties.

"Do you have any comment about these photos?" They flashed a few more that were more or less the same. "They are causing quite the uproar on the internet right now."

Van hadn't looked. She didn't need to know what anyone was saying about her and Clay. Instead, she felt a blush rise to her cheeks that she hoped her makeup wouldn't hide. "The thing with Clay is, I've had a crush on him since I was fourteen. That was before my dad married his mom. And it turns out he's had a crush on me too. It's actually pretty exciting that something's starting to happen between us. It's been a long time coming."

Van heard one of the producers sigh and say, "That is adorable." Van shot her a grin.

"What exactly is something?" the reporter asked.

Van only shrugged and motioned toward the pictures. "That only happened yesterday. You know as much as I do, but I think whatever it is could be really, really good." Van looked to Phoenix again, afraid she'd see Phoenix scowling. Instead, her friend was wiping a tear from her eye and motioned for Van to keep going. "But, as much as I'd like to keep gushing about Clay, I agreed to come on this show to talk about the legal drama with my former manager, so let's get back to that."

Phoenix nodded and gave a silent slow clap.

The reporter looked shocked, then schooled her face back into her trademark saccharine smile, then continued, asking Van why she kept up with the allegations against Bishop when the police wouldn't pursue the case—and that was Van's moment to shine.

"I'm so glad you asked. This is something I feel really strongly about. So many people already feel like they don't have a voice when they go through something similar to what happened to me. And I think you'll agree I have a fantastic platform. I have my own show, a gigantic Twitter following. I am working on my third album. Millions of people have access to my voice. People know my name, know my face, and for the most part, they listen when I talk. And I really think it says something that so many people can trust me with so much else, but when it comes to what happened to me, everyone automatically assumes I'm making it up for promotional purposes."

Van looked directly at the camera instead of the reporter. "I want to be super clear. Sexual assault is not a joke. It is not a stunt. Henry Bishop raped me, and I will not let that slide, and I will fight to be heard, and I will fight for other voices to be heard too. The 'Me Too' Movement did so much for awakening us to those voices and those experiences, but the way people have reacted to 'The Van Birch Incident' tells me that we still aren't listening. With all the influence I have, I am still not being heard. My security team is fielding death threats and rape threats daily. I now have round-the-clock, 24-hour security. My dad's house is locked down tighter than the White House right now, but I will not be intimidated, and I will not be quiet. I will keep talking until we hear survivors and start believing them when they tell us they've been hurt."

The screen flashed to a photo of Van taken by the police, the ones Phoenix had brought just for this purpose. The photos showed Van in nothing but her black panties and black bra with bruises all over her hips and thighs, a dead look in her eyes. A gasp came from the studio audience, because nobody had seen these photos yet. Nobody had seen the bruises or the handprints that clearly indicated violence, not desire. "The L.A. County Sherriff have these photos in evidence. And I'm lucky enough to be able to identify my assailant, but there are people all over the world who don't even have this much. Or they don't have the resources to come forward, or their rape kit is sitting in a closet somewhere, untested. And that's something my friend Phoenix Lambert and I are working to change starting today. Because our voices deserve to be heard."

Van outlined the foundations she and Phoenix had contacted in the last two days and how they were working with them to press for change. The reporter cut Van off pretty quickly from there—but that was fine. It was out there. Other journalists—real journalists—would be blowing up Phoenix's phone in a matter of minutes for more information.

And maybe, just maybe, they'd pushed all the right buttons with Bishop.

Red Alert! Sexy Scandal Unfolding!

Van Birch has a sex tape with Bishop!

How long were these two getting it on behind our backs? This tape is dated from February. Was this perhaps their Valentine's Day tryst? It is certainly H. O. T. Hot! Check out the full unedited footage at the link below.

21

*C*lay was attempting to enjoy a leisurely lunch on the back porch with Pebbles when Robin plopped down in the wicker chair next to him. He handed Clay an open beer and said, "Well, it's out there."

"What is?"

Robin only huffed out an exasperated breath and watched Pebbles bound across the yard in her clumsy puppy steps.

"The tape."

Clay snapped his head around so fast his neck popped. "The *sex* tape? Did Bishop release it?"

Robin nodded and looked pale. He held a beer in his hand too, but he hadn't touched it. "Did you watch it?" Clay asked. But he'd known it was a stupid question, even as Robin shook his head. His eyes had gone vacant.

"I guess not," was all Clay could say, Robin didn't answer.

Clay didn't want to think about anybody seeing that vulnerable, private part of Van but himself. Clay certainly wasn't planning to watch the video, because to see her that way with Bishop would make him want to kill things. Specifically, he might actually kill Bishop. Clay couldn't imagine the turmoil all this caused Robin, not being able to help or protect his daughter from someone who continued to prey on her.

"I hope a shark bites his dick off," Clay said then downed half his beer in one gulp.

"I was hoping for a straight up disemboweling. Not picky about how."

Clay let out a ghost of a laugh and wondered how Robin felt about Van taking their bud of a relationship public but didn't have the courage to ask. Clay was still wrapping his mind around it himself.

He'd waited in her room the other night, hoping to spend some time with her. Had he had sex on his mind? Yes, but he'd also wanted to work on the song they'd started. Clay had never shared anything he'd written before, and he'd never written with someone else, and he wanted more.

Clay had played the song over and over again as he'd waited for her. His eyes had grown heavier every minute from the lack of sleep. He didn't remember laying down, but he remembered making room for her to join him. Clay woke a few times in the night just to run his hands over the skin exposed from where her shirt had ridden up and press her closer to his chest. It had felt so right to have Van lying there beside him. Clay wanted her there all the time.

In the back of his sleep-fogged mind, Clay had planned to roll over on top of her once the sun began to rise and show her how much he enjoyed sleeping with her, but when he'd woken just before dawn, she'd been gone. And not just out for a run or downstairs making breakfast. She'd been on her way back to L.A. to "take care of things" for a few days. She didn't say when she'd be back. There were no words of encouragement or endearment, just a "stay tuned" and her usual epigraph, *Love, Van B.* The same signature she used when giving autographs to nameless fans.

The impersonal note plus the interview she'd done had left Clay with a squeezing in the middle of his chest, as if his lungs had lost the capacity to inflate. He was damn proud of her for going on camera and speaking with so much conviction and so much confidence. Clay had never seen her be so bare and honest and vulnerable in public. Van always wore the good-time girl persona as a mask. She'd used Bryant and her reality show and her publicity stunts as a shield for so long, it was a relief for the world to see the Van he'd always seen.

His pride didn't stop him from being afraid. Even if she moved forward with honesty and transparency, Van's life would always be centered out of L.A. Her life was there. She and Phoenix would move back to California full-time in a few weeks, and Clay would have to figure out what he was even rebuilding his house for.

Was it even worth staying in Wellville? If he couldn't have Van with him in Kansas, would he be willing to move to L.A.? Or would it be better to give up entirely and move somewhere else where he was less well known. Where the whole town didn't know that Van Birch, pop star, was his stepsister and almost-lover. Could he even escape that stigma with those photos of them kissing out in the world?

He certainly wouldn't be able to if he signed on for that stupid reality show.

And yet.

Part of him wanted to do it.

It was a selfish, hopeful part of him. Not only would Clay get to build his house exactly the way he wanted to, but Van would be a part of it. She would stay with him while the house was built, and a tiny part of himself that he didn't even want to acknowledge believed that if he could convince her to stay for just a little while longer, he could convince her not to leave at all.

"This is what you wanted, though. Right?" Clay asked.

Robin had confided a little of the strategy he and Phoenix had been working on before. Apparently Phoenix hadn't spoken to Robin since the morning at the police station. Robin had been walking around the house, picking things up, then putting them down again as he wandered from room to room. He was like Pebbles when she couldn't figure out where she'd left her rawhide. But now, the vacancy in his expression. The stillness of defeat radiating off Robin, recalled the days after Clay's mom had died. Clay wasn't sure how he felt about Robin being that upset at arguing with Phoenix.

The beer bottle clanked against the wood as Robin set it by his feet and buried his hands in his hair, then scrubbed them over his salt and pepper beard. "It's been a rare thing in my career to gleefully plan a strategy or an argument on paper and not take just as much pleasure when it all played out. But this situation with Van— everything that's happened since that tornado touched down—has been nothing but a disaster."

Clay nodded with a grunt of agreement.

"I agreed with Phoenix that this was the best way to tackle the problem. Van needs to be bold, and she needs to be strong, and she needs to use her voice. But I hate the way it's left her exposed. When other women go through nasty breakups, the whole world doesn't discuss it in front of them. Doesn't blame them for it."

The word "breakup" tipped Clay's already simmering temper. "This wasn't just a regular old break up, Robin."

"I know that." His words landed on the ground between them. Heavy and sharp like he'd thrown a knife between Clay's feet, like a man looking for duel.

But Robin didn't say anything else, and neither did Clay. Pebbles bounded up the porch, a thick stick in her mouth. Clay played tug of war with her for a minute before she relented. He tossed the stick across the expanse of Robin's mostly brown backyard. The sun had been too hot, the rain too rare, this season for any grass to survive.

"I want her to enjoy some semblance of normalcy— but all I've ever been able to give her—" Robin cut himself off and was gazing toward the back door, as if expecting Van, or perhaps Phoenix, to poke their heads out of the kitchen and offer him some bit of comfort.

"You've given her everything thing she needs," Clay said.

Robin only shook his head, and Clay wondered if he was thinking about his first wife. Van's mom, who had died when Van was only ten. So young and so vulnerable, but already filled with desire to fulfill her mother's musical aspirations. Then Clay thought about his own mother. How she'd raised him from birth to the age of sixteen completely by herself, and how happy she'd been on the day she'd married Robin.

They'd lived in an apartment near downtown. Not a bad part of town necessarily but an inexpensive neighborhood. Their apartment had been old, with creaky pipes and the kind of water heater you had to warm up by running the kitchen faucet for five minutes, then wait twenty minutes or there wasn't enough hot water to take a shower. Clay had been a total shit as a kid, breaking stuff on purpose when he was angry, picking fights at school, messing up his clothes when he knew his mom didn't have any money to buy more. He'd been better after he'd met Bryant, who also didn't have a dad. By the time she'd met Robin, Clay had been happy for her. He'd been glad that she wouldn't have to worry about money all the time anymore. But when he realized who her new boyfriend was, Clay had grown surly. When they'd told him they were getting married right as Van was about to start high school, and it would have finally, finally been okay for him to ask her out, Clay had been livid.

He'd never told his mom why he'd behaved like a prick all those months, but looking back, he thought she'd known. She'd even tried to throw them together. Suggesting he drive Van to play practice or track practice or take her and whoever her best friend was that week over to the mall. He thought she'd been torturing him at the time. Making him spend time around the girl he wanted but couldn't have. Trying to get him to act like the brother he never wanted to be—not to Van at least. But these days, he sometimes thought maybe, in her own subtle way, his Mom had been trying to let him know that it would be okay if he spent time with Van like that.

Grief hit him in a dark, heavy, unexpected wave. Over the last two years, he'd gotten used to not having his mom around. It wasn't always easy, but the pain of missing her didn't always bite so hard as it did now. Clay's mom had been the most loving, accepting person he'd known in his entire life. And whatever her problems had been with Robin, Clay knew she'd loved him with a fierceness that he'd only ever seen mirrored in the way Clay felt about Van.

"What did you argue about?" Clay asked.

Robin frowned at him. Clearly confused by what Clay was asking.

"The night before the crash. What sent Mom to my place?"

Robin's face crumpled. If he'd been defeated by what was going on with Van and his argument with Phoenix, Clay asking that question had pushed Robin over the edge to devastated. This time he grabbed the beer bottle from the porch floor and chugged it. Clay hadn't seen anyone do that in years, maybe not since he was on active duty.

"I would have thought she'd told you," he said, after he wiped his lip with his bare wrist.

Pebbles was back with her stick, wagging her entire rear end with excitement as she bounced between Clay's knees, eager to play. He went through the motions of tug of war and tossing the stick again before she chased after it. He waited until she was frolicking with her prize through the yard to say, "She said she wasn't ready to talk about it. So I ordered us a pizza, poured her a glass of wine, and we watched some rom com on TV."

Robin chewed his lip before saying. "She asked me for a divorce that night."

Clay sat up straight, his temper roiling. His heartbeat was so loud in his ears he barely heard anything else. He remembered how Robin had been looking at Phoenix like he craved her, how often they'd been drinking wine together in the evenings lately, how he'd followed her downstairs a couple weeks ago like a lust-driven dog on the trail of a bitch in heat when he didn't realize Clay was looking. "What did you do to her?"

Robin shook his head and took another sip of his beer. "I didn't do anything."

Obviously that was a lie. Clay's mother had loved Robin. She had worshipped him. Moving in with him had made their lives so much easier. He'd never seen her happier than when she and Robin were first married. It was as if the burden of being a single mom had been lifted off her shoulders, and she was finally allowed to just be herself. She'd blossomed in the years after she and Robin married. She'd cultivated her garden. Sold fresh flowers every week at the farmers' market. She'd put so much effort into her little plots around Robin's yard. The plots that he paid somebody to maintain now.

"Then why would she want a divorce?" Clay asked.

Robin shook his head almost imperceptibly. "I wish I had something more to tell you, Clay. But it was nothing more than that we'd grown apart."

"You didn't cheat on her with a younger woman?"

"You're asking if I started sleeping with Phoenix before your mother died?"

"It seems like a valid question."

"No. Until last Christmas, Phoenix was just a friend of Van's."

Anger surged again. "And since when were *any* of Van's friends acceptable choices for your bedmates?"

Robin leaned forward in his chair, and Clay realized

he had done the same. They were nose to nose on the deck, glaring at each other. Clay had no doubt that his face was just as flushed and sweaty as Robin's.

"I have never once looked at any of Van's friends inappropriately." Clay could hear the wrath, the venom in Robin's voice.

"Until Phoenix."

Robin's eyes turned steely. His jaw clenched and Clay could almost hear the wood under Robin's palms groaning as he squeezed the arms of his deck chair. "Phoenix is different."

"I'll bet," Clay said.

Robin gave a cruel, humorless chuckle and leaned back in his chair. "You don't know anything about it."

"Then enlighten me."

Robin laughed again. "For a man who's trying his best to crawl into my daughter's bed, you have a lot of nerve."

Robin had never spoken to Clay like this before. Like a stranger. Like a threat. Like an arrogant ass. The Robin that Clay had always known had been a compassionate, understanding man. He'd known Robin could be ruthless, but he'd always just assumed Robin left that person behind when he left the courtroom. Clay never expected to feel his bite. The shock had him pushing to his feet.

"I'm not just after a quick lay, Robin. You know me better than that."

Robin cocked his head to the side. His voice was cold when he said it. "Do I?"

"Dammit. I'd marry her if she'd let me."

Clay hadn't realized they'd been yelling until his voice cut off, and the silence was long and deep as Robin studied him. Clay couldn't read his expression. He was caught between trying to figure out what Robin was thinking and berating himself for voicing that deep, dark desire aloud. It was something he'd never even allowed himself to think before. He just sat there, his eyes on Clay's for a full two minutes until he said, "I guess you won't know until you ask her."

"Wait. What?"

Clay hadn't realized he'd spoken the words out loud until Robin said, "If that's what you want, you'll have to ask her and see what she says."

Clay plopped back in his chair, wishing like hell it was later in the day so he wouldn't feel guilty about knocking back another beer. And maybe another after that. Instead he asked Robin, "You'd be okay with that?"

Robin lifted one shoulder and let it drop. Something Van did often too. "It's not up to me. And you know Van wouldn't listen to my opinion either way."

"But you'd be okay with it. If I married Van, you wouldn't disown us or anything?"

"Why would I do that?" He sounded legitimately confused. Just as Clay was about to bring up how he and Van had legally been siblings at one point, Robin waved him off. "You mean because I was married to your mother? I think we're all old enough to see past that. It might have been different when you were teenagers, but now, what does it matter?"

"I imagine all the gossip shows would have a field day with it—probably are already. I've been afraid to look."

"Phoenix won't let it get too out of hand," Robin said, then looked down into his empty beer bottle, like he might find Phoenix at the bottom of it. Poor Robin, he had awful luck with women.

At least Phoenix was still alive.

Clay shook his head. He was getting ahead of himself. He shouldn't be talking about marrying Van when she didn't even know how he felt about her. He wasn't entirely sure how she felt about him. Sure, she'd publicly acknowledged kissing him, but for all Clay knew, they were both just living out old teenage fantasies and that's as far as it would go.

Instead of continuing down that road, Clay asked Robin if he'd heard anything about what to expect with Bishop. He should have paid more attention, but Robin only repeated what Clay already knew, that they were countersuing on grounds that he incited the incident at The Fox.

All of the animosity of the previous few minutes was forgotten as they spoke. Though Clay was left thinking about his mother and if she hadn't been as happy as he'd believed her to be. And what did it say about him that he hadn't noticed she'd grown unhappy? Then every few minutes, worry and fear spiked as he thought about what Van must be going through right now.

Clay pulled his phone out of his pocket and shot Van a quick text, the first they'd exchanged since she left. Clay wasn't sure she wanted to hear from him, but *he* needed to check in with her.

CLAY: *How you holding up?*

He watched the three dots pulse, then fade. Clay imagined her checking her phone, seeing it was him and then discarding her phone in favor of whoever was more interesting, more glamorous, in L.A..

He'd put his attention back on what Robin was saying about how, with Clay's and Bryant's history in the military, it was likely that they would be able to build sympathy with the right judge. When Clay's phone vibrated in his hand, it startled him.

VAN: *Well, the dude bros have nothing but compliments about how I look naked, so there's that.*

A smile cracked over his lips. That typical wry optimism from Van settled the ball of anxiety that had been living in Clay's chest.

CLAY: *You know what I mean.*
    VAN: *How would you feel knowing half the world had seen your lady bits?*

Rage. That's the only word for the fire that ripped through Clay, surging up from his toes and turning his face red.

CLAY: *If I think about that part too much, I might kill somebody.*
    VAN: *That's a level of possessive I don't think I can tolerate in a partner, but I appreciate the sentiment.*

. . .

Partner. The word doused Clay's rage like he was participating in that ice bucket challenge. He might have actually shivered. It was only then he noticed Robin had stopped talking legal-ese and was tapping out something on his own phone.

Good. He wouldn't notice how Clay's heartbeat had just ratcheted up to unhealthy levels of hopeful and anxious.

CLAY: *Partner?*

Van didn't reply right away, and Clay tried not to stare at how the dots started, stopped, faded, and did it all again.

In the end, her message left him just as anxious as he had been before, but for an entirely different reason.

VAN: *I'm home Thursday. We'll talk then. But whatever this thing is between us, it's so much more than just sex, don't you think?*

CLAY: *It is definitely more than sex, especially since there hasn't been any sex yet.*

VAN: *Thursday. I promise.*

Now Clay just had to make it through the next four days without losing his shit on someone.

Error: Video No Longer Available

We have been informed that the video we posted earlier today was filmed without the consent of one of the participating parties. Therefore, we have taken it down. We apologize for any part we had in its distribution and apologize to our favorite starlet, Ms. Van Birch, in particular.

2 2

*P*hoenix plopped down next to Van on the
sofa on her patio. It was one of those long,
low things that was uncomfortable as hell, like someone
had tried to upholster a pew, but it looked gorgeous
next to the split-leaf philodendron and the haint-blue
walls.

Phoenix was nothing if not superstitious.

Phoenix dropped a water bottle into Van's lap and
dipped hers back, chugging down half of it like a frat boy
at a keg party. They'd just come back from a session with
Stark. He'd pushed Van extra hard, since she was going
soft and eating junk food in "Hicksville." But only Van for
some reason. Phoenix had gotten off light. She'd walked a
leisurely pace on the treadmill the entire time Stark had
been kicking Van's ass, and Van might have been just the
tiniest bit resentful.

Her muscles barely allowed her to twist the cap off the
bottle. Actually raising the thing to her lips might be
beyond her capabilities. She was going to just sit on

Phoenix's overpriced patio pew and sweat out the rest of her water supply. It would be fine. Nobody panic.

Honestly, Van was glad for the physical exhaustion. It was a relief after the nervous anxiety of the past few days. Her phone hadn't stopped blowing up since the interview had gone live, and then the tape came out, as predicted, and the hounds of media hell had broken loose.

Phoenix had released one short, terse statement shaming Bishop and making it clear the video had been filmed without Van's consent and condemning it as another violation. Van's lawyers had filed suit; the video had been taken down, and now they were lying low, waiting to see which way the social media winds blew.

Tomorrow Van would spend some time in the studio. The record company wanted to hear what she'd been working on so far. She didn't have much to show them, only two songs, but one was catchy enough that they might be able to use it as a teaser until the new album was ready.

Then they had a few meetings that they'd been supposed to skype in to from Wellville rescheduled as in-person meetings since they were now in town. One of those meetings was with the production company, and Van knew they'd want to know if the show with Clay was a go-ahead. Her schedule was so full, Van was looking forward to heading back to Kansas and pretending her only responsibilities were writing songs and filming her reality show.

And she missed Clay. The little text conversation had left her in mind of what it had been like to have his body hovering over her and how much she wanted to press her chest against his and grind her hips over the bulge in his jeans. Van's skin flushed as she remembered the hardness of him teasing her. At least she could blame that on the workout.

Phoenix hadn't noticed. Her eyes, like always, were on whatever screen was in front of her face. In this case, her phone. She'd been frowning at it all weekend. What was unusual was that Phoenix had just been staring at the screen. Normally Phoenix was all flying thumbs and soft *tsk*s when she worked. Now she was just staring.

Van nudged Phoenix's knee with her toe, the only part of her body Van could currently move. "What's up with you?"

Phoenix dropped her phone in her lap and finished her bottle of water, crumpling it with the force of the Hulk on a bad day. "I don't know what you mean," she said as she tossed the bottle over her shoulder and into the flowerbed.

Van's heart might have stopped. Phoenix didn't waste anything. She didn't buy single-use plastic, even. Stark had forced the water bottles on them before they'd left. That was the only reason Phoenix had it in the first place. She'd had solar panels installed on her roof and invested in wind farms. She did not toss plastic into her rosebush for anything. "You just littered, Fe. Something's wrong."

Phoenix sagged back against the arm of the sofa, if you could call the fabric-covered brick an arm, and sighed. "The only communication I've had with your dad since we got here has been through the lawyers."

Van almost laughed out loud, but she knew better than to cross Phoenix when she was mad. Phoenix's hippy parents probably knew somebody who raised pigs. If Van kicked Phoenix when she was down, they'd never find Van's body.

Instead, she asked, "What's wrong with that?"

Phoenix met Van's eyes with a hard, annoyed glare that said, *Don't patronize me.*

Van shrugged. "I thought I wasn't supposed to know."

"That was Robin's idea. I've been dying to tell you for months."

Van sat up so fast, she felt like she'd left her skeleton behind like in an old cartoon, but then it slammed back into her, and all she felt was the pain from our two-hour long torture session with Stark. "Months?"

Van wasn't stupid. She'd been living in a house with the two of them sneaking into each other's beds for a weeks now, but she hadn't realized it had been going on any longer than that.

"Exactly how long have you been boning my dad?"

Phoenix's nose rose into the air as she said, "It started at Christmas."

Van's mouth gaped like a fish out of water. "I— But, what, how do you mean 'it started at Christmas?' We were only there for two nights."

"Exactly that," Phoenix said. "Remember when we all waited up for Clay on Christmas Eve because he was supposed to be back at nine?"

Cold sick trickled over Van's tired-ass bones. Yes, she remembered that night. That was the night he'd chosen ditzy Daisy over his family. No—that name wasn't fair to Daisy. Or was it Darla? Van was sure she was a plenty nice lady, but she had been Clay's girlfriend at the time, and he'd chosen to spend the night with her instead of coming to family Christmas, so she had been the focus of Van's wrath that night. Sure, Van would have been nice to her if Clay had brought her along like he should have done. Instead he'd hidden her away at his house where it is only natural that they participated in all of the most humanly pleasurable activities that Van hadn't been able to stop picturing in her head, over and over and over again. That was the night she'd started calling Clay "Man-whore" in her head. Which wasn't fair either.

It wasn't his fault Van remembered the name of almost every single girlfriend he'd had over the last four years, even though she hadn't met most of them. Or any of them really. Clay never brought girls around.

She did remember how her Dad had insisted they wait for Clay before doing gifts and going to bed. She remembered she'd given up around ten-thirty. It had been fun, drinking eggnog and spiced wine and eating cheese and crackers with Fe and Dad and Bryant and his mom. Bishop had been there too and followed Van up to her room, but Van was choosing not to remember that part of the evening.

"How long did you 'stay up and wait for Clay?'" Van asked, putting finger quotes around the end, making a euphemism out "wait for Clay." Which was cruel considering Van was counting down the days until she got back to Kansas so she could maul him.

Van had to suppress a shiver as she remembered how close they'd come to consummating whatever was going on between them a few days ago. The promise of that impressive hardness he'd been pressing against her, the kissing on his front stoop had all been so exquisite. Van's achy muscles nearly liquefied right there on Phoenix's uncomfortable patio furniture.

Phoenix wouldn't meet Van's eye. "We gave up waiting at midnight."

"And you two drank all of the wine so there wasn't any Christmas morning." Van remembered now how they'd had to make do with whiskey-spiked cider on Christmas afternoon after they'd spent the morning playing Santa Claus at the Children's Hospital two hours away. Phoenix had been nursing an awful hangover, and Robin had been a little green around the gills as well—and he never, *never* drank to excess.

"Okay, so I get the first time, that was because you had too much wine. Explain to me how it kept going?"

Phoenix raised one shoulder and let it fall, still not meeting Van's eye as she said, "Neither of us wanted it to be a one-night thing from the beginning."

Woah.

Woah.

"Oh God. Have you always had the hots for my dad? Has our entire friendship been a lie? Have you been working your ass off for me for five years only for the chance to hop into bed with a middle-aged lawyer from Kansas?"

Phoenix glared at Van. Good. That was better than being all weird and looking anywhere *but* at her. "I don't go after married guys. You know that."

She was right. Van did know that.

Van patted her shoulder. "It was a joke, Fe."

"Yeah, well. It's not funny. I never thought of Robin like that until I did, and after, it was impossible to go back."

Van nodded; maybe it was a little exaggerated. She was having a little trouble understanding how anyone saw her dad as anything other than a reasonable middle-aged guy with a graying beard, but she supposed he wasn't in bad shape? She didn't know. Her mind couldn't go there. "So you two have been sneaking back and forth from L.A. to Wellville for the last eight months?"

"More him than me, but yes."

"My dad has been in L.A., and he didn't even call me?" Van was not gonna lie; that hurt a little bit.

Phoenix could see the look of betrayal on Van's face. "It wasn't just sex—or at least I didn't ever think it was. Then everything happened. He said some hurtful things."

Van raised her eyebrows, nonverbally asking what kind of hateful things.

Phoenix pursed her lips, "He defended Clay in front of me . . ."

Van didn't want to make this conversation about her, and despite Phoenix's hang-ups with Clay, Van was able to see the excuse for what it was. There was something else going on between Phoenix and Robin that Phoenix wasn't ready to talk about. That was fine. Van would be there when Phoenix was ready. For now, she only said, "Clay's not that bad, you know."

Phoenix snorted. "It's not even about that. He knows. He knows what happened to me, and he said the exact same words my mom used to say about Kyle, after he said some other really shitty things. And he's acting like I'm the one who screwed up."

Van hugged her then. This wasn't about Van and Clay, but they were going to have to talk about that soon. "Does he know that?"

Phoenix shrugged. "He knows the basics."

"You should tell him why what he said bothered you," Van said.

"Maybe." Phoenix pulled out of Van's arms. "I don't know. I feel pretty stupid right now. I mean, how much of a future can I really have with a guy who's twenty-five years older than me? I shouldn't even be upset about it."

Van refrained from saying, "Exactly!" She could see the pain her friend was in, and while Van couldn't pretend to understand how Phoenix felt, Van did know her dad. He wasn't a cruel man. Whatever he'd said to hurt Phoenix's feelings, it had probably been practical, because he *was* old enough to be Phoenix's father. He definitely hadn't purposefully said what he had about Clay to hurt Phoenix's feelings.

"Give him a break. He's not your mom or your stepdad, and Clay really isn't Kyle, so while I totally respect your Mama Bear tendencies, I feel like you're over-reacting."

Phoenix's eyes flared in anger, and Van knew she definitely didn't have the whole story.

But Phoenix mastered whatever it was and said, "You'll understand if I respectfully disagree about Clay. With his track record with women—"

"I'm no better with men," Van cut her off. "And he and I talked about everything that's happened, Fe, and he is so good. You've got to trust me on this."

Phoenix inhaled heavily through her nose, and Van knew she was annoyed and reluctant, but she didn't argue any further. "After Bishop, I don't think I'm going to trust any man ever again."

"I know the feeling," Van said, laying a hand on

Phoenix's knee, "But I do trust Clay. And I really, really need you to trust me right now."

Another sigh and a tentative nod. "Your dad is an ass, but I always trust you," Phoenix said, then socked Van playfully on the arm. "Can we eat now? I'm fucking starving."

And just like, all the tension between them was gone. Phoenix was still upset with Van's dad for whatever reason, but Van knew they were going to be just fine.

Buckle Up Ladies, Bryant Wilder is On The Market

Everyone's favorite Hollywood boyfriend is a boyfriend no longer. Van Birch spilled the beans in an interview today that she and Wilder passed through Splitsville months ago but remain good friends. While Van seems to have moved on to the next hunky contractor in line (Does she have a type, perhaps? Check out the steamy photos below), this means Bryant Wilder is currently single and available. Who's up for a trip to Wellville? We bet we could fog up those glasses.

*V*an's phone had not stopped exploding for five days. It was a relief to turn it off on the plane ride home. She couldn't handle the slut-shaming any more. The men who had called her a whore before had only become more vocal, as if the physical evidence that she'd had sex before was not only proof that she was the worst kind of slut but proof that she deserved punishment.

It didn't help that Bishop had playfully swatted her ass at some point during the video and now they all thought she *liked* to be beaten like she was some kind of masochist. The threats she'd received had only ratcheted up in the last few days. Several more death threats had been passed along to the police via Phoenix and the lawyers, but Van didn't expect to see anything come of it. It was becoming a full-time job just getting her dad's address taken down from random websites.

They'd hired more security for the house in Kansas. Van was more worried for her dad and the others than she was for herself. What if somebody did something stupid to the house? But with persistent threats of harm to her person, Van had stopped arguing with Butch about being escorted everywhere she went with a bigger entourage than the President.

Truth to tell, Van was almost glad for the protection. She'd thought having that video of herself out there would be inconvenient and embarrassing, but she didn't anticipate how raw and exposed she would feel. It was a different kind of vulnerability than before. Ever since she'd watched edited footage of herself in Bishop's bed, she'd felt like someone had run over her in a gravel lot— repeatedly. Then she and Phoenix had watched the entire video with her lawyers present. If that wasn't one of the most uncomfortable scenarios in her entire life, she didn't know what was. The only thing that could have actually made it worse was if her dad had been in the room with them.

The lawyers didn't have any trouble remaining detached and professional throughout the whole thing, but Van was about to sever Phoenix's fingers, she was squeezing her hand so hard. Van remembered the interlude. She *had* recalled it fondly—or as fondly as she could after the stupid asshole broke everything good that had ever happened between them. Knowing now that all the time he'd taken to pleasure her that night, that the worship she'd felt from him, had all been a cover so he could film her without her knowledge turned Van's stomach in a way she hadn't thought was still possible.

Even after The Incident.

That could always be blamed on a moment of passion. Even in her head, Van still sometimes entertained the

possibility that things had gotten out of hand that night—
that he really hadn't meant to hurt her. He hadn't meant
to scare the shit out of her. Maybe they just hadn't been
communicating well. Perhaps there was something *she*
could have said or done that would have changed things.
Maybe *she* could have done something where *she* would
have had more control of the situation, more control of
him. Van had known he'd been drunk. And she knew he
was stubborn, even belligerent, when he didn't get his
way.

But no.

Because all of that put the blame back on Van
somehow, and she was sick with herself for even thinking
it.

There was not a damn thing she could have done to
change the situation. She had fallen in love with a man
who absolutely did not give one goddamn about her—
only how he could use her. The relationship she'd thought
they'd been building had been nothing but a charade. He
would have boxed Van in, chipped away at her confidence,
and made her rely on him and only him until she was
nothing but his puppet.

Watching him hover over her on that video and tease
the ticklish spot at the base of her neck with his tongue so
that she giggled and writhed against him made her
stomach sour. Van had been ready to give her whole self
to this man, and the making of this video had been
premeditated. It had been a card he'd kept in his back
pocket in case Van misbehaved and he needed a way to
rein her back in.

Joke's on you, buddy. Van Birch was a woman who had

made a career out of behaving badly, and she wasn't about to stop now.

By the time Van and Phoenix had boarded the plane back to Kansas, the video had been taken down from all major websites, and all the television networks that had aired clips of it had issued apologies. Van's team had threatened legal action against every single one of them for airing a video that had been filmed without Van's consent and that could be used as evidence in an ongoing legal battle. The news networks couldn't take the footage down fast enough, but once a video was out there these days, there was no real way to make it disappear for good. Copies had been made, and though Van's team had people seeking out as many as they could on file-sharing websites, Van knew that video would probably crop up at unwanted times for the rest of her life.

She'd known all of this going in, but it didn't make it any easier when it actually happened.

Van hadn't had a panic attack since that night in the hallway with Clay. She hadn't always been doing well with her anxiety but keeping up with Stark's intense workout schedule and practicing meditation with Maggie on the daily had helped keep her sane. Still, Van's soul felt like it wanted to vibrate out of her skin the whole flight back to Kansas. She'd brought her guitar on the plane under the pretense of writing songs in flight, but all she was capable of doing was plucking listlessly at the strings as she watched the clouds slide beneath the wing of the plane.

The gentle *tap tap* of Phoenix's fingers over the keyboard felt more like the harsh gong of her heartbeat in her ear, until she set her guitar aside and broke out the anxiety app Maggie had prescribed and did a few breathing exercises. Van was so proud of the work she'd done over the last few days, but somehow she was still about to have a panic attack on the plane.

Would she ever outlive this?

Would there ever be a time in her life, in her career, that she wasn't the woman who accused Henry Bishop of rape? Would she ever not be just another starlet with a sex tape?

Suddenly, the pressure to create an outstanding album that outshone all of this was too much for Van to handle. It felt like an Acme anvil weighted down on her chest, and she spent the whole second half of the flight counting one on the inhale and two on the exhale and tried to think of Clay.

He'd never called her, and she'd never called him. They hadn't video chatted. Just texted. To Van's great pleasure, most of Clay's texts had been dirty.

He'd described in detail what he wanted to do to her. Everything from licking her in intimate places to teasing her nipples to pulling her hair to coming inside her as she scratched the hell out of his back. And God help her, but Van wanted it all. She wanted his hands running over her knees and up her thighs, then between them. She wanted him on top of her, behind her, under her. She wanted his fingers tweaking her nipples as she rode him—and she wanted to feel the hot pulse of him when she finally drove him over the edge.

Both of their phones probably needed a good wipe down, because Van gave back as good as she got. She hadn't quit texting him each day until he'd texted her some variation of *Fuck, Van. You're gonna kill me.*

Even though the dirty texts were fantastic, the ones that made it worth all the other shit that was bombarding her phone were the ones where he just checked in. He asked if she'd been talking to Maggie. He sent photos of Pebbles with captions claiming the dog had missed her. With a little goading, he'd even sent her a couple selfies. One was of him shirtless in bed on Wednesday morning, because Van could be persuasive as hell. She was never getting rid of that picture, which put his defined pecs and arms on full display. His chin was tipped up and there was fine dusting of stubble over his jaw.

The other selfie was just of Clay, sitting on his bed, with his guitar in his lap, looking a little sheepish, like taking the photo embarrassed him.

They'd been working on the song, texting little low-quality audio files back and forth. Van hadn't written any lyrics yet, but the music was coming together with two distinct guitar parts, and Van wanted the song to have two singing parts as well, but she was waiting to spring that idea on Clay in person where she could be a lot more convincing about making him say yes.

Convincing him to do a reality TV show with her was one thing. At least he got a house out of that. Convincing him to sing on her album was something else entirely. He wasn't stupid. He would know exactly what that meant, how much a person of interest he would become. That he might have to tour with her. Be interviewed. Surely, he knew that being in a relationship with Van came with all that anyway? Didn't he?

Writing with Clay felt natural in a way that Van had never expected. After years of distance and reluctant acknowledgements, the gulf between them had closed as if it had never been there. Van wasn't sure what to do with the way giving space to the part of herself that had always loved him made her feel. Grounded. Calm. These were never words she'd used to describe herself. She'd been an anxious mess most of her life. Van had never been able to sit still. There had always been more to achieve, a goal to chase after, something she hadn't attained yet. But sitting in quiet with the knowledge that her feelings for Clay were legitimate and right gave Van room to stop running from everything else.

She remembered that there were good things in the world. Not just death threats and people on Twitter trying to convince other douche bags to mobilize against her. There was sweet guitar music and a grown man blushing at her texts and room for love to grow.

On one level their relationship felt inevitable and long overdue. On another, there was always the fear that maybe it wasn't the same for him as it was for her. Maybe for Clay, instead of giving in to long-held feelings, maybe it was the fulfillment of some fantasy, and once they finally got down and dirty, that would be the end of it.

Clay must have been thinking the same thing, because the night before, a night when Van knew he had plans to hang out at The Fox with Bryant, he texted her again.

Clay: *What are we doing here, Van?*

Van: *Mastering the art of sexting? You get an A+.*

Clay: *Is that all?*

Van: *I hope not. I'd be a little disappointed if I didn't get a practical demonstration.*

. . .

Okay, so Van was being a little bit of a shit, because his questions were making her nervous, and she was avoiding having him tell her that once they finished the song, once they gave each other a few fantastic orgasms, that they'd go back to being awkward sort-of family that never talked.

Clay: *I want more than sex from you.*

    Van: *I want more too.*

    Clay: *How much more?*

    Van: *You wanna be my date to the Grammys?*

    Clay: *Aren't those in January?*

    Van: *Kind of part of the point, babe.*

    Clay: *Glad we're on the same page.*

    Van: *But we're still on for that practical demonstration, right?*

    Clay: *Maybe. I'll see you tomorrow.*

Between thoughts of Clay and the breathing app, Van was measurably calmer by the time they landed, but she wasn't sure she was ever going to be whole again. Butch escorted them off the plane. Bryant plus two other giant dudes were waiting for them, and instead of annoyance, Van felt comfort in their presence.

Van ran for Bryant. He scooped her up and swung her in a circle, before placing a kiss on the top of her head and setting her feet back on the floor. Cameras flashed in her peripheral vision, and Van laughed up at his gigantic smile.

This greeting was going to confuse the hell out of

everyone. It had taken a few days, but Van's public breakup with Bryant had finally caught up with the sex tape news. There had been a surge of bloggers claiming they'd never been duped and had known all along that Van and Bryant hadn't been in a relationship for at least a year. Van only laughed at them. It didn't matter what they thought. It never had. Bryant was her best friend, and Van would love him until the end of time. And she wasn't going to hide how excited she was to see him after a week away just because it might keep fueling the VanBryant ship.

Ending the fake relationship had been the right thing to do. Smiling up at Bryant, Van felt the last vestiges of her panic recede. This, allowing the two of them to just be who they were together. Good friends.

"Glad you're back," Bryant said as he stepped back.

"Me too. How have the cameras been?"

"My house is swarmed. Your house is swarmed. Clay's lot is swarmed."

"Clay's lot?"

"Anywhere that's got a tie to you, there are cameras."

"Damn it." She'd known those pictures of her and Clay were going to cause trouble.

"Where's Dad?" she asked.

"At the office. That trial is taking over his life."

Van nodded. There had been very few times in Van's life when a trial hadn't been taking over her dad's life. He'd always been attentive and supportive, but he was just as much of a workaholic as Van was. This particular trial, about water or drainage rights or something to do with agriculture, could be huge for him.

Van searched Phoenix out; she was chatting with

Butch. She almost even had a smile on her face. They hadn't talked any more about Phoenix's relationship with Robin, but Van understood why she was upset with him—even if Van thought Phoenix was being a little irrational about it.

Van couldn't wait to see her dad. After all the shit they'd endured over the last week, she needed some quality piano time. Maybe some daddy-daughter breakdown time.

That sounded just about right.

Doxed!

We've all known it wouldn't be difficult to find Van Birch's family home in Wellville, Kansas. The big, white Victorian home has become an icon of idyllic midwestern living, but Van Birch's security team has been working around the clock to keep her address from going public. Birch's camp released a public plea this afternoon to media and fans alike to please not share the location of the family home as the starlet continues to receive multiple threats against her safety on a daily basis.

Birch, who normally travels with minimal security, was photographed in L.A. last week with three personal bodyguards, and the most recent photos of the family home in Wellville look like it's more heavily guarded than Area 51. We hear the razor wire is arriving next week.

*V*an was trying to kill him.

That morning, before she'd gotten on the plane to come back home, she'd sent him a selfie of herself as she'd gotten out of the shower. Her hair was down, and mostly dry, but her skin glistened with water and her towel was slipping down over her left breast. If the camera had taken a second longer to take the picture, it might have been an actual boob shot.

That probably would have killed him. Clay couldn't get the image of her in only a towel out of his mind as it was, and he had to work all day trying not to think about what her skin would feel like, wet and warm, pressed against his chest.

It was a miracle he hadn't cut a finger off or nailed his hand to a two-by-four.

Van texted him that she was home while he still had about four hours of work to do.

But those were the words she used.

Home.

She was home.

Clay tried not to read into that word. That Van was thinking of Wellville as home again. She'd been here for almost two months after living here most of her life. It was easy to slip back into those words, that Kansas was home, after living in California for so long. But the words warmed a place in Clay's chest he hadn't quite let her touch yet.

Clay texted her back that he was working late, but that he'd see her tonight and to keep working on the song. Clay wanted to goad her about her use of the word "home." He wanted to nudge her to specify whether she meant Wellville or Robin's house or . . . he couldn't even think it—not yet.

Clay knew that the past week without Van around had been slower, quieter, emptier, than the couple weeks before had been, even though not all that much had changed. Work was the same. Busier even. Clay was managing more guys, struggling to meet tighter deadlines. But it was still satisfying work. He had Bryant and Robin and Pebbles for company, even though the other two had been moody as hell. Robin, Clay understood, between his big case and Phoenix blowing him off; it made sense. Bryant, Clay still couldn't figure out, though he insisted it wasn't because Van had broken up with him on television without telling him first.

They'd had a long conversation about it at The Fox. Clay had admitted to his feelings for Van, that he planned to see if she would have him. Forever.

Bryant gave Clay the most sincere smile he'd been able to manage in the last few days and clapped Clay on the shoulder. "I'm happy for you two. Really. If you'd only figured this out when you were nineteen, you would have saved us all a helluva lot of trouble."

Clay wasn't exactly sure what he'd meant by that, but he took the endorsement and ran with it and tried not to let himself be driven to distraction by the texts Van was sending him in the meantime.

Goddamn, her texts.

They were going to be the death of him.

Anticipation built as he finished up his last project for the day and packed up the tools. The paparazzi had increased at the end of the drive at the construction site, and they were even worse at Robin's house. Though Clay was pleased to see Butch and a couple of additional security guys patrolling the garden.

Clay and the guard at the back door exchanged nods as Clay all but ran inside. The sound of the piano greeted his ears, then Van's voice; then shortly thereafter Robin's voice joined hers. It was a song they'd sung together a million times. One Clay purposefully had never learned the name of because, though it was a beautiful duet, it was a song that Van's mother had loved. And though Clay's mom had never had a problem with it; it had always made Clay a little uncomfortable. He didn't want his mom to feel like she didn't belong.

And if his mom hadn't belonged here, Clay had always been afraid there wasn't a place for him in this house either.

That wasn't the case anymore though.

The truth was, Clay didn't want to move out on his own. He liked having breakfast with Robin and driving to the job site with Van. He didn't even mind the stupid cameras that much anymore. He liked hearing Van's music all throughout the house during the day and watching her play with Pebbles at night.

Clay had never given much thought to what the life of a family man looked like—outside the fact that he knew it would be his eventual future. But now that he had Van— or at least now that he was close to convincing Van to giving him a shot—everything else was falling into place.

Clay didn't want to build the same two-bedroom house he'd had before. He didn't want the same half-acre plot he'd had before either.

He wanted a big house, on a big tract of land. He wanted room for a carpentry shop and a house full of people. He wanted noise and music and kids to run around with the dogs and to teach them how to grow vegetables the way his mother had taught him.

As Clay swiped a couple of cold slices of pizza from the fridge and washed them down with water from the tap, a seed of an idea germinated inside his mind. He only hoped Van—and her production company—would go for it.

He sneaked up the back staircase so he didn't interrupt the father-daughter jam session and hopped into the shower. By the time he pulled on a clean t-shirt and a fresh pair of jeans, Clay had a plan of his own.

He grabbed a legal pad and a carpentry pencil from his room—it was the only kind of pencil he had. It wasn't as pretty as the leather journal Van kept to jot down lyrics in, but it would do.

He slung his guitar over his shoulder by its strap and hid himself away in Van's room for a redo of the night before she'd gone back to L.A.. Hopefully, tonight Clay wouldn't crap out and fall asleep at ten o'clock like he had last time. But since he hadn't spent last night pacing a jail cell, he liked his chances for tonight a lot better.

Bishop had been lying low since the sex tape had come out. He probably had such a heap of legal troubles dropped on his lap the second the video went live, he didn't have time to do anything but conference with his lawyers.

Clay hoped that motherfucker spent every cent he had on digging himself out of his own shit pile.

At least he hadn't come near Van.

Clay flexed his fists as he remembered what it had been like to bash the asshole's head into the wall. If he came near Van, Clay might very well actually kill him the way he'd wanted to at Christmas.

Yes, Christmas. Not when Van came home after the tornado. Clay had only wanted to kill him slower then.

At Christmas, Bishop couldn't keep his hands off Van, especially at Christmas dinner, when he both Bryant and Clay were there,like he was laying claim to her.

Watching them had made Clay sick. As if they all didn't already know Van and Bishop were fooling around. What Clay didn't appreciate was how Bishop aimed most of his lewd comments about Van—always outside of her hearing of course—not at Bryant, whom she was supposed to be in a relationship with, but at Clay. As if Bishop knew.

He had no clue about *how much* Clay didn't want to care about who Van was sleeping with. Clay was still sure that all Bishop had known was that Bishop had slept with Van and Clay hadn't and that maybe Clay would like to someday. Clay was fairly certain Bishop saw Clay as his main rival for Van's affection because Bishop saw a glimmer of himself in Clay. The ambition that had driven him into the Army, the need to start his own company when he got out.

You'd think it would be Bryant that Bishop taunted, but Bishop was such an idiot, he couldn't even see Bryant's quiet strength. Bryant was bigger than Clay—in height at least. They'd both kept up their workouts after they'd left the Army, but Bryant's glasses and the paperbacks he always kept in his back pocket had fooled Bishop somehow. Or maybe Bishop just thought that Van walked all over Bryant enough for the both of them.

Clay had wondered why Bryant was putting up with the affair but assumed it had been because Bryant had his fair share of indiscretions over the years.

Clay didn't view that as a weakness on Bryant's part like Bishop did. Clay didn't discount Bryant because he would do anything for the people he loved. His willingness to self-sacrifice, even if it was to his own detriment, was a one of his friend's biggest strengths. It was Bishop's own fault that he mistook he and Clay for being alike.

Nobody was going to get Bishop and Clay confused anytime soon. They were about the same size; Bishop might have had an inch or two on him, but that was it. They were both strong, muscular. But Bishop had long auburn hair where Clay's once red hair had faded to almost blonde over the last ten years. Bishop wore an over-groomed beard while Clay usually kept himself clean cut. And of course, Clay wasn't an abusive asshole.

Clay ran a hand over his jaw, feeling a day's worth of stubble there. It was too hot in his line of work to wear a beard. Especially in the summer. There were some days in the winter where he'd considered it, but mostly he couldn't get past the fourth day of stubble. It would itch too much during the day, and he'd go home and shave.

Clay balanced his guitar on his knee and strummed, then winced at how out of tune the D string was. His mind strayed as he tuned. Clay knew what Bishop saw in him to rival. It was the same thing Phoenix feared in him. Clay was not a man easily deterred from what he wanted. Both Bishop and Phoenix had categorized him as a predator. But Clay wasn't like Bishop.

He knew what it was like to be vulnerable. He'd seen his mother struggle with what had been done to her, with what it meant to show love to a son she hadn't wanted and didn't ask for but had raised anyway. She'd been stretched so thin during his childhood. He remembered her putting herself through school. He still had pictures of her at her college graduation, when she'd finally earned her teaching degree. Clay had only been seven, but he'd shared her triumph. Clay had watched her blossom when she'd fallen in love with Robin.

Clay had been struggling with the idea that his mother had wanted to leave Robin. But maybe, when she'd asked Robin for the divorce, it had just been time for her to do something for herself for the first time in her life. Robin had seemed to think it was a simple matter, and Clay had watched Robin mourn her death. So maybe the why wasn't important. Maybe it was just enough that his mother had known what she wanted.

Clay was so sorry she hadn't had the chance to move forward.

That was the difference between Bishop and Clay. Clay might not be afraid to go after what he wanted, but if

Van told him no, he would let her go. No matter what. He'd spent half his life letting her go already. Clay had one last chance to make her an offer, and he was going to take it. In the end the choice was hers.

The doorknob turned, and Clay stopped strumming his guitar as Van stepped into the room.

@xXxChad4Lyfe: @VanBMusic bitch your bodyguards don't scare me. I know where you live and I'll cut your slut throat.

25

*V*an followed the sound of Clay's aimless strumming down the hall, past his room, and toward her own. Van tried and failed to suppress a smile as she pushed the door open—only for Clay to cease playing as she stepped inside.

"Don't stop," she said. Her voice was quieter than she'd expected but clear after singing with her dad for the last couple of hours.

Playing with her dad was like taking a spiritual bath. It had washed away all the stink and soil of the trip to L.A. and all the icky experiences that went with it. She was home with people who didn't see her as a money maker or as a famous singer or a TV star or as another attention-seeking whore with a sex tape. Her dad and Clay just saw her as Van. Itsy bitsy Vanessa Birch who never went anywhere without her guitar.

Clay's smile was worth the time away. It was broad and genuine, and it melted her heart down into her toes at the same time as driving her stomach up into her chest so that it was hard to breathe. That dimple on the right side of his cheek did her in every single time. Van wanted to lick it.

He strummed without breaking eye contact, then settled into their song. She watched his strong hands on his instrument for a minute before she picked up her guitar and joined him on the bed, picking out the melody she refused to write words to.

And then she was surprised when Clay sang.

His voice was clear and strong and deep, like he could front his own rock band—or maybe a country outfit since that's what he listened to. But Clay wasn't singing country right now.

He was singing for her.

Van wanted to stop and listen and watch him, but she forced herself to keep playing, picking out the tune while he played the rhythm part. She was helpless while he sang though, a complete puddle of want; she was so dazzled by his voice.

I dreamed of you in the desert
  Heard you from another shore
  I did what my head demanded
  Even though I wanted more

He was quite possibly the most beautiful man Van had ever seen—and not because he was in her bedroom playing her a song he'd written. Though that seriously upped the hotness factor. Van had never dated a fellow musician. The guys she'd met in L.A. who were in the music industry were

more about playing the game than the actual song writing—
or they were married, and as much as Van didn't apologize
for her sex life, married guys were strictly off limits, no
matter how much they offered to boost her career.

I saw you in the distance
   Though you shimmered out of reach
   I followed you to the oasis
   And laid myself down at your feet

Clay closed his eyes as they came to the part where the
chorus repeated, and Van felt his words down beneath her
bones, between her cells, as the song welled up from
within her. Van joined him, even though she didn't know
the words he was going to sing next, she knew the sounds
the melody called for and what the harmony part would
be, and Van sang it because it felt right.

He felt right.

This felt so right.

Clay's eyes met hers, and he tried and failed to
suppress a grin as he sang. Van met his smile with one of
her own, no doubt big and goofy, and went right back
into improvising the harmony, even as she felt his grin
and his lyrics heat her core. Van hadn't felt this settled or
this calm in years.

She didn't think any man had ever been more perfect.

I loved you in the moonlight

By day it wasn't right
To steal away your shine
But I could love you in the moonlight
And imagine you were mine

The last chords reverberated through the room as silence slowly descended on her bedroom. Van forced herself to wait for Clay to meet her eyes.

When he did, she said, "You wrote me a song."

His cheeks turned red, and the only thing sexier than a singing Clay was a bashful, self-conscious Clay. Van had definitely never seen this man look like that before. She was going to eat him alive like a praying mantis if she wasn't careful.

"I wrote you a song," he said, his cheeks flushing even deeper.

Van set her guitar on its stand, then took Clay's guitar and set it against the wall next to hers. He grabbed her hands as she approached him and interlaced his fingers with her, pulling her in between his legs.

"You're home," he said.

Van couldn't keep her smile growing. "Did you miss me?"

He nuzzled his nose into her t-shirt, his face conveniently right at chest level. "You and your wicked phone have been driving me crazy."

Van used their joined fingers to wrap his arms around her waist, then ran her fingers through his short blonde hair. The light from the lamp highlighted the strawberry strands still mixed in with the yellow. "What are you going to do about it?" she asked, scraping her nails over the base of his scalp and down his neck.

His fingers pulled the fabric of her t-shirt taut and his teeth closed over the tip of her left breast, sending a current of electricity through Van's entire body that practically melted her bones.

"That's it?" she teased.

Clay harrumphed even as his fingers slipped under her shirt and skimmed around her hips to her belly before pulling the shirt up and over her head. Van thought he'd go straight back to her breasts. She had worn her favorite black lacy bra for him. She didn't have a ton to work with in the boob department, but she knew how to rock some lingerie and what Van did have looked fucking fantastic.

And the poor bastard was completely missing it. He was so distracted by the bare skin at her stomach that he was completely missing out on the magnificence that was her artfully wrapped tits.

As his fingers roamed up and down her stomach, Van's offense at his attention grew less intense as desire bloomed from his steady stroking, building the fire inside her. His hands were the perfect texture. Callused and strong, just rough enough to cause friction, but not hard or bruising.

Clay's fingers dipped below her waistband, and her breath hitched. His dimple appeared along with a knowing smirk. "I have been dreaming about this," he whispered.

"Since you were in the desert, apparently," she said as his fingers traveled up her ribs.

He shushed her as he skimmed the band on her bra then traced back down to skim a little bit farther beneath her jeans this time. Van shivered under his touch. One hand still clutched his shoulders. The other dug into his hair, trying to find purchase in the short strands before he made her float away on a wave of her own desire.

Clay leaned forward and placed a soft, slow kiss right over her navel. Van's eyes drifted shut as the connection to him washed over her. What they were doing here wasn't a fling. It wasn't a lust-addled fuck against the wall. This, right now, was the start of something real. That kiss was a promise.

After one last pass of her fingernails through Clay's hair, Van sank to her knees in front of him, which put her face level with his crotch, but she was ignoring that for the moment. Clay's hands skimmed over her arms and up her neck so he cupped Van's jaw. His eyes met hers, and she knew he wanted to kiss her. Van wanted him to kiss her too, but she had something she needed to do first.

She gave him a gentle smile as her hands snaked under his shirt and tugged it up. He took her cue and pulled the gray t-shirt up and off. Van allowed her hands to roam down his shoulders and over his abs. She traced the fine, blonde hair down his stomach then leaned over on her toes and placed a soft kiss just above his belly button, just like he had done to her.

Clay's hand fisted in her hair and angled her head back as Van rocked back on her heels.

"Van."

His voice was barely there. A whisper of a whisper as one finger stroked over Van's cheek then around her lips. She swallowed at the unbridled emotion shining in his eyes. Yes, she'd been riling him up with dirty texts all week, but he wasn't playing around. Van recognized adoration in his eyes. Worship. Love.

Clay Noble loved her, and he was about to show her just how much.

Van rose onto her toes again pushed up into the circle of his arms so that her chest rubbed against his. When she was level with his face, Van brushed her lips over his, a quick mimic of the kiss she'd placed on his belly. "What is it, Clay?"

"You are so amazing," he said, the same reverence still hushing his voice to a whisper.

"I'm just me, Clay."

His hands ran down her back, tracing the outline of her spine until he reached her waist. He circled the dip with his fingers then grasped Van's hips and pulled her against him. "And you're perfect."

"I'm not," she said, even as she writhed against his chest, needing the feel of the friction of his skin against hers.

"To me, you are."

"Shh." She placed a finger over his lips. "Not yet."

It was one thing to feel the weight of his love, but Van wasn't ready to hear the words. She wasn't ready to say them back—or even think them. She knew there was no going back after this. Maggie and Van had talked about it all week—how the text messages were a way to avoid telling him how much she felt for him. To avoid having those kinds of forever conversations Van knew were in their future, because they were ones she wasn't ready to have yet.

Van wanted to be with Clay, yes. That wasn't going to change. But she wanted to have everything with him. Van wanted to remember their first kiss. (Boy howdy, would she ever.) She wanted to date him and to get to know each other sexually without all that expectation looming over them. She wanted to put her whole self into this act tonight—showing him in her own way that she loved him too.

Van removed her finger and lowered her lips to his. The switch flipped from sweet and reverent to desperate. Clay's hands tightened on her hips. Their tongues met for a quick clash before Van pushed him backwards onto the bed. She squirmed against him, loving the feel of his skin against hers, his callused hands on her back, and his hard stomach against her own.

His fingers unhooked her bra and Van slipped it down her arms and flung it off. They both moaned as she flattened her breasts against his at the same time she ground her mound into the bulge in his jeans. God, she needed him inside her now. She'd had a week of sexting foreplay and humping her bed while she thought about the way he'd felt between her legs when she'd straddled him on his front stoop. Van didn't need any more teasing. She was ready.

Apparently, Clay felt the same way, because he flipped her onto her back and repositioned them in the middle of her bed. He lowered himself on top of her for a rough battle of teeth and tongues, then with a nip to Van's bottom lip, he sat back on his heels and took in his fill of her bare torso.

A single finger traced the underside of one breast, then up and over the nipple, causing Van to suck in her breath before he skimmed over her breast bone and did the same to the other side.

"Clay," she begged as he rolled the nipple between his thumb and forefinger. "Please."

Heat pooled in her core, and the need couldn't be ignored. She was desperate to take him inside her. For his weight on top of her. She needed him now.

Clay let his finger wander over the bumps of her ribs and down the plane of her stomach to the waistband of her jeans. Van couldn't keep her hips from meeting his touch, and they rolled up all on their own when he dipped his fingers behind the material of not just jeans, but lacy black panties as well.

His dimple appeared then, pleased with her reaction.

"Please," Van said again.

Clay dipped his head down and kissed her, just above the belly button before flashing her a mischievous, confident grin and working the fly on her jeans.

A thrill of heat and a trail of sparks sped through Van's bloodstream. This. This was so different than any encounter she'd ever had.

Clay pulled her tight jeans down her legs, standing to pull the skinny leg over her heels and toss them across the room.

Van was so lost in watching the bunch and pull of his muscles as he moved, she didn't notice that he'd tossed a string of condoms onto the bed until he was reaching for one. Apparently all that delicious rippling of muscle had been him shedding his jeans and briefs.

Clay was naked in her bedroom. He was hard and erect, and Van wanted to lick every inch of him.

She plucked one of the foil packs out of the pile that must have been in his back pocket. "Someone's feeling confident."

Clay smirked as took the packet from her, then rolled the condom over his impressive erection. God, could the motion of his hand over his cock be any sexier?

"After the text messages you've been sending me all week, we're going to need them," he said as he settled his weight over her body. "Jesus, just the one of you in the towel is enough to keep me hard for a week." He ground his stiff length over her seam for emphasis and Van bucked against him.

He captured one of her nipples between his teeth. The pinch of pain followed by the velvet softness of his tongue had her panting and writhing against him.

"I seem to recall. That I wasn't. The only one sending dirty messages," Van said between pants.

Clay adjusted his hips and instead of grinding against her pelvis, the tip of his cock slipped along the slick folds of her pussy, teasing her entrance. Van's legs automatically closed around his hips, trying to guide him inside her, but he stilled.

"You're on board then?"

Van squeezed her thighs and dug her heels into his ass. "If you keep building things up like this, I'm going to expect at least three orgasms tonight before I let you finish."

"I was thinking four or five." He laid a kiss to her sternum between every word for emphasis.

Van dug her nails into his shoulders and bucked her hips, teasing his tip with her wet heat. "Jesus, Clay. Just fuck me already."

"Is this you talking dirty?" He angled his head up so his lips brushed hers as he spoke.

"If that's what it's going to take to get you to finally

make love to me," Van said, the frustration straining her voice in a way she knew her vocal coach would have a fit about.

Clay kissed her hard then, his lips and tongue confident and seeking all at the same time. Van opened her mouth to him at the same moment she allowed her legs to relax around Clay's middle and that was all he needed to slip inside. They groaned together when he sank all the way into her, breath and body pausing to get used to the feel of each other.

"I don't—" he said, but didn't finish the thought as he moved over her, easing out a fraction of an inch before sinking back in and grinding, as if he were trying to fit as much of his body inside of Van's as he could at once.

It was delicious.

Van met him at the top of each thrust with a swivel of her hips meant to drive him crazy, and his grunts of appreciation were worth it.

When his fingers found the small of her back and encouraged Van to arch up into him, it was a whole new experience as he somehow sank even deeper. They moved together, not just joined, but as one. The base of his cock rubbed against her clit, and with each undulating wave of their bodies, Van could feel herself start to clench around him. She rode the waves of descending pleasure that pulsed in time to the movement of their bodies. The friction and heat from Clay and the pleasure inside her coalesced into a shower of pure white light that burst from her core along with a string of curses from her mouth.

Clay covered her lips with his, swallowing her too loud cries as his thrusts became erratic, then slowed. His breaths came in pants in her ear. She found she needed to catch her breath too. She hadn't even realized she'd lost it. Breathing hadn't seemed necessary when he'd been inside her.

Van turned her head and kissed the spot where the dimple appeared on his cheek when he smiled.

"Why didn't we do this ten years ago?" Van asked.

His dimple showed up as he eased to the side and discreetly discarded the used condom. "Somehow, I don't think it would have been nearly as good then."

"Speak for yourself. I've always been fantastic at sex."

Clay pulled her into the crook of his shoulder. "I don't doubt it." He kissed her temple. "What did your dad tell you when Mom and I moved in?"

Van squinted at him, trying to remember. "We didn't really talk about it. He just told me he was getting married, but since I already knew you guys, it was just a given to whom. He asked me if there was any reason I would be uncomfortable with you living here, and I said no and that was the end of it."

"Hmm."

Clay was quiet for a moment.

He was quiet for a long time. "Why?" Van asked.

"My mom, Robin, and I had a very different conversation about what it meant to become someone's older brother—even if it was just a stepbrother."

"So they really emphasized the brother part."

"And the part where it was my job to look out for you. That some men saw pretty young women and liked to figure out how to take advantage of them, and that it was now part of my responsibility to keep you safe."

"Um. Wow." Van said. "Is that why you pulled those guys out of my room?"

He shrugged. "That and I was jealous as hell."

Van snuggled further into him and squeezed. "Funny. I was trying to make you jealous."

He flicked her nose, but settled back into a contemplative posture, his lips turning down into a slight frown.

"Do you think—" Van asked. Then stopped. "Do you think what happened to your mom—"

"Yes." He said but didn't let her finish. "I think she was afraid someone would hurt you, because you are so open and trusting-"

Van snorted. She didn't feel open and trusting, but "She was right."

Clay ignored her. "And I think she was always afraid I was going to turn into my father."

Van stroked a hand over his chest. "No she wasn't, Clay."

He shrugged.

"Mary Beth loved you."

"She watched me sometimes, like she was just waiting for him to jump out at her."

Van squeezed his shoulders. "Or she was marveling that you were such an amazing person that it was a miracle she had the privilege of being your mother."

A reluctant huff of a laugh wheezed from his throat. "She used to call me her miracle baby."

Van kissed his chin. "See."

Clay turned onto his side so that he faced her. He

propped his head on his elbow and tangled the fingers on the other hand in her hair. With sad, solemn eyes, he said, "I have that violence in me, though."

Van kissed his thumb as it traced over her lips. Her hand gripped his short hair so she could scrape her nails over his scalp. Clay's eyelids shuddered, and Van made a note of how much he like the nape of his neck scratched.

When his eyes met hers again, sleepy and sad and still dark with desire, Van placed a soft, chaste kiss to his lips with her eyes open.

"No you don't. Not even a little bit. You are the embodiment of your last name." She placed another quick kiss on his lips, but this time Clay held her close, not allowing any space between them. "You are Noble through and through."

He kissed her then. Hot and urgent as he rolled her on top of him. Good. It was Van's turn to blow his mind.

Wellville Police Department: Threats Against Van Birch are Serious, Priority

In a statement released this morning, the Wellville Police Department has stepped in to help investigate the numerous death threats against Van Birch as they fight to keep the starlet's address off the internet and guarantee her safety in the wake of her allegations against former manager, Henry Bishop.

While Bishop is currently in Wellville to win back his former lover's heart, the police do not consider him a person of interest. The police have set up a barricade around the house, moving the media line beyond the edge of the property. Only residents of the home and pre-approved visitors are allowed to pass.

We've compiled a few of the so-called threats that have been publically sent to Van Birch today via social media. You tell us if you think they're serious or just internet trolls blowing smoke.
WARNING: Not for the faint of heart.

26

"I haven't had Skittle's pizza since high school," Van said, then moaned as she took a gigantic bite of pie with cheese oozing off the side.

They'd used four of the six condoms Clay brought to her room. And though he was tired and maybe even a little sore, that moan stirred a longing inside him to hear her come again. Clay needed to pace himself. Van wasn't going anywhere—not yet anyway. And they both needed rest.

They'd fallen asleep after their third round, sometime after midnight. The nap hadn't lasted long. Clay wasn't sure who woke up first, but their bodies were aware of each other, even in their sleep. He was barely awake enough to remember the condom they came together so fast and so hard and lay together sweaty and panting when Van's stomach growled loud and long.

"When was the last time you ate?" he asked.

Her response was to shrug and say, "I had peanuts on the plane?" like it was a question.

Clay had dressed her in his t-shirt and pulled on his jeans and ordered a pizza from the one place in town that had 24-hour delivery. He'd been surprised when Race had delivered the pizza to the door. Apparently, he was the officer on duty that night. Clay had known the police had become involved in Van's security since the tape had come out, but he hadn't realized how much until Race had given him a grim smile and told him to enjoy his night. Clay had been expecting a lewd comment or two from his old friend. With Clay's lack of shirt and mussed hair, it was more than obvious what he'd been up to; that Race didn't say anything was sobering.

"That's because your trainer only lets you eat edamame and kale."

She cocked her head to the side. "How do you know what edamame is?"

Clay frowned and narrowed his eyes at her. "I might not be from L.A., but I'm not an idiot, Van."

She took another too big bite and said, "I didn't think steamed soybeans were a big part of your diet, that's all."

Clay grabbed his first slice only after Van had finished one over-sized piece from tip to crust. Skittle's pizzas were gigantic, with slices bigger than his face. The quality wasn't great, but at three in the morning after an eventful evening, it was pretty delicious.

"You haven't been eating enough lately," he said and washed down his bite with the fancy sparkling lemon water Van had pulled out of the fridge.

She shrugged. "I haven't had much of an appetite, what with everything that's been going on."

"And you work out too much."

"I'm just following Stark's schedule."

"Stark can go to hell."

Van scrunched her nose and watched Clay as she chewed. Maybe he was pushing her boundaries a little too hard a little too soon.

"I like working out," she said in a small voice. "It helps with the panic attacks."

Well, didn't that make him feel like an ass. "I just want you to take care of yourself. You'll be one of those celebrities in the hospital for exhaustion if you're not careful."

Van snorted a laugh around her mouthful of pizza. "You know no one ever actually really has exhaustion, right? That's code for rehab?"

Clay only gave her an annoyed look and refocused his attention on the pizza. Really though, he was glad she was feeling playful. And if the game tonight was "pick on Clay," he was down with that. He let them lapse into silence as they ate.

"Are you still having panic attacks?" he asked after a few minutes.

The person Van had been showing him since the night at Tessa's had been calm and confident. Troubled maybe, but even and maybe a little silly sometimes. The person she showed the press was nothing but calm and measured —a calculating vixen with a wild side.

Van's chewing slowed, and Clay could see she didn't want to answer. Tension tightened over his ribs, squeezing them so that it was hard to breathe. He didn't want Van to be reluctant to share with him, but the way her eyes grew wide and she sucked back a huge gulp of fizzy water, Clay could tell that she didn't want to talk about it.

"Not often anymore," she said.

"But you are still having them?"

She lifted one shoulder and let it fall, then dropped the second half of the slice of pizza she'd been eating back in the box.

"Some days it all just seems like too much."

"What seems like too much, exactly?"

Van chewed her lip as she held his gaze, as if she were debating how much she was going to tell him. Then she said, "Hold on just a sec" and disappeared up the stairs.

The stairs creaked under her weight, but her bare feet didn't make a sound. Clay realized how used he'd gotten to hearing Robin clomping around in the last week and had missed the quiet reminders that Van was in the house.

Her return wasn't so quiet. She rushed down the stairs, almost breathless by the time she pulled to a halt in front of him at the kitchen island and dropped her phone into his hand. The screen was already unlocked and clogged with notification banners.

"You have over five-thousand Twitter notifications." Clay tapped the banner, and the app loaded.

"And that's just since ten o'clock."

"Jesus." His curse was intended for the amount of social media interaction she had to put up with, but then he saw the actual tweets. "Fucking hell," Clay scrolled through some more of the messages. They were almost all the same. "They're tweeting this address."

"I know. Phoenix is already on getting it taken down —again."

Clay didn't doubt that Phoenix was. She was probably awake right now chewing someone's ass. But it was the other tweets that held Clay's attention and made his blood ignite in rage. "These are death threats."

"And rape threats and gang rape threats and murder fantasies." Van's voice sounded bored. Like she was used to this sort of shit.

"It's been going on for years," she said, reaching for her phone. "It's mostly talk."

"And that guy who broke into your condo last year was just talking, was he?"

"Hey, I called in Butch, didn't I?"

Clay ran a hand down her small, smooth arm and pulled her close. "I'm glad you did. I'm not ready to risk not taking those douchebags seriously."

Van nodded against his shoulder. "I haven't shown anyone these, though," she said, holding up her phone again.

Clay creased his brow but took the little device again and scanned the screen. He was looking at text messages, declarations of love and pleading of misunderstanding peppered in amongst veiled threats that Van was making things more difficult than they needed to be. Clay stepped away from Van as he realized that all of them were from Bishop. He scrolled up. They went back and back and back and back. Clay scrolled until they changed from pleading to lascivious teasing—to the time from before.

Bishop had texted Van almost every day since he'd raped her. He hadn't stopped telling her that she was overreacting, that she misunderstood, and that he loved her. Would never hurt her. He pleaded for her to drop the charges. Insinuated that he would have to retaliate to punish her. It was all sick and teasing, and just the glimpse of the previous texts—the one from when they'd been a couple—made Clay's stomach turn.

He'd had her trust. Hell, he'd had her love. The most precious thing in the entire world, and he'd abused it—abused her. And he hadn't stopped being an asshole since. Clay was damn sure he hadn't started being an asshole to her the night he decided to overpower her. He had to have been manipulating her in some other way for years. Hadn't he?

"You haven't told anyone about this?"

Van shuffled from one foot to the other. "I mentioned one or two to Phoenix, showed a few to my dad, but no. Not really."

Clay was going to kill him. He handed Van back her phone before he crushed it. The adrenaline pumping through his system would have given him more than enough strength.

"He wasn't supposed to contact you at all during the investigation."

"I know." Her voice was so weak. So helpless.

"He violated that. It could have an impact on how it moves forward."

"It doesn't matter anymore. They're never going to prosecute him."

"He's still a threat to you, Van."

"I know. Why do you think I'm still having panic attacks? It doesn't matter what crazies on the internet say; he's the one I'm in danger from."

Clay pulled her into his arms, as if that would protect her. He held her until he felt her tension start to relax. "You need a restraining order."

"What's the point?"

Clay pushed her to arm's length so that he could look into her eyes. She moved as easily as a rag doll, and he hated how vulnerable all of this had made her. She had been so confident on TV this past week, but really, she was still scared and hurting. "The point is making sure that you stay safe. That he doesn't have the power to hurt you again."

"Butch is here. The local police know what's up, but they refuse to do anything until he's an immediate threat. Dad's got a PI following him, so we at least know where he is."

"Wait. Robin knows where he is?"

"He's been at the Triggert Hotel this whole time."

The Triggert was the one fancy hotel they had in town. It was an historic affair downtown with spiral staircases and a cage elevator. It had mostly survived the tornado intact, though Clay took satisfaction in knowing the penthouse suite was under construction so Bishop would be forced into a less luxurious accommodation. It was also where most of the TV crew was staying.

"I would have assumed he would follow you back to L.A.."

She shook her head. "He's still pressing charges against you and Bryant."

Clay snorted.

He knew that. He just hadn't figured Bishop would stick around for the court date. Stupid bastard was only costing all of them money. Clay didn't care if Bishop had it to burn, it was a fucking waste of time and energy. Robin was confident there wouldn't be anything that really came of it. Bryant and Clay were vets, and Bishop had bated them and allegedly raped someone they cared about. What was a broken nose and a concussion in the grand scheme of things, really?

An assault charge on Clay's record might be worth it.

Clay ran his fingers up and down her spine, then zeroed in on a knot behind her shoulder blade. She gave a soft whimper and melted into Clay's chest. "What else can I do?" he asked.

"Just stay with me," she said onto his skin.

"I'm not going anywhere."

Local Shop-Keeper Refuses to Serve Celebrity

Henry Bishop hasn't made it a secret that he's made the trek to Wellville to try to win back the affections of estranged lover, Van Birch.

But when he tried to stop in a local watering hole—Revival Coffee and Books—for a cup of morning joe, the proprietress, Minneapolis Halvarson, daughter of Denver Developer, Jonas Halvarson, enlisted the help of her staff, customers, and two of Van's own security detail to bar him from the building.

When reached for comment, Halvarson's only response was, "He's not welcome here."

Revival is the known haunt of Phoenix Lambert, rumored to be where she's been running the Van Birch empire since the operation moved to Wellville over the summer. Think what you want about the feud between Bishop and Van Birch, but we think Minneapolis has balls of steel.

27

*V*an stood off to the side while the photographer and his assistant rearranged Minnie's shop to create the best atmosphere for the photo shoot. Deciding to capitalize on their new relationship, and since they'd been writing together every day, Phoenix had arranged a photoshoot of Van and Clay together with their guitars. Van was mostly excited because it meant that Clay had to stand around all day in nothing but a worn pair of jeans. No shirt, bare feet. She wanted to lick him like a popsicle. Depending on how the photoshoot went, maybe she would—even if it grossed Phoenix out. She still wasn't completely supportive of the Van and Clay boning scenario, but she was rational enough to know good promo material when she saw it.

It had been one week since they'd returned from L.A., and it had been the most stressful and most fulfilling week of Van's life. Clay and Bryant were still working long hours to keep up with the reconstruction, but Clay didn't seem to have any less energy for her when he got home. He'd shower, grab a bite to eat. Then they'd write together for a couple of hours, then they'd screw each other's brains out before falling into an exhausted sleep. He'd wanted to get up with Van for her run this morning, apparently not trusting the three—THREE!—security guys she had with her at all times now to keep her safe. But he hadn't stirred when she'd gotten out of bed, so she'd let him sleep. He was still sleeping when Van finished her full body workout after her run and showered. She'd had to shake him awake in order to get to the bookstore on time—a lot of good that did. They'd been mostly standing around all day.

The makeup artist was trying to touch up the powder that Clay had sweated off his forehead, and he was batting the girl and her brush away.

Van found herself smiling and schooled her face into what she hoped settled for general amusement. She was having trouble not making googly eyes at him. The last few days had been so perfect, at least as far as Clay was concerned. A thrill shot down her spine and warmth pooled in her belly, and the annoyance in his eyes softened to something tender when he caught her watching. Van almost pinched herself just to make sure that this was real. That this was actually happening. She almost didn't believe it, even though she'd been living it.

Van only realized she was giving Clay a sappy smile when he returned it. And she only snapped out of it when a couple of cameras flashed over her shoulders. Crap. She knew the news of her and Clay was out there, but there were some things she wanted to keep private. Sappy grins were not for public consumption.

Van had stopped answering questions about her

relationship with Clay except to say that she was in one. That's one of the reasons they were doing this photoshoot, to satisfy public curiosity and control the conversation. She and Clay were still figuring out where they were—who they were together. Right now, she was just stunned by how good she felt. The other stuff was still there. The lingering fear and anxiety that had followed her since Bishop hadn't just magically evaporated, but the heartbreak that had been so keen at the beginning had faded. She was beginning to understand that though what she'd had with Bishop had been intense, it definitely hadn't been healthy.

She hated that she'd let Bishop dazzle her for so long. She'd had a crush on him from the moment they'd met, but in a total schoolgirl sort of way, she didn't ever think a man ten years older than her would want anything to do with. When he'd started looking at her differently, like he wanted her instead of just the business of Van Birch, she'd been so excited that he was noticing her that Van put up with more than she should have. She put all her trust in him and went in completely blind as to why he wanted to pay attention to her.

Not anymore.

Being with Clay showed her how different real love was.

Even her dad and Phoenix were giving them space to see how they fit together. They both knew what was happening, but both had been making themselves scarce —probably to avoid each other as much as they were avoiding Clay and Van. Whatever was between Phoenix and Van's dad seemed to be over.

Maybe as they filmed the rebuilding of Clay's house,

they could ease into the relationship on camera. That would give them almost a year before the footage went live to figure out how they were going to work long-term.

Not that Van had any doubt that they would be long-term. In her mind, there was no going back, but they needed a little space to figure that out by themselves first.

The headlines were still fascinated with the "Plot Twist" Van had thrown at them by telling them that not only was she not with Bryant, but that she was actually dating her brother.

Her brother.

The gossip sites loved that phrase and how incestuous it made her sound. Van wanted to scream, "CLAY IS NOT MY BROTHER!" every time she saw it. But she didn't. Someday she would explain that Clay had never been her brother. He'd just always been the guy she didn't think she could have. And that had been stupid of her, because now that she wasn't avoiding her feelings for Clay any more, she'd never felt so comfortable in her own skin.

The photographers were finally ready for them, and Van took the seat she'd been eyeing, on the floor with her back to a bookcase, colorful spines acting as a backdrop. Clay dropped down beside her in all his barely clothed glory. He looked fantastic. Van was decked out head to toe in black from her black tank top, to the skinny jeans to the black flats on her feet. She was even playing her black guitar today while Clay played his regular blonde one.

At first it was like they were back in Van's bedroom playing together if she could tune out the flashes. After that, Phoenix and the photographer kept moving them around and positioning them so that it was stupidly impractical to actually play, until they finally got rid of the guitars altogether and had Van and Clay posed against the exposed brick wall, holding one another.

As much as Van enjoyed being pressed up against Clay's bare skin, she'd never done a shoot like this before. It felt too intimate, and Clay was having trouble relaxing.

After an hour and a half of posing against cold brick, Van suggested they all take a break. She could tell Clay was getting frustrated at realizing at how much the visual aspect of her job was engineered, and maybe a grueling photo shoot wasn't the best way to inaugurate him into true celebrity. Besides, Clay's jaw had started to tick fifteen minutes ago. Van was afraid he might break a tooth from the effort of not lashing out, and she needed some water and maybe a bagel before she could endure anymore posing.

They escaped out the back door the second the photographer snapped the lens cap on her camera. The moment the alley door closed with a slam behind them, Clay had Van backed up against the limestone wall, arms framing either side of her face, in a pose not altogether different from the one they'd just abandoned inside, only now he wasn't playing shy.

"How do you do this all the time?" he asked as he eased against her, pelvis first, then rolling until his entire front was pressed against Van's, his lips tracing a light trail up her neck.

His kisses tickled, and Van squirmed underneath him. "Usually when I do a photoshoot, there's free stuff involved. This time all I get is you."

He hummed against her throat. "I'll have to make this ten minutes worth it then."

But before Van could push him away and get out the

"Ewww. Gross!" that was on the tip of her tongue, Clay snort-laughed at himself and pushed off the wall.

"Sorry," he said, still chuckling. "I obviously can't pull that off."

Van shrugged and socked him lightly on the shoulder. "The first part was hot. But I am not having sex next to a dumpster."

He grabbed Van's wrist and pulled her close again, planting a swift, hard kiss on her lips. "Glad to hear it."

His smile was gone when Van opened her eyes, and he was staring at her in an intense way she couldn't quite interpret. "Thanks for doing this," Van said. "I know you kind of get swept up in the Van Birch machine sometimes when all you want to do is hammer stuff."

Van barely refrained from adding "like me" to the end of her sentence.

It brought his smile back anyway. "I see the lure, and I'm not going to take it," Clay placed another kiss on her nose. "Because lewd jokes aren't my thing." He wrapped his arms tight around her waist and squeezed. Van took his cue and hopped up, wrapping her legs around his waist as his hands settled under her backside to support her.

"And yes, while I would rather be building things," he said, "I will pretty much do whatever you ask me to. Always have."

He was right. He'd always shown up when she'd asked him to. Except— "Except last Christmas."

His arms stiffened around her and he bowed his forehead so it touched hers. "Asking me to watch that sorry excuse of a man paw at you was more than I could handle."

"That's not why I wanted you around," Van said, allowing her fingernails to scrape over the back of his neck in slow circles.

His breathing deepened even as his grip on her ass tightened. "I know. But I've never been able to watch you with another guy. Even seeing you cuddle up to Bryant has always made me sick to my stomach, and I *like* Bryant."

Van scraped her nails harder, and he sucked in a breath. "I see. So what you're saying is, that you've luuurved me from the start."

Van's back eased against the limestone wall as Clay pressed her into it. He angled her hips so she could feel the hard bulge in his jeans. Van arched against the dark spiral of pleasure his arousal sparked through her. Clay already had her rethinking her "no sex in stinky alleys" rule.

Using the wall to support her, Clay raised one hand to Van's chin and tipped it up so she met his eyes. "Yes, Van. I love you. I have loved you for a long time. And that's not going to change, no matter how many stupid photo shoots you drag me to."

Van kissed him then. Her tongue seeking entrance into his mouth immediately, because she needed to be a part of him in this moment. Clay loved her. She'd known, probably on some level she'd known he'd loved her since the first time he'd asked to kiss her, but they'd always ignored it.

When they broke apart, panting a minute later, Van traced the artful two-day stubble he'd been instructed to grow for the shoot and asked, "How about if I want you to do that reality show?"

"We're doing the show," he said, sharing a mischievous grin with her.

"And how about if I tell you I want you to come on tour with me."

He furrowed his brow. "Why?"

"Because that song we've been working on? I think we should make it a duet."

His frown deepened, and Van decided she really liked the dark and broody Clay. "Come on." She arched her back into the wall so that she rubbed against the bulge in his jeans again and he groaned. "You know you wanna be up on that stage with me."

Clay pressed Van into the wall, pinning her with his hips. He set a slow, rolling rhythm, pressing his ridge into the apex of her thighs just hard enough to tease her. It was Van's turn to moan as he said, "That's where you're wrong. I have absolutely zero desire to perform in front of people."

Van scratched the back of his neck, and he let his head fall backwards as she grazed his scalp. "But you'll do it?" she asked.

He didn't answer, just squeezed Van tighter—and maybe he would have kissed her again, but the back door opened just then.

"Good Lord. I know you two are new, but do you have to—" Phoenix broke off and waved her hand in their direction— "be so gross about it?" She finished with a look on her face like she was smelling something foul— which, given their proximity of the cafe's dumpster, she probably was.

Van giggled into Clay's neck, because Phoenix was directing her scowl squarely at Clay, and Van could tell by the way his muscles had grown taut and tense that he was glaring right back at her.

"We've been waiting for you," Phoenix said, tapping the face of her smart watch.

Van patted Clay's shoulder, and he lowered her feet to the ground. He stood behind her, gripping her hips, likely trying not to be a total dick to Phoenix for interrupting their sexy negotiations—and Van appreciated his restraint. She gave Phoenix a cheery smile and said, "Sorry. We'll be right in."

Phoenix scrunched her nose again at the smell. "Well, hurry it up. I'm sending Butch. It's basically a miracle the paps out front haven't found you yet."

Van cringed. Rookie mistake. Van knew to be aware of the paparazzi, but when Clay was around, Van tended to forget that she was famous—which was ludicrous because her fame basically defined her life. Avoiding paparazzi, posing for cameras, designing her appearances, and engineering an entertaining reality show. Everything Van did was in the public eye.

And yet, with Clay, in Wellville, Van just felt like she was at home.

"Right. Give us a sec."

Phoenix rolled her eyes but let the heavy door slam shut behind her. Clay's hands on Van's hips loosened, but he still grumbled, "I may never get along with her," in her ear.

"Give her some time," Van said and broke free of his grasp. "Come on, let's get this thing finished."

"Fine," Clay said and followed her inside. He grumbled under his breath the whole time they were setting up the next few shots. The man was grumpy as hell today. Van asked Phoenix when the food was supposed to show up, because she had a feeling Clay's mood would improve once he ate. She'd noticed that about him in the last week. The man didn't do well when his blood sugar dropped.

With reassurances that they'd break for lunch in an hour, Van and Clay posed for another half an hour straight before every phone in the room started going off at almost exactly the same time. Phoenix's buzzed across the table. Van's played Jeff Buckley from inside her bag. Clay's phone rang in his pocket with a classic ringer tone. The security team all pulled their phones out of their pockets. Even the photographer's phone played a classical dity.

When Clay pulled his phone from his pocket, it was Bryant. He frowned but answered, and Van could see Phoenix was chatting, then pulled her phone away from her head to squint and frown at *another* incoming call.

"What's up?" Clay asked. Van couldn't hear Bryant's reply, but something had to be up. She crossed to where her messenger bag sat, slung over the back of a chair, and fished her phone out of the side pocket. It was her label— and Van wondered who Phoenix was talking to. They usually called her first—well, they'd called Bishop first in the past—but now that Phoenix was basically running the whole Van Birch show, they'd *been* calling her the last couple of months. They almost never called Van directly unless some serious shit was going down.

Even when the sex tape dropped, they'd called Phoenix.

"Hello?" Van said, but the room was so loud with the cacophony of ten separate phone conversations all happening at once that she could barely make out Mark's words on the other end of the line.

"Hang on," she said when all she caught was alley and something that might have sounded like "fucking insect," and she wondered if Bishop had done something else— but she couldn't figure out what could be worse than what he'd already done. As far as sexually demeaning someone, Bishop had pretty much taken the cake, hadn't he?

Once she was outside, Mark's connection wasn't any clearer. It sounded like he was in the car, maybe, but without having to listen over everyone else's voice, Van could finally hear what he was saying.

"What the fuck are we supposed to do with this, Van?" was the first clear sentence she could make out after the heavy back door shut behind her and she was once again in the stinky, yet quiet, alley.

"I'm sorry," I said, "you'll have to start over. I couldn't hear anything there for a minute."

Van could almost hear Mark's teeth grind. "I'm talking about the photos that gossip rag just dropped. From this morning. Of you and Clay basically fucking in an alley. What the fuck is that about, Van?"

Van's whole body flushed. "We were just talking," I said.

He scoffed, "You'll forgive me if I decline to believe you."

"There might have been some kissing."

"You were pressed up against the building with your legs around his waist."

Yup. Yup, they were. And she had no defense. "Clay and I are together, not that it's any of your business."

Mark uttered a few lines of something that was

between flabbergasted gibberish and really filthy swearing. "It's too soon for this. The whole goddamn world still thinks you're blood related, and now you two are fucking in alleys."

See, this was why the label usually contacted someone that wasn't Van. Mark, though an excellent rep to have on her side when getting an album made, was not someone she enjoyed time with any other time ever.

"I have always been clear that Clay was my stepbrother. If people think otherwise then that's not my problem."

More gibberish swearing reached Van's ears. She rolled her eyes and tapped her foot, aware that she probably needed to get back inside. Whoever had taken those pictures earlier could still be hanging out. Damn modern technology.

"Listen," Van said. "Talk to Phoenix. She already has a game plan. We'll just have to step it up is all."

"I tried calling Phoenix, but she was already on another call—probably your production studio losing their damn minds."

"Well, if you could stop losing yours and say, 'Oh Van, I'm so happy you're putting your life together after the guy I put in charge of managing your career nearly destroyed you,' that would be great."

There was a moment of silence, and Mark said, "Look, I never would have—"

But Van cut him off; she didn't really need to hear it. "I know. I'm sorry. I don't blame you at all, even if you are a prick."

That got her a dry laugh. "Have Phoenix call me? We might need her in person for this one, you got me?"

"She'll give you a call—"

Something heavy hit Van from behind, knocking the phone from her hand as she landed on the ground with a cry. She pushed back up on her elbows when a sharp pain bloomed from a blow to her head, and everything went black.

Van Birch is into PDA and So Are We

Ooo La La. Van Birch wasn't joking when she said she was getting together with her hottie stepbrother and contractor, Clay Noble. Check out these photos of the couple possibly getting busy in an alley in Wellville. And prepare yourselves, ladies. Clay does not have a shirt on.

*C*lay hung up from a short conversation with Bryant warning him about the photos of him and Van from earlier to check that that was the only emergency. Clay was ticked about the photos. That had been a private moment—the first time he'd told Van he loved her out loud. He'd rather the memory not be marred by being made to look like something sordid, but otherwise, Clay wasn't too bothered. Van and he were together. He knew the brunt of the burden of correcting public perception about Clay and Van would fall on Phoenix's shoulders. Clay had no qualms about forcing Phoenix to say nice things about him in public. He felt a perverse surge of pleasure at the idea.

But when he checked the room to see if Van was stressing, Clay didn't see her. Phoenix was in the corner speaking rapidly while thumbing through something on her iPad—likely the photos. The photographer and the assistants were all off the phone but huddled together talking over each other. All three of Van's security team were in their own little huddle, talking about Lord knows what. Minnie was lingering near one of the bookshelves with her baby on her hip. She'd been around but had been working in back while they'd been taking over her shop.

She met Clay's eyes and seemed to come to the same realization he had just a few moments ago. Van wasn't here.

Clay couldn't tell if it was his panic mirrored on Minnie's face or some panic of her own that showed there, but either way, both of them knew that Van should have been in the room.

Clay crossed to Minnie, making his way across the room in about three steps. "Did you see where she went?" he asked.

She shook her head. "Is everything all right?" she asked.

"Just some paparazzi gossip rag bullshit. Do you think she's in the bathroom?"

Minnie shook her head again. "I just came from there."

Clay cursed and ran his fingers through his hair. He needed a haircut, but the makeup artist this morning had raved over how it was the perfect length for looking purposefully disheveled. Clay didn't want to look disheveled. He wanted to look calm, orderly, in control. Because his panic wasn't subsiding. He didn't know where Van was, and he knew there was nowhere else she should be.

Clay turned around and found Phoenix scanning the room the same as he had done a few seconds ago.

Again, he crossed the room with his feet barely touching the floor. "Where did she go?" Clay asked as

Phoenix tried to keep looking for Van around his body as Clay closed in on her.

"I don't know," she said. "I thought she was with you."

"She was, until everyone's phone rang."

"Maybe she stepped outside?" Minnie asked. "I came out to see what all the noise was about."

Clay hadn't noticed that Minnie had followed him until then.

"The alley," Phoenix and Clay said at the same time. And he was already making his way for the back door before he'd even stopped speaking.

Clay burst through with such force that the heavy metal door banged open and bounced off the limestone wall behind it.

Empty.

The alley was empty.

That didn't stop him from jogging from one end to the other, calling for Van.

Her crack security team was filing out the door. Butch wasn't with them today. Good. Van liked him, and Clay didn't think she'd take kindly to when Clay insisted she fire him. The rest of these guys, though... He'd bet all his insurance money that they were goners, judging by the fiery rage in Phoenix's eyes as she turned on them.

"You're not supposed to let her out of your sight!"

The two more oafish ones hemmed and hawed, but the third was crouching over something on the other side of the dumpster. Clay charged over, but the guard's hand flew up to stop him from stepping into something.

Clay hadn't seen it at first, because it wasn't large, and

the whole alley was a mess of grease spots and loose asphalt, but there, just out of sight of the alley entrance and the back door to Minnie's shop, was Van's phone, cracked screen face up on the ground. About a foot away from it lay a broken brick.

Clay crouched next to the security guard he thought might be Alvin.

"Is that…"

"Blood," he nodded.

Clay swallowed. There was blood on the edge of the brick, and a few droplets on the concrete. He followed the path it made. It had fallen fast and swift for about six feet and then just stopped.

"Probably put her in a car," Alvin said, and Clay had to stop himself from bellowing into the sky.

"Where the fuck did they take her?" He knew it was an irrational question, but all of the tweets Van had showed him came rushing back into his mind. The stalkers, the death threats, the rape threats. Her address. The way the fucking paparazzi knew where they were going to be at every turn.

"Goddamnit!" Clay yelled, crouched to scoop up a loose piece of pavement and hurled at where the car must have been.

Clay heard Phoenix already on the phone with 911, and the security guy guarding the scene was on the phone with Butch. The two other guys were scrolling through something on their phones.

Minnie showed up next to Clay's elbow. "She hasn't been gone long," she said. "They couldn't have gotten far."

Clay knew she was trying to be reassuring, but right now, he needed more than reassurances. He needed physical proof that Van was alive and unharmed. Clay needed to be the one to find her. He'd only finally just figured out how to be honest with her—and himself—about his feelings for her and now she was probably at the mercy of some fucking men's rights activist with some stupid chip on his shoulder because he blamed women for his being a narcissistic prick.

"You don't have security cameras, do you?" he asked Minnie.

She shook her head. "But the bank might," she said, nodding her head toward the big building on the other side of the alley. It was a building down from hers, but the car that they'd put Van in would have parked right behind it. At the very least they could get some plate numbers or a make on the car.

Clay turned to tell the only security guy here he liked, but he was already saying into the phone, "Check in with the bank, Butch. See if they have cameras in the alley that would pick anything up."

Clay could hear sirens in the distance, but Phoenix was still on the phone, even though she wasn't speaking. Her eyes on the spot of ground where Van's phone still lay.

"Have you called Robin yet?"

She shook her head, her eyes never leaving Van's phone. "I'm still on the line with the dispatcher."

It took all of Clay's energy not to sneer. She wouldn't even call Robin to tell him that his daughter was missing. The woman clearly needed to get over herself.

Taking a deep breath, and then another, Clay pulled his phone from his pocket and pulled up Robin's number with shaky fingers. Did he even know about the pictures yet? Did he know about any of this? Clay knew he'd been consulting on the case against Bishop, but how much did he know about the death threats?

Clay could hear his heartbeat echoing in his ears as Robin's phone rang once. Twice. Part way through the third ring, Robin picked up. "If you're calling to apologize for making out with my daughter in public—and we're going with making out, because the alternative—I warn you Clay, I think of you as my son, but if it was the alternative—I will kill you."

Clay believed him. He'd had a rough summer as a parent, and here Clay was, about to make it even worse. Guilt sank into Clay's bones as he realized he was partly to blame too. He'd stopped paying attention to Van right along with everyone, even though he knew exactly how much danger she was in.

"Robin—"

"It might be better if you and I don't speak right now."

"Robin, I—"

The lump in Clay's throat cut off his own speech this time, and Clay could feel Robin's mood shift.

"What happened?" he asked, worry and panic replacing his anger.

"She's missing." Clay said; then the next words tumbled out of his mouth too fast. "All of the phones started ringing at once, and we were all dealing with the news of those pictures going live, and I guess Van couldn't hear or something because she went out into the alley to take her call, and no one noticed her go, not for a few minutes, and she's not here."

"How do you know she didn't sneak around the corner for a taco?"

Clay almost smiled. That would be something that Van would do. Probably had done a million times before. "Her phone's still here. In the alley. And—" Clay couldn't bring himself to tell Robin about the blood they'd found on the ground while they were on the phone, not when he was at the office. "There's signs of a struggle. Someone took her."

The lump in Clay's throat overcame his speech again, and he realized he was having trouble breathing. Clay might be having a panic attack. He wasn't sure. He swallowed and gasped out, "I'm so sorry, Robin."

Clay heard papers shuffling over the phone line and knew Robin was packing up so he could leave. "It's not your fault, Clay. I'll be right there, and we'll find her. Okay? We'll get her home safe."

Clay nodded, even though Robin couldn't see him. He knew Robin was saying what he needed to believe to make the short trip from his office to Revival. Clay needed to believe it too. He *needed* Van to come home safe.

Breaking: Van Birch is Missing!

Van Birch has been abducted from where she was on location doing a photoshoot in Wellville. Updates to come.

29

The first thing Van felt was pain. Her head pounded so hard that she didn't want to open her eyes. It was like her worst hangover times a billion. She couldn't think about anything other than how bad her head hurt. Van was not sure how long it took her to realize that there were voices in the background. At first they were just tones, a semi-melodic backdrop of male voices until slowly, so slowly, they solidified into actual words.

They were talking about her, about how pretty she was all tied up. That's when it occurred to Van to see if she could move. She tried to move her arms and legs, but sure enough, restraints kept them from obeying her commands to move. She jerked against the bonds. Her head flashed with each movement, and it was like being knocked out all over again without the lovely falling into the blackness that had happened the first time.

Van stopped moving and concentrated on figuring out where she was. She kept her eyes closed, because they hadn't figured out she was awake yet, and it didn't feel like she had a blindfold on. She was gagged however, and she was on something soft, with her limbs pulled wide, which had her thinking she'd been bound prone on a bed. Clothes still on.

There was that at least.

It was then that Van realized she recognized one of the voices. The first voice, the one that she didn't recognize, the one that had been talking about how pretty she was all tied up had been interrupted by someone she knew, but her brain wasn't making the connections to who it could be. She recognized the voice, but he wasn't someone she saw often.

Then he started yelling about how this wasn't the plan and why he was filming her and what the fuck was he doing having her all tied up.

The new guy said that was the only way to make sure she didn't fight back.

That had Van's eyes flying open whether she wanted them to or not. It took a second for her vision to adjust to the fucking spotlight that was trained on her. And every movement of her eyes in her sockets sent a new spark of pain to her already throbbing head.

That's when the fighting really started, and the shouting made it more difficult for Van to focus, but she had to. There was no way she was going to let them keep her tied up. She was not becoming anyone's victim again. She blocked out how her fighting and scratching hadn't helped her before. How Bishop had so easily held her down and used her.

The recognition of the voice registered the moment before her vision cleared. Michael. It was Michael Astor that was arguing about not following the plan with the guy who tied her up. Whatever the plan had been, Van glad it had been derailed, because the other guy was arguing that it was the only way Van was going to learn her place in the world and that it was women like her who gave men a bad name when women were the ones who were sluts.

The words, "I mean, you saw it man; she'll fuck anything. Even her own brother. Why not me?" had Van pulling at her bonds. Panic rising. No. No. No. This was not happening. Not again. They were not going to hurt her.

"Jesus Christ, man," Michael said. "You were supposed to pretend to tie her up. Maybe scare her a little bit into submission."

Michael loomed over Van on the bed. "Is that blood? What the fuck man?" Then Michael knelt over her, and Van stilled, remembering the last time she'd seen him and he'd tried to force himself on her. Michael was no better than the guy he was yelling at, and really, he sounded a little unhinged, talking about a plan to kidnap her.

He ran a finger down her cheek. "Sorry about this, Vanessa. He wasn't supposed to touch you. He was supposed to just pull you off the street for a minute so we could save you. But I promise, you aren't in any danger."

Van flinched away from his touch. Her stomach turned as his finger skimmed over her chin and down across her collarbone.

The door banged open, and Van flinched again, the noise too much for her head. Michael's hand fell away, and she let out a breath, only to have trouble catching another when she heard the voice she'd feared for two months say. "What the fuck, Michael?"

Bishop.

He was here, in the room with her, and she heard his heavy footsteps cross the creaking floor, and she couldn't breathe. She tried to pull in a breath, but it wasn't enough. She was going to suffocate from sheer fright as Bishop came into sight overhead.

"Aw, Ness. What did they do to you?"

She knew her eyes were wide with fear and panic as they met his. The familiar brown warmth they displayed did nothing to ease her fear. He was going to touch her again, and there was nothing she could do about it.

"I'm really sorry about this, baby," he said. "This is what I get for going along with Michael's nutso ideas. Absolute fucking chaos."

Then, he was pulling at her wrist, and her whole body clamped up until she realized what he was doing. He was untying her. Oxygen actually made it into her lungs then. She was going to be set free. Bishop was going to let her go.

"This wasn't how it was supposed to go. But we can start over. You just do your bit and play your part, and we'll get this whole mess wrapped up and figured out, and then we can go home to L.A. and pretend this whole summer never happened."

What the fuck? Van's head hurt too much to figure out what he was saying, and she tried to say that she wasn't going anywhere with him, but the gag had dried out her tongue so much that she barely made a sound.

When one of Van's wrists was free, he rubbed at the

marks on her skin, his fingers gentle, almost loving, as he helped to restore the blood flow to her wrist and hand.

When she remembered she could move her left arm, she yanked it back out of his grip and then sent it flying toward his face. He still had the remnants of the black eyes from where Bryant had broken his nose. Van aimed for his nose again, but it was her left arm, which had never had much strength to it, and since her other three limbs were still tied down, she had barely any power to it. Bishop caught her arm and pinned it to the bed.

"None of that now, Van. You need to promise to be a good girl before I untie you."

Van tried to tell him to go to hell, but she choked on the gag.

That was when she heard footsteps, heavy and loud, like a herd of bison were stampeding toward them down the hallway. Then there were shouts of hands up and the police were there and then a gunshot rang out and everything went beautifully black.

Social Media Plot Uncovered; Bishop, Astor, Blogger in Custody

Authorities have been tight-lipped so far about starlet Van Birch's abduction and subsequent rescue, but we have photos of Henry Bishop, Michael Astor, and an outspoken YouTuber taken into custody in downtown Wellville this afternoon, just after the pop star was rushed to the hospital, where she is being treated for minor injuries.

Our hearts are with the Birches tonight, and we all wish our favorite pop star a speedy recovery.

30

Clay wasn't allowed to see Van until eleven that night. None of them were.

She had a severe concussion and was having trouble keeping conscious. Luckily, other than a nasty cut on the back of her head and some bruising from the restraints, she was fine. They were worried that too much excitement might make her hyperventilate again like she had been when the police had arrived.

Clay had never seen a more satisfying sight than when Robin, with his private investigator, and Bryant and Phoenix had arrived outside the hotel where Bishop and Michael had been staying just in time to see the two jackasses escorted outside in handcuffs along with their pathetic little stalker accomplice.

In the hours since, they'd been filled in on the basics. Bishop and Michael had come up with a master plan to get Bishop out of the dog house with Van and back into being a hero in the public eye. They'd hired some crazy off the internet to kidnap Van, and then they were going to rescue her on camera while at the same time allowing the guy to get away. All he'd wanted was $50,000 and a lock of Van's hair, apparently. He hadn't gotten either.

They'd waited together, silently, in the private hospital waiting room once the police left. Butch and a police officer guarded Van's door while Bryant and Clay sat in chairs flanking the waiting room door so they could peek out and check the hallway in front of Van's door periodically. Clay already knew he and Bryant weren't going to trust anyone they didn't know around her for a long time.

Robin and Phoenix sat on opposite sides of the room. Phoenix kept her eyes down, so she didn't notice the way Robin stared at her every now and then. For once though, Phoenix had zero devices on her. She sat with her arms folded, staring at the corner. Robin sat slumped over in his seat, his elbows on his knees. Every few minutes he ran his hands through his hair and cursed.

Minnie sat by herself in the middle of the room, somehow swept up with all of them, but she refused to leave, and Clay kind of respected that in her, even if she and Bryant were ignoring each other the same way Phoenix ignored Robin.

They could only see Van one at a time, and no one argued when Robin went in first, but Phoenix was adamant she be the second. Then Clay told Bryant to go, that he would watch out for everyone while Bryant saw her. Then Clay told Minnie to take her turn. She wasn't gone long, but she thanked Clay when she returned.

Clay couldn't put it off any longer. It was his turn. He was afraid that maybe she'd blame him too—for the alley,

500

for the photos, for all of it—when he should have been with her.

But she was asleep when he entered her room. She had an IV, and a few sensors hooked up to her, but besides looking pale, she just looked like Van. Maybe a little less eyeliner than usual, but she was there, and she was breathing, and she was beautiful. He took the hand that only had a little machine clamped to her finger and kissed the back of it. Then he traced the bruises on her wrist, so like the bruises she'd had that first night she'd come home.

"I'm so sorry, Van. I should have been there to protect you from all this."

Her arm twitched in his hand, and he looked up to find her eyes open. "Don't be stupid," she said. Her voice came out a breathy rasp.

Clay couldn't help it when a wide, slow smile spread over his lips. "You're awake."

"Barely."

He laughed. "You should rest."

"And you should give yourself a break." Her voice was already growing weaker.

"Only if you promise to come home to me soon."

"Only if you promise to marry me once all this mess is over." she said, then squeezed his fingers.

Clay choked on his own breath. "You're delirious."

"I know what I'm saying," she insisted, even as she could barely keep her eyes open. "Well?"

"Of course we're getting married, but let's talk about it when you're less concussed, alright?"

"Fine." There was just enough of Van's usual attitude in

that word that Clay smiled and squeezed her hand. Then, barely moving her lips, Van said, "I love you, Clay."

His heart stopped. He wasn't sure he'd even heard the words, but he said them back anyway. "I love you too, Van."

But she was already asleep.

31

Two Months Later

"This is it?" Van asked when Clay pulled up to an empty field in the middle of nowhere. "This is what you wanted to show me?"

Clay pulled his keys from the ignition and hopped out his door with a flippant, "This is it."

Van checked over her shoulder. Nothing in the truck bed, nothing hidden behind the seat. So he hadn't brought her out to an abandoned field for a romantic picnic and sexy times. For which she was kind of thankful. It was almost Thanksgiving and cold as hell in Kansas. They were already talking about expecting snow.

Clay opened Van's door and held out a hand to her.

She only stared at him. "You're not bringing me out here to kill me, are you?" she asked.

"Get out of the car, Van." Clay said.

She made a show of removing her seatbelt and pulling her scarf tighter around her neck before taking his hand. "I know we were in L.A. for two weeks longer than I promised, but you know I can't control how the legal system works. And you can't kill me because it turns out you like living in California more than you thought. It's just not fair."

They'd spent most of the last two months in California. First they'd been recording her new album. Well, their new album. It was still technically billed as Van's record, but Clay had helped her write most of the songs and sang on about half of them, enough to justify taking him on tour with her next summer. Not like she needed an excuse to take him with her; she planned to be married to him by then. But Van was all about hedging her bets these days.

Clay kissed the top of her head and pulled her into the arctic forty-mile-per-hour wind and dragged her until they were so far into the field that Van could barely make out Clay's truck parked next to the side of the road. All she saw in every direction was dead grass. The drab brown complimented the dingy gray skies nicely.

"Here," he said. Clay dropped her hand and held his arms out, a giant, expectant smile on his face.

Van turned in a circle. "'Here' what? There's nothing here." She kicked at the dead grass. "Is there an X marks the spot under here or something? Are we digging for buried treasure with the invisible shovels you brought?"

"God, you're so dense." Clay said. He wrapped an arm around her shoulders and laid a kiss on the top of her head to soften the insult. "This is where I'm going to build our house."

Van scrunched her nose as she looked into his eyes. The light was getting too dim to see if they were dilated or not. "Are you high?" she asked.

His response was to laugh. "Because if you were high, I would totally expect you to choose an empty field and start building a house instead of binging on gummy bears like a normal human."

"I promise you, I was completely sober when I bought this land."

"Holy fuck, you aren't joking."

Clay tried to school his smile, but he couldn't. He looked like his joy was going to split his whole face in half. "Nope. This, and the forty acres around it, are ours."

"How?" Van asked. "When?"

"I started looking back at the beginning of September. Asked Robin to help get my old lot on the market and then went to the producer myself with the idea of building a whole new house for us. You know, a big one. That we can grow into."

"You bought forty acres without telling me?" When he'd told her he'd invested the advance he'd gotten from the album, she'd been thinking stock market, not barren wasteland.

"You bought a house on the beach without telling me," he said.

Van spluttered. She had done that. But the house *next door* to Phoenix had gone on the market, and it was a cozy craftsman that was way bigger on the inside than it looked like from the beach. And it was *on* the beach *and* next door to Phoenix. "How often do you get the chance to live right next door to your best friend?" Van asked.

Clay rolled his eyes. "Because you don't spend ten hours a day together already."

"And now we'll be able to watch each other's kids, too!" Van said, offering Clay a wide, toothy smile. Kids was the one issue they were still negotiating on. He wanted them yesterday. Van, who was only twenty-five, wanted to wait a few more years. So far, they compromised to revisit the issue after they finished the summer tour. The prospect of kids was still her best bargaining chip, and Clay knew it.

"It's only fair that if you got to pick our California house, I get to pick the Kansas house," he said, ignoring her comment about kids outright. Which was fine. Given what Van now knew about Phoenix's relationship with her dad, there was a possibility that any kids Phoenix had would also be Van's siblings, and that was something she didn't want to think about too hard unless Phoenix and Robin ever actually got back together.

Van crossed her arms and shivered. The temperature was dropping below freezing as the sun started to set. "Okay, but how big are we talking, because you know how I feel about McMansions."

"I was thinking ranch style, because of the wind," Clay said. "With a big front porch and an even bigger deck in the back. An airy interior, a barn out that way," he motioned vaguely behind them, "chickens in the yard, livestock in the pasture, a horse or two."

"A woodshop?" Van supplied.

"And a woodshop." Clay wrapped Van in his arms, and she snuggled into his warmth.

"I always knew you secretly wanted to be a farmer."

He chuckled. "So you're on board?"

"Would you sell the land if I wasn't?"

Clay squeezed her in closer. "Would you sell the beach house?"

"I'm in, but the next time there's an extravagant purchase in our future, can we please discuss it before hand?"

"That's probably the responsible thing to do," Clay said.

They stood together for a few minutes. Van tried taking in the expanse around her that was going to be her future home. She couldn't see it yet. All she saw was an empty hay field, but she trusted Clay's judgement. She'd just spent an entire summer watching him transform a disaster zone back into a quaint neighborhood. She was certain he could make these few acres into a happy place.

"You ready for next week?" Clay asked in her ear.

Next week was the first of the hearings that would eventually lead up to Bishop's trial. After her kidnapping had been such a public ordeal, L.A. County had finally indicted him. It was going to be a long, hard road, one that Van didn't particularly want to walk, but one that she would.

"No, but I'll make it through."

Clay kissed her neck. "We'll make it through."

Cold though she was, Van rotated in his arms so she could stand on her toes to lay one on him to show her appreciation. Clay turned her cold, quick, closed-mouth kiss to a soft, warm, languid one when he tangled his hands in her hair and dipped his tongue past her lips. Van almost started shivering for an entirely different reason.

Eventually, Clay pulled away and tapped her on her cold, pink nose. "You're cold."

"Really? What gave me away?" She sniffed so she didn't drip snot on his fingers.

"Just, one more thing before we go, okay?"

Van stomped her feet, pretending her toes were cold, but she was wearing her fur-lined boots. Her toes were just about the only toasty thing about her.

"You are way too used to California winters," Clay laughed and placed a kiss on the tip of her nose this time.

"Yeah, yeah, and it's not even winter yet, I know," Van said. She couldn't help it if she was cold-blooded. She needed sun and a rock to bask on, and she was not ashamed of it. "Is there a rock or something out here I need to see as I turn into an ice sculpture?"

"Kind of," Clay said. His hand disappeared into his coat pocket and reappeared holding a black velvet box.

Van cocked her head to the side. They'd never made a formality of their engagement. Their family understood that they planned to get married someday. She and Clay had been planning for a future together in an abstract sort of way, but they hadn't spoken much about specifics. Hence each of them purchasing property without consulting one another.

As Clay opened the box, he said, "We should make this official, don't you think?"

He held the ring out to her, and Van did the cliché thing and covered her mouth. The ring was perfect. It was small, with an organic cluster of mini stones set into rose gold. "It's black diamonds from a jewelry artist based out of Kansas City," he said. "I thought you'd like it."

Van took the box from him and plucked the ring out. "It's gorgeous," she said. "And it won't weigh my hand down."

"Can I?"

She offered him the ring, then spread the fingers on her left hand so he could slide it on for her.

"I feel like I should get you something," Van said, admiring the way the cluster of jewels sat against the base of her ring finger. "This is so perfect."

"All I want is for you to chose a wedding date."

"And to have the wedding here," Van said.

Clay shrugged. "That part goes without saying."

Van rolled her eyes. Of course he would just assume. While she'd toyed with the idea of having a beach-front wedding, she'd also always had her heart set on getting married in the Rose Garden in Wellville. And if she wanted to marry him before the tour started, that pretty much meant they *had* to get married in May.

They'd be done filming the house-building show by then, but the tour wouldn't kick off until the end of June. They might have just enough time for a honeymoon if they timed everything right.

"I can do that," she said, "but you have to take me someplace warm right now, or I won't be alive come May to actually marry you."

Clay's dimple made an appearance as he entwined his fingers with hers and pulled her along on a mad dash back to his truck.

Wedding of the Century

We've been waiting with bated breath for the wedding of the century since Clay Noble proposed to his stepsister (we'll never get tired of printing that), singer and reality star Van Birch on the inaugural season of his show, Contractor, in February. And this couple hasn't stopped surprising us since their antics last fall. First the photos of the not-quite-siblings getting hot and heavy in the alley, then recording an album together, then testifying against former manager Henry Bishop at his trial last month. The surprise proposal was the perfect cherry on top of the absurd sundae that has become the improbable romance between the two reality-TV moguls.

You can imagine how offended we were when the wedding was going to take place on private property with security tighter than the President's. But! We have the first exclusive photos of the happy couple on their big day. And if we're not mistaken, we think the bride's sporting a bit of baby bump. Do you see it too?

THANK YOU FOR READING!

I hope you enjoyed reading *The Van Birch Incident*. I first developed the concept for The Incident Series in the spring of 2018, and I was first entertaining the idea of becoming an independent author. I wanted to enter the market with a series of books that really turned romance tropes on their heads, so I identified some of the tropes I thought I enjoyed the least, and developed a story I hadn't seen anywhere yet. In the process, I learned that I liked a lot more tropes and different kinds of romance stories than I thought I did. *The Van Birch Incident* is the fifth full-length novel I've published, and I am so glad I took the time to develop the story. Look for Bryant's and Minnie's story in *The Deception Incident* as well Robin and Phoenix' story in *The Betrayal Incident*, both coming in 2020. Or learn how Van got to be where she is in the prequel novella, *Love, Van B.*

Want to Connect with Me?
I am @marlaholtauthor on Instagram. I'd love to see your bookstagram posts or just chat about the book. I can't wait to meet you!

Finally, leaving reviews is one of the best ways you can support the Indie Authors you love. I'd be forever in your debt if you took the time to review *The Van Birch Incident*

As Van would say, be outrageous you beautiful bitch.

ACKNOWLEDGMENTS

First, thank you to everyone who has read this book and supported me as I have written it. I have been a complete basket case. That's what happens when a project starts with the simple idea of a backwards fake relationship, but really it's the stepbrother she's in love with trope and sort of turns into a romance with a lot to say about fucking the patriarchy.

Thank you to my husband, of course, for putting up with my intensity and single-mindedness while working on this project. You were also so instrumental in tracking down the most loathsome and disgusting of the social media posts I used as templates. And I still think your idea of making each one a Chad was solid gold.

Thank you to Erin who gave me a zillion pep talks over the last few months, and for your beautiful insight and unending encouragement. Thank you to my beta readers who helped make this story stronger. Thank you to Jackie. Your editing skills saved this manuscript from being a hot mess. Thank you to Tia, who designed the best set of covers a girl could ask for. Thank you also for your help with making the blurb absolutely perfect. Thank you to all my friends on Instagram for constantly being not only an inspiration, but also for your hilarity, your irreverence, and your photos of hot dudes with rockin' abs in gray sweatpants. I couldn't have asked for a better community.

And finally, a big thank you to anyone who has ever had the courage to say, "I won't keep quiet so you can be comfortable." This book is for you. (And if you've had to keep your silence to keep yourself safe, this book is for you too.)

THE INCIDENT SERIES

Love, Van B: An Incident Series Novella
The Deception Incident (Coming Soon)
The Betrayal Incident (Coming Soon)